NO CRONES ABOUT IT

A SPELL'S ANGELS COZY MYSTERY BOOK 2

AMANDA M. LEE

WINCHESTERSHAW PUBLICATIONS

PROLOGUE

*T*he wind howled like a wounded feral animal. It shook the small shack in which we'd taken refuge for the night so hard I was convinced the roof would be torn off or cave in on top of us.

Of course, I'd just heard the story about three pigs, and there was a lot of huffing and puffing in that tale. The woman with me — she wasn't my mother, but I was instructed to call her that in public in case anyone questioned why we were together — said talking pigs weren't real. As for talking wolves, they were a different story.

I didn't understand. The woman said it was normal because I was too young. Age didn't mean much to me. She said I was four, almost five. I could count. However, the passing of time meant very little to me. I only knew that we were constantly moving ... and hiding.

It had been that way as long as I could remember. We never stayed in the same place for more than a few nights. I didn't have a home. I wasn't even sure what that word meant. We were children of the stars. That's what she said, the woman I was with. The wolves were children of the moon and we were children of the stars.

"Are there others?" That's what I asked as we huddled before a fire barrel inside the shack. The windows had been opened for venting, but the smoke was still thicker than I would've liked.

She shrugged as she placed a blanket over my shoulders. She wasn't my mother, but she cared for me as if she was. She made sure I was fed — we rarely went hungry for more than a day — and she did her best to keep me warm. The chills that often pervaded my body were from fear, not cold.

It was cold tonight, though. We were in an area thick with trees ... and wind. I couldn't get warm. She seemed to sense that, because she sat next to me, wrapped an arm around my shoulders and lent me some of her warmth.

"Other what?" she asked, her head cocked to the side as she listened to the wind. She kept one ear on my chatter — which she said was important because if I didn't ask questions I wouldn't find answers — but her focus was clearly elsewhere.

"We're the children of the stars," I repeated. "Wolves are children of the moon. Are there others?"

A small smile played at the corners of her mouth. She seemed amused by the question. "You're getting ahead of your lessons, little one. You're not ready to hear about the others."

"You told me about the wolves," I persisted. "I want to know about the others."

She sighed, the sound long and drawn out. Weariness permeated her every mannerism and expression. She held strong, though. She always held strong.

"There are vampires," she started. "They are children of the night."

I knew about vampires, but I had been warned that the ones we saw in movies — a rare treat — were not real. "They can't go out in the sun, right?"

She nodded. "Very good." She gave me encouragement regularly, but it didn't feel like love. It felt like responsibility, and I could never figure out why. I saw other children playing in parks when we passed, laughing and joking.

That was not my life.

"And they drink blood." I wrinkled my nose at the thought. I didn't care how hungry I got, I couldn't imagine drinking blood.

"They do." She bobbed her head. "There are also children of the earth. Do you know who they are?"

I screwed up my face in concentration. "Witches." I wasn't sure how I knew that. It was something I'd picked up along the way.

"And what do we know about witches?"

"There are good and bad."

Her smile widened. "Very good. You must always be sure. The bad witches are your enemies. The good witches are your friends. You must always be mindful which you're dealing with because good witches will help you."

I was still confused. "Am I a witch?"

She hesitated, as if debating how to answer. "Yes ... in some ways. You're more than that, though. You're not a child of the earth, at least not specifically."

I was a child of the stars. I knew that. She'd told me over and over ... and yet I still didn't understand. "What are children of the stars?"

"They are ... more." She shook her dark head and rubbed the spot between her eyebrows. It was clear our travels — we'd trekked a great distance the past few days — were starting to catch up with her. "You're not ready to understand what you are," she explained. "You're too young."

She often said that. I found it frustrating. "Maybe I'm not too young."

"You're too young," she repeated. "You can't understand."

"When will you tell me?"

"When I'm sure you can understand."

That didn't help ease my agitation. "But ... ."

"No." She extended a finger by way of warning, which immediately shut my mouth. She rarely yelled and never struck me by way of punishment. But she did have her limits. "You're not ready to understand. I hope to be there when you are ready, but if I'm not I have faith you will figure it out on your own."

I huddled deeper into the blanket when the wind howled again. "Why does it have to sound like wolves?" I'd been taught over and over — since before I could talk perhaps — that wolves were my enemy. They were something to fear, aside from the claws that could rip out my throat and the glowing eyes that haunted my dreams. They were more dangerous than even that.

I'd seen wolves before. The human kind, I mean. The ones that walked as men and women during the day and killers at night. They were the creatures we ran from now. There were other creatures to run from at different times — monsters with strange names that I didn't remember — but most often it was wolves.

They terrified me to my very bones.

"That's how they hide," my companion explained, brushing my flaxen hair from my face with gentle fingers. "They can't stop from screaming at the night, but they cannot hide like they used to in olden times."

"When they hid among the Indians?" I asked.

She smirked. "Native Americans," she corrected. "Basically, though, you're exactly right. The first wolf tribes in this land were born among the native people. They did not come into creation to do evil. They were good people who needed a way to protect their own ... hence they took the form of one of their spirit animals to act as protectors."

It was a heavy conversation for a four-year-old, but I'd been told on numerous occasions that I was wise beyond my years. I wanted to understand. I couldn't help feeling that if I understood, perhaps I would be able to help and we could stop running. That's all I really wanted ... an end to the movement.

No, that's not entirely true. I wanted a home like other children. I was fearful it would never happen. In my gut, that was the desire that haunted my dreams even more than snapping teeth and rivers of blood. Children of the stars weren't supposed to have roots, yet I yearned for them.

"Why did the wolves change?" I asked finally. This was key to understanding our enemy, yet I always struggled. I couldn't understand how something could start out good and turn evil. To me, everything should always be good.

She worked her jaw before answering. "I'm not sure you can understand."

"I can."

She patted my head. "Fine. I will try. The thing with wolves is that not all of them are bad. There are some that are good. They remember why they came into existence, the persecution they faced, and they're genuinely good people.

"There is a fringe element that is bad, though," she continued. "It's growing. The children of the moon — the bad ones, at least — want to obliterate the children of the stars so they can shine brighter.

"Think about the night sky," she pressed, gesturing toward the window. "The moon is the biggest element, so it immediately catches your eye. The stars, however, are numerous and together their power can eclipse the moon. The moon never wants to be eclipsed and that's what these wolves are fighting."

"That's why they chase us?"

"Essentially. They chase you harder than others because you can eclipse the moon harder and faster than most. Your birth was foretold years before you arrived ... and the wolves heard the whispers. They are afraid of you."

My eyes widened. "They're afraid of me?" My voice was a raspy whisper. "But ... why? I don't want to hurt them. I just want to be left alone."

"They don't know what they fear. They know you're powerful and, to them, that's enough reason to want to kill you."

And I was back to not understanding. "But ... ."

"No." She shook her head, firm. "That's enough questions for one night. You need rest. We will leave tomorrow."

I feared she would say that. It wasn't that I was overly fond of the shack —

quite frankly, it was something straight out of my worst dreams — but I was sick of the wandering. I wanted just a few days of peace. We never got it. I was about to point that out to her when the howling wind shifted. This time the noise outside was different, more intense.

The hair on the back of my neck stood on end and small bumps broke out on my arms and neck as a chill ran through me. I instantly knew we would be leaving much sooner than we planned ... and for once, I was fine with it. "They're here," I whispered.

The woman was instantly on her feet, her eyes daggers of hate as she turned her attention to the windows. "Pack," she ordered. "We must leave ... right now."

I didn't own anything other than the blanket, a locket that was tucked away in my pocket and a small bag. Essentially, I was always packed. Wordlessly, I shoved the blanket into my bag and slipped the straps over my shoulders. I was used to this. The wolves always found us.

"Will we hide the stars?" I asked. "Is that how we will get away?"

She nodded without hesitation. "Yes. We will hide the stars. It must be fast."

I instinctively raised my hands. She might've ordered the spell that needed to be cast, but I provided the power. It was always that way these days. I was strong. I realized that. I might not have understood why or the reason for the running, but I grasped the fact that it was necessary.

"We should go now," I insisted, magic sparking from my fingertips. This child of the stars was ready to run even though I wanted a place to stay so badly it caused me to ache. "They're outside. I can hear them ... and sense them ... and feel them."

She arched an eyebrow, intrigue lighting her sharp features. "You can feel them? How long have you been able to do that?"

"I don't know. I ... ."

She waved her hand to cut me off. "We'll speak of it later. For now, you must shroud us. There are too many to fight."

I'd figured that out myself. If we stumbled across one wolf — sometimes two — we destroyed them. It was easier. There were at least five outside the shack. Too many.

"We're already under," I informed her. "We're safe."

She didn't question me. She didn't poke her head out and play it safe. Instead, she shoved me in front of her and we walked into a world of snapping teeth, essentially hidden from their senses, yet vulnerable all the same.

I didn't understand, but I knew there would be no looking back.

I BOLTED TO A SITTING position in my bed, a light sheen of sweat coating my body. The dream was fresh in my head — there'd been blood and growls enough to cause my mind to want to implode — and like all the dreams from when I was a child, I wondered if it was real.

"Children of the stars," I muttered, dragging a hand through my long blond hair. "What a load of hooey."

Even as I said the words I wasn't sure I believed them. The woman from the dreams — I couldn't always remember her face as clearly as I did this evening — evoked feelings of regret and sadness. It was as if I missed her even though I couldn't remember her.

At some point I became Scout Randall. The little girl in the dream — if she was real at all — was nothing but a fragment. Everything from before I was found in front of a fire station was a blank. The only hints of that life came to me in dreams, and I could never be sure I was imagining what I thought must've happened or fighting memories that wanted to take me over.

I didn't understand.

There was a war going on in my brain, and although I'd managed to fight the dreams to the point they no longer overwhelmed me — a regular occurrence when I was a teenager — they still snuck up on me more often than I liked. I wanted answers about my past, but I was willing to forego them if it meant the semi-regular dreams would end.

All I truly wanted was peace.

As if on cue, the wind howled and caused me to shiver. That must have triggered the dream, I rationalized as I slowly got to my feet. The cabin I called home — a perk of my job with the Spells Angels, the biker gang that fought monsters the world over — was rustic, but in much better shape than the shack in my dream. I'd been working on it steadily since arriving in Hawthorne Hollow, a hamlet in northern Lower Michigan. Before arriving here, I was stationed in Detroit. I thought I would miss the city. It turned out, I didn't.

Because I knew sleep was probably something I wouldn't be able to claim again tonight, I padded to the window and looked out. The trees whipped back and forth, and I almost expected to see lightning split the sky. But it was quiet ... other than the wind.

It howled, shaking the walls, and causing shivers to run down my spine.

Then another type of howl joined the song. This one belonged to a wolf.

How close it was, I couldn't say. Not so close I worried, even though the dream remained at the forefront of my brain.

Another howl joined in ... and another. There were at least three wolves in the area, hiding in the wind. I understood it on an instinctive level, and while I no longer felt fear as I did as a child, I remained unnerved.

Something bad was about to happen. I could feel it.

ONE

PRESENT DAY

"*D*uck and cover!"

Marissa Martin used a detached tree branch to cover her head and dodged behind a large maple as a wall of water descended on us.

I remained rooted to my spot and deflected the small tsunami with a bit of magic, re-directing it toward the lake where it had originated. I was not amused.

"Knock that off!" I growled, extending a warning finger in the direction of the red-haired woman standing in about two feet of water. She had weaponized the water, which seemed to bother Marissa more than me.

"Oh, well, that's going to work," Marissa drawled. If it was possible, she seemed even farther away than she had moments before. I didn't look over my shoulder to see if that was the case. "Just tell her to knock it off. I bet she's quaking in her shoes."

The woman standing in front of me was a siren — which meant she essentially lived in the water — so I was fairly convinced she wasn't wearing shoes. Of course, to be fair, I wasn't all that familiar with sirens. During my time with Spells Angels – we're talking years here – I'd fought many a monster. Sirens were a new one for me.

"What are you even doing in Michigan?" I barked at the woman, who was swirling her hand in such a manner I was convinced she was about to create another water cyclone. "Don't even think about doing that."

She ignored the warning. "I happen to like Michigan," she shot back. Her hair was so red Lucy Ricardo would've been jealous. "Who are you to tell me where I can and can't live? Last time I checked, it was a free country."

I growled as she shot another fountain of water in my direction. This time I barely managed to get my hands up in time to ward off the water. I was annoyed with Marissa's insistence on hiding instead of helping — we were supposed to be partners on this assignment — so I felt zero guilt when I directed the water toward her.

"Hey!" I could hear her sputtering and, even though I knew better than to turn my back on the siren, I couldn't stop myself from glancing in my so-called partner's direction. I wasn't disappointed. She looked like a drowned rat, her hair plastered to her face and the leather of her coat shining in an unnatural way.

It took everything I had to swallow my laughter. "Sorry," I offered in a voice that lacked sincerity. "I didn't see you there ... standing ... way behind me."

"Oh, whatever."

I turned back to the siren, expecting another assault. Instead, she remained rooted to her spot, curious more than murderous. "What?" I was genuinely baffled by her reaction.

"What are you?"

The question caught me off guard. "We're with Spells Angels," I replied out of habit. "We're here to take you into custody."

She laughed. I didn't blame her. Even I thought I sounded ridiculous.

"Spells Angels? Is that like *Charlie's Angels*?"

It was a fair question. "Not even remotely."

"It's totally like *Charlie's Angels*," Marissa countered, her fingers busy as she tried to comb at her hair. "I'm Farrah, in case you're wondering. I'm only staking my claim because you're blond and you might think I should be Tanya Roberts or something. That's not going to happen. Everyone wants to be Farrah ... and I'm her."

That was the exact opposite of what I was thinking. "Um ... I want to be Kate Jackson."

Marissa made an exaggerated face. She was in her forties, but told everyone she was in her thirties (and often acted like she was in her teens when it came to competing with other women) and it was clear that our frosty relationship wouldn't be warming anytime soon. I was convinced that's why Rooster Tremaine, the head of the Hawthorne Hollow branch of Spells Angels, assigned us to this case together. There were plenty of other members of the group — any other members really — I would've gotten along with better in the face of a crisis.

That's not how Rooster rolls, though.

"No one wants to be Kate Jackson," Marissa shot back. "She was the most boring Angel. I mean ... she didn't have perfect hair. She wasn't sexy."

"I think she was sexy," I shot back. "Besides, she was the smartest one. I'd rather be the smartest than the prettiest."

Marissa rolled her eyes. "Whatever. I can't believe Gunner has been flirting with you. I mean everyone knows Farrah is the best angel."

My cheeks colored at mention of Gunner Stratton, Hawthorne Hollow's golden boy and another member of Spells Angels. He was a wolf shifter — something I hadn't much considered despite the dreams that were amping up in my new environment — and we had something of a flirtation going on. He was insistent that we were going to date, although I wasn't so sure. Would I even stay in Hawthorne Hollow? That wasn't a foregone conclusion. I didn't want to get attached to him until I made my decision. It was something I had to give serious thought to. In fact ... oh, wait. The siren was still staring at me.

"Who is Gunner?" The siren looked almost gleeful. "Is he handsome? I love handsome men."

I narrowed my eyes. I didn't like her attitude. If she'd kept her activities under the radar in the first place, our presence at this lake — however pretty — wouldn't have been necessary. "Don't worry about his looks. It doesn't matter."

"He's totally handsome," Marissa volunteered, ignoring the furtive look I shot her. "He's one of those guys who looks as if he should be on a fashion runway. You know ... like Harley-Davidson, but pretty."

The siren snorted. "He sounds like he's right up my alley. Send him my way."

"I don't know that he likes redheads," Marissa countered. "Well, redheads like you, I mean. He likes redheads like me ... and apparently blondes." She shot me a disdainful look. "He prefers softer redheads, though. We were well on our way to a romance for the ages before Scout here showed up and ruined everything. She's the new element — although hopefully not for long — and I figure he'll be over his infatuation pretty quickly and then it will be business as usual."

It didn't surprise me that Marissa was hopeful I would vacate the area. I had news for her, though; I never left an assignment before it was finished and I had no doubt this one would drag on a bit longer. Part of me was gleeful ... if only because I knew it would drive her insane.

"Is that true?" The siren's voice was wheedling. "Is Gunner going to trade you in for the old one here?"

Marissa's mouth dropped open. "I am not old!"

"Sure."

Marissa's eyes were accusatory when they landed on me. "Tell her I'm not old."

Ugh. This is not how I saw my day going. I was convinced there would be an opportunity for a nap somewhere in my afternoon. I'd gotten only a few hours of sleep thanks to the dream, after all. I had big plans ... and the current predicament didn't fit into them.

"She's young and spry," I automatically answered. Hey, giving in to Marissa's whims was better than engaging in a fight. "We all wish we could be as spry as her."

"And hot," Marissa added. She was a vain creature that I didn't fully understand. I mean, don't get me wrong, I understood about using my looks to get what I wanted out of men on a professional level, but I couldn't fathom why it was necessary to base my self-worth on how others regarded me ... especially when it came to something as simplistic as one's exterior.

"She's totally hot," I echoed, holding the siren's gaze. "Speaking of hot ... you're pretty smoking." I felt weird saying the words, but I was trying to appease the woman so it wouldn't come down to a battle royale. I was fairly certain I would win — like I said, I'd never taken on a siren before so I couldn't be completely sure — but if there was another way to get rid of the creature, I was all for it. "I would think you would do better in a beach environment ... near an ocean." Which would make her somebody else's problem, I silently added. "You can't keep hanging out here and killing boaters."

The siren adopted an innocent expression. "Me? I'm not killing boaters. Why would you even think that?"

As far as acting talent went, the redhead was sorely lacking. She was like a bad soap opera actress, which was saying something. "Six bodies have washed up on the shore in the past two weeks," I explained. "All of them had their virtue sucked from them. That's a siren thing."

"Oh, well, that's terrible," she drawled. "What does a siren look like? I'll be sure to keep my eyes open and tell you if I run across one."

That was slightly better ... but only slightly. "They look like you." My affect was calm, flat. "They can manipulate water, like a tsunami, and they sing songs to lure men to their deaths. People have reported hearing singing on the water."

"I love a good song." The siren beamed. "As for the rest, I'm afraid that I'm unaware of what you're talking about. I'm just a woman who loves the water."

Yeah, speaking of that ... . "I thought sirens were drawn to saltwater."

"I'm not a siren, so I can't speak to that. If I was a siren, though, I might point out that saltwater is very drying. Though it has healing properties, saltwater can wear a body down. I much prefer fresh water ... which I'm sure this siren you seek can relate to."

I couldn't hide my smile. She made me laugh. Sure, she was a killer who had wreaked havoc on the area for weeks, but she was kind of funny. A sense of humor was highly underrated in situations like this. That didn't mean I had time to waste on her. I really was in need of a nap.

"You need to go." I folded my arms across my chest and pinned her with a serious look. "You can't stay here. If you do, we'll have to kill you."

"And who are you to kill anyone?" The siren's voice turned accusatory. "What makes you so high and mighty? Perhaps this siren you seek is just doing what comes naturally and you should mind your own business."

It was an intriguing thought. Unfortunately, I had a job to do, and I was nothing if not a stickler. I always finished every task placed in front of me. "You're not going to leave, are you?"

"I see no reason to leave. This is my home. It sounds to me as if you're new to the area. That means it's not your home. You're not the boss of me."

I rolled my neck, frustration bubbling up. "I'm going to have to kill you if you don't willingly leave," I warned. "I'm serious. You can't keep killing innocent men. That's not how this works."

She let loose an unladylike snort that was filled with disdain. "Innocent? Please. My song can only call those who aren't pure of heart and you know it."

I didn't know that. I made a mental note to research sirens while keeping my gaze pinned on her. "I thought you weren't the siren."

Realizing her mistake too late, she narrowed her eyes. "You should turn around," she threatened. "I find you amusing and am willing to let you leave ... just this once."

"That's funny. That was the same warning I was going to give you."

"I'm not leaving." She was adamant. "This is my home. You can't make me leave. I'm simply fulfilling my destiny. Singing is what sirens were always meant to do. It's not my fault you can't understand that."

I frowned. "If you won't leave of your own volition, we'll have to make you leave."

"Yeah," Marissa echoed. She was still behind me, which I found more amusing than annoying. I wasn't worried about taking the siren. Instinctively I knew I had the strength.

"I look forward to the attempt," the siren taunted.

I groaned and rubbed the tender spot between my eyebrows. Apparently this was going to get messy after all. "Okay, but don't say we didn't warn you."

"Bring it on."

TAKING DOWN THE SIREN WAS messier than I'd envisioned. By the time we'd finished, we were covered in dirt, water and sea grass that was so gross it made me shudder. I wasn't thrilled with the outcome — she didn't go easily — but Marissa was positively apoplectic.

"I'm not going on an assignment with you ever again," she complained as we moved toward the dirt circle where our bikes waited for us. "I'm serious. You're a menace."

I wasn't exactly hurt by her words. "I killed her, didn't I? I don't see what you're complaining about."

"You don't understand what I'm complaining about?" Marissa was incredulous. "You used an elemental spell. I mean ... an elemental spell." She was practically shrieking, which did nothing to alleviate the headache threatening to overtake me.

"It was interesting," I agreed, amused despite myself.

"Interesting? She exploded. She left this ... stuff ... all over us." Marissa grabbed a handful of the sea grass — seriously, who knew that sirens had that inside of them? — and heaved it at me. "You're not supposed to make our enemies explode. That's not how this works."

"That's funny. I didn't realize there were specific rules to fighting."

"Well, there are." She glared at me a moment longer and then turned back to what could loosely be described as a parking lot. "I'm seriously going to talk to Rooster about having you transferred."

Rooster wasn't the sort of guy who kowtowed to others, so I wasn't exactly worried. "You do that. In fact ... ." I lost my train of thought when I realized we were no longer alone. Three men stood at the far edge of the parking lot, huge Harleys resting in the shadow of a weeping willow. How had we not heard them arrive?

"Can we help you?" I asked, focusing on our new friends rather than an old argument that was bound to give me a headache.

The center man of the trio, a huge individual who reminded me of an oak tree, smirked as we approached. His hair, largely covered by a bandana, was salt-and-pepper by his ears. "Hello." His exterior was amiable enough, but I didn't trust him.

"Hello." I had no idea who he was but I sensed a hint of power the closer I got. I also sensed something else. "You're a shifter."

He arched an eyebrow. "Excuse me?"

He was playing a game that I recognized well. "It doesn't matter." I wasn't in the mood to deal with the testosterone trio ... and that's exactly what they were. They were here to flex and I was still in desperate need of a nap. "We should be going." I directed Marissa toward her motorcycle, and even though she wasn't the sort to follow orders, she didn't put up a fight. She was clearly as uncomfortable with the situation as I was, probably the only thing we'd ever agreed upon.

"Don't leave so soon," the leader countered. "We're just getting to know one another."

Getting to know him sounded like pure torture. "I think we're fine not knowing you."

"Oh, really?" Laughter bubbled up as the man looked to his two younger companions. "See, boys. I told you this was the area for us. The women here are feisty, something you were worried about. This place is perfect for us."

For some reason I couldn't identify, his words made me uneasy. "You're moving here?"

"We're definitely considering it." He stepped forward and extended his hand. "I'm Cyrus Marsh. This is my son, Flint." He gestured toward a younger man who boasted the same eyes but lacked the size. "This is Drake Frost. He's a good friend and he's scouting the area with us."

Unlike Flint, who had a weak chin and flat aura, Drake was something else. His aura was fiery red ... and he had chiseled cheekbones and onyx eyes. His black hair framed one of those faces that belonged in an action movie. He was so good looking he was almost breathtaking, something that wasn't lost on Marissa if her sharp intake of breath was to be believed.

"Oh, my," she muttered as she fanned herself.

Drake was the sort who realized he had an effect on women. He smiled, showing off a hint of a dimple that only made him more appealing ... if that was even possible. Despite his handsome countenance, he remained as closed off emotionally as the others.

I didn't trust him.

"It's nice to meet you." I perfunctorily shook Cyrus's hand and then moved toward my bike. "I hope you find what you're looking for in the area ... I mean a house or whatever." It was only after the initial words were out of my mouth that I realized it sounded like an invitation I didn't want to extend.

Drake chuckled, his lips curving. "I'm sure we will find what we're looking for."

I held his gaze for an extended moment. There was something charming about the man, almost winning, and that was on top of his looks. There was also something chilling. He was more than he pretended to be. "We should be going."

Marissa, still entranced with Drake, had to be shoved toward her bike. "Welcome to the area," she murmured.

"You shouldn't leave yet," Flint called out. "We need a private tour and I'm guessing you're just the women to provide it ... I mean, if you're not logistically challenged or anything. I know women have trouble with directions, but I'm willing to put up with a few wrong turns if you'll show us around."

Whatever merriment had been coursing through me moments before evaporated and I didn't bother to hide my glare. "You're big, strong men," I countered. "I'm sure you can find your own way."

"Or you could find your way with me," Flint shot back, puffing out his chest. "I think I have what you're looking for."

His self-assurance was a turn-off, mostly because it was wrapped in ego and simplicity. "I already have what I'm looking for," I called out, briefly holding Drake's gaze before climbing on my bike. "Have fun looking around. It's a beautiful area."

"Stay away from that seaweed stuff on the beach," Marissa called out. "It's ... toxic."

I smiled at her unhappiness. "You should definitely stay away from the seaweed. Otherwise, welcome to Hawthorne Hollow. I'm sure we'll be seeing you around."

Drake's gaze never wandered from me. "You can count on it."

TWO

I made sure to refrain from looking over my shoulder as I drove
away from the parking lot, which was basically a circle of dirt that
had once been lush and green. Enough locals visited the area during spring
and summer to turn it into something else. I was still bothered by the idea
that the three shifters had managed to sneak up on me. Normally I was much
more aware of my surroundings.

I kept my eyes forward until I hit the main road and then I pulled over,
keeping my bike idling, so I could study the three men from an elevated position. They shouldn't have been able to hear my bike, but that didn't stop one
of the figures – I was fairly certain it was Drake – from slowly turning until
he faced me.

I sat there for a long time. I refused to turn away and let him win the
staring contest that wasn't really a competition. Eventually, though, I had no
choice but to turn back to the road. I couldn't waste an entire day watching
them. My actions would give them power, and there was nothing I hated
more than giving an enemy power.

And, yes, I was certain at least one member of that group was my enemy.
Which one, though? That was the question.

Marissa didn't bother to wait for me. I couldn't really blame her. She was
long gone when I returned to my drive. I maintained a lazy pace for the dura-
tion of the trip back to Hawthorne Hollow ... and then I immediately pointed
myself toward a local watering hole, The Rusty Cauldron. Even though the

Spells Angels had a home base, it was the bar that served as our meeting place, and I knew other members of our group would be there. That somehow seemed important given what happened.

By the time I arrived at The Cauldron, Marissa was already in the middle of a recitation about how we'd spent our day. It took only a few seconds for me to realize I didn't come off all that well in the telling.

"She cast an elemental spell," Marissa screeched. "Do you have any idea what happens when a siren explodes?"

I took a moment to glance around the bar, exhaling when I realized the only individuals present were members of the group. That's not to say the establishment didn't have non-paranormal visitors. For some reason, however, they mostly avoided the place until the dinner hour had elapsed.

"I'm actually curious what happens when a siren explodes." Bonnie Jenkins, her dark hair pulled back in a simple ponytail, sipped from a beer and let her eyes bounce between Marissa and me. She was the enthusiastic sort, and that was on display today. "Is it gross?"

"It's beyond gross," Marissa replied. "A bunch of seaweed comes out and lands on you. It smells like sewage, to boot."

From his spot behind the pool table, Gunner cocked an eyebrow. He had a cue in his hand and looked to be in the middle of a game with Rooster. They were obviously listening.

"Seaweed?" Bonnie made a face. "I don't understand how that's possible."

"Join the club." Marissa was positively apoplectic as she jerked her thumb in my direction. "This one felt the need to talk the siren to death and offered her a way out if she would just leave, by the way. Someone might want to inform her that's not the way we do business."

The "someone" she was referring to was Rooster, and the look he slid me was questioning. Ah, well, I guess I was going to have to make up an excuse.

"I figured if she left I wouldn't have to deal with her," I offered. Lying might've been easier, but I wasn't the sort to take the easy route. I owned my actions. Er, well, most of the time. "She was kind of funny."

Marissa shot me a withering look. "She was not funny."

"She looked like Ariel from *The Little Mermaid*," I countered, refusing to back down. "Well ... if Ariel smoked two packs a day and lured men to their deaths. I just thought it would be easier if she left."

Rooster worked his jaw. I could practically hear the gears in his mind working. On one hand, he didn't want to agree with Marissa. That would only further inflate her ego, if that was even possible. On the other, it was obvious he wasn't happy with my reaction to the situation.

17

"She's killed at least six men that we know of," he said finally, choosing his words carefully. "Three men have also gone missing on that lake. Their bodies have never been found. It's not much of a stretch to imagine she had something to do with those disappearances as well."

I couldn't really argue with the statement, so I didn't.

"We can't simply allow behavior like that to slide," he continued. "It was necessary to take her out."

"I took her out."

"With elemental magic," Marissa hissed.

"I expect my orders to be followed," Rooster offered, ignoring the persnickety redhead at the bar. Whistler, the bar owner and most seasoned member of the team, handed her a beer without comment. "If you can't follow orders, you're not any good to us."

The words rankled. "I took her out," I repeated. "What more do you want?"

"I would prefer you not offer murderers a free ride out of town," he replied, not missing a beat. "You're a powerful ally, Scout." His lips quirked as I rolled my eyes. "But you have to follow the same rules as everybody else."

Even I couldn't argue with the verbal smackdown. "I'm sorry." I held up my hands in capitulation. "I wasn't thinking. She was just ... funny."

"She was not funny!" Marissa's tone was scathing. "She was tossing around water in an attempt to drown us."

"How could you tell from where you were standing?" I shot back. "You were hiding behind a tree while I was talking to her."

Marissa's eyes narrowed to slits. "I was gauging the situation. Not all of us have elemental magic to fall back on."

"Speaking of that ... ." Gunner cleared his throat to get my attention. He'd been silent since I'd entered. Our relationship – if that's what you could call it – was a work in progress. There was a lot of flirting, but for every step forward we took, two steps back were almost immediately necessary. We were both acting like blind dates sent to prom together. It was beyond weird.

"Speaking of what?" I asked innocently. I knew what subject he was about to broach, but I wasn't in the mood to discuss it.

"I didn't realize you had elemental magic in your bag of tricks," he pressed. "That's not really normal for a witch."

I hated that word. *Normal.* I'd never been normal. I couldn't remember my childhood before the kind-hearted firefighter found me, named me and made sure I was taken into custody by the proper authorities. I recognized "normal" was never a part of it.

"Well, I don't know what to tell you." I offered up a partial shrug. "I used the spell I thought would be best to take her out. I've never fought a siren before. We don't have them in Detroit."

"We don't have them here either," Rooster admitted. "I'm not even sure what you use to take out a siren."

"Beheading is best," Bonnie offered. She seemed fully engaged in the conversation. "I tried for a Florida office before coming here, but the waiting list is years long. I didn't think sirens liked fresh water."

"According to the dead one, saltwater is harsh on hair and skin," I explained, throwing myself into one of the comfortable chairs and leaning my head back as I exhaled on a groan. Lack of sleep from the previous evening was starting to wear on me. That nap was sounding better and better. "Is the lecture over? I might need some downtime."

Gunner's gaze was keen as it latched with mine. "You don't look as if you slept very well."

From anybody else, that might've been an insult. Concern etched itself through the lines of his face. He had a good heart ... even if that wasn't the part of his anatomy that caused my brain to fuzz at times when we were talking. "It was a restless night." I said the words more to myself than for his benefit. "I thought I heard wolves in the wind."

"Wolves?" Whistler shifted behind the bar. "Are you sure?"

I nodded. I saw no reason to lie. "Yeah. I heard the howling. Then, of course, we ran into a few down by the lake. I'm assuming they were the source of the howling ... although I'm not sure if it was them or others with their group."

Apparently my words had a profound effect on the men in the room because Gunner and Rooster abandoned their game and moved closer to me.

"I think vital information has been left out of the story," Rooster intoned. "What shifters?"

The atmosphere crackled with electricity and thoughts of a nap quickly dissipated. Something very interesting was going on here. I opened my mouth to answer the question but Marissa beat me to it.

"Three shifters were in that dirt circle thing when we left," she explained. "It was as if they were waiting for us."

"Did you recognize them?" Rooster queried.

"I didn't. They were pretty boring. Well ... one of them was pretty far from boring. Drake Something-or-Other. He was all kinds of hot. Of course, he only had eyes for Scout." Her gaze was dark when it linked with mine. "I'm starting to think that she's using elemental magic for more than just blowing up sirens. I think she might be casting love spells, because every good-looking man in town instantly melts into a puddle at her feet."

The comment was pointed toward Gunner – and he appropriately scowled – but it was obvious he wasn't angry about being called on the carpet. His ire was directed at Drake. "Did you get full names?" he growled.

This was getting more interesting by the second. "Cyrus and Flint Marsh. The other guy was Drake Frost. They said they were interested in moving to the area."

"Did you believe them?"

I shook my head. "They were watching us. I'm not sure how much they saw. I didn't hear them arrive."

"That's because you were blowing up a siren," Marissa hissed.

I pretended I didn't hear her. "We didn't spend a lot of time talking. Cyrus was obviously in charge. His kid was mouthy and full of himself, but he would probably wet himself in a fight. As Marissa said, Drake was the most inter-esting ... although I didn't think I was quite as enamored with him as she was."

"Oh, puh-leez." Marissa threw her hands up in theatrical fashion. "You two were staring at each other as if you were the last eggrolls on the plate. It was disgusting. He didn't even look in my direction."

"Perhaps that's because he saw Scout using elemental magic to take down a siren," Bonnie suggested. "They were probably curious but afraid. I mean ... she is pretty terrifying."

"Oh, you have no idea." Marissa slammed half her beer. She was practically breathless when she continued. "I thought I was going to die. I've never been so terrified." The look she shot Gunner was right out of a romance novel. "I'm just happy I got a chance to see all of you again."

Gunner merely rolled his eyes. "It sounds like a terrifying ordeal." He ran his tongue over his teeth and then slid his gaze to Rooster. "I guess we should've known they would show up here eventually."

My curiosity was officially piqued. "You know them."

"We know Cyrus," Rooster corrected. "At least I do. I've crossed paths with him a time or two."

"And I know him through my father," Gunner added, referring to the local police chief who walked a fine line when it came to the human and para-normal elements crossing paths in Hawthorne Hollow. "I haven't seen him since I was a teenager. There was a pack gathering – this was before the pack split – and there was a big shindig at one of the area resorts."

It seemed I was behind on local politics. "You had a pack split?" I was up on pack law enough to know that was never a good sign. It meant that two factions were warring. I very much doubted this instance would be any different. "Was there a war?"

"There was a fight," he replied, rubbing the back of his neck. "In the end, our pack – which I'm no longer active with – stayed here and his pack moved to mid-Michigan, somewhere near where that college was razed last year. I wonder if that's the reason he's back."

I tilted my head, considering. I'd heard about the college. It had been there one day and flattened the next. The human news referred to it as an "act of God." They said a sinkhole opened up and swallowed the entire school. That was utter nonsense, but non-paranormals often needed answers, whether they were ludicrous or not.

"Covenant College," I offered, my mind busy. "It was a hotbed of paranormal activity before it was destroyed."

Gunner couldn't hide his surprise. "Did you ever visit?"

I shook my head. "I kind of wish I'd gotten the chance, but it never worked out. They say a mage was involved in taking it down. I've always wanted to meet a mage."

"Apparently the mage involved is temperamental and terrifying," Bonnie offered. "I would prefer not meeting her ... though you might be able to take her on." Her expression turned thoughtful. "Maybe you're part mage."

The idea had flitted through my mind a time or two. I was well aware that I was stronger than most witches. Heck, I was more powerful than five standard witches combined. I was not, however, properly trained. I worked on instinct. Even though I wasn't the sort to doubt myself, taking on a mage was outside my comfort zone.

"I don't know and it hardly matters," I said finally. "I'm just want to know what you can tell us about our new friends."

"Not much," Gunner replied. "Cyrus is known as the type who would rather fight than negotiate. It was a miracle that the pack leadership got him to leave the first time without blood being shed – or at least a lot of blood – and I've never heard the full story on what went down. Maybe I'll have to bug Dad about it again."

"That sounds like a good idea," I encouraged. "What about the kid? He had 'tool' written all over him."

Gunner snorted, amusement flitting across his handsome features. "That's the best way to describe Flint. He's a jackass, to boot. He's garnered a reputation as a womanizer – something he promotes – and he's known to sexually harass any woman he comes into contact with." An idea lit in the back of Gunner's eyes. "He didn't harass you, did he?"

It was kind of sweet that he was worried. It was also kind of annoying. "No. But if he had, I'm capable of taking care of myself."

He grumbled something under his breath that I couldn't make out. Then he straightened. "What did you say the other guy's name was?"

"Drake Frost. He seemed ... separate from them, though I'm not exactly sure why."

"He could be part of the pack they built down there," Rooster noted. "It's interesting that he's back in town but didn't alert anyone to his presence. I wonder what he was doing by the lake."

That was an important question, but I didn't have an answer. Even if I did, it would've fallen by the wayside thanks to the door flying open to allow our resident sidekick – Ruthie "Raisin" Morton – entrance. Her hair was wild and full of waves as she rushed in, paying no mind to the way Whistler rolled his eyes.

"Guess what?" she announced, breathless.

I smiled as Gunner moved to shut the door. "You found a boyfriend? What's his name?"

Raisin shot me a death glare. "This isn't about a boy. I'm not the sort of girl who gets giddy about a boy. Though ... I might one day." Her eyes lingered on Gunner for a long time. It was no secret she had a crush on him. But he was fourteen years older than her, so she didn't have a prayer. Still, he doted on her, showering her with the attention she seemed to so desperately need. It simply wasn't romantic attention. "What was I saying again?"

"You have big news," I supplied, grinning. I couldn't help but like the kid. She had a special ... something. It was impossible to identify. Her abusive father was sitting in the county jail, charged with attempted murder for an attack on her grandmother, and she'd been officially removed from his custody. Now, she lived with the grandmother, and the girl's life seemed to be settling in a comfortable groove.

That was good after the life she'd been enduring. She had a home she wasn't afraid to return to every night. Everyone should have that.

"Oh, right." Raisin rubbed her hands together, her eyes sparkling. "Guess who got cast in the school play. We're not talking about a small role either. We're talking about the lead."

There was no need to guess. I had no idea that Raisin's interests ran to theater. "I'm guessing you."

"Me!" She rolled up to the balls of her feet and made a giddy noise. "I'm going to be Little Red Riding Hood."

I stilled, surprised. "How is that a play?"

"It just is. It's a modern and updated take."

"Well ... fun." I didn't know what else to say. "When is your big debut?"

"I'm not sure yet. We have to practice first. You guys are going to come, right?" She was vulnerable when asking the question. She looked her age rather than the wise-beyond-her-years urchin I'd met when I first arrived. "I mean ... everyone else will have big families there. I don't really have that."

"Of course we'll come," Rooster replied smoothly. His tone told me that anyone who put up a fuss would be on the receiving end of a brutal diatribe, much worse than what I'd received when he'd found out I'd offered the siren a way out. "We wouldn't miss it for the world."

"Great." She did a little hip-wiggling dance. "I'm so excited. But I'm also afraid. What does it feel like when you're going to pass out?"

I laughed. She wasn't going to pass out. Youth was an extraordinary thing. Two weeks before she'd been fighting for her life at her father's hands. Now she was looking forward to a future she probably never thought possible.

THREE

$\mathcal{M}$y plans for a nap went awry. After leaving The Cauldron, I headed straight home. All I could think about was climbing out of my pants and crawling into bed. Apparently that wasn't in the cards.

Merlin, the cat I'd somehow adopted (even though I wasn't sure how) had been on a rampage in my absence. There was toilet paper scattered from one end of the cabin to the other, and as far as I could tell it was still attached to the roll.

"You little ... ." It was hard to yell at the kitten. Not impossible, of course, but difficult. I never considered myself the mothering type, but there was something about the little scamp that melted my heart. Of course, admitting that was out of the question. "I think you might be my own little form of karma," I complained to the one-pound wonder of black and white fluff.

For his part, Merlin merely sat in the middle of his mess, eyeing me with what could only be described as disinterest. There were times I almost expected him to shoot back a snarky response. He never did, of course. That didn't mean I would've been all that surprised if it happened.

"You should be thrilled I even gave you a home," I complained as I started gathering the toilet paper. Merlin perked up when he saw what I was doing and gave chase. "Stop that," I scolded, frustrated when he yanked at the end of the toilet paper. "You're making a mess."

The kitten grinned — no, seriously, he let loose an evil smile — and continued attacking the paper.

"Fine. You win." I threw my hands in the air, tossing the toilet paper like confetti in the process. "I hope you have an absolutely fabulous time with your mess." I stomped toward the bedroom. I had no idea who I was putting on a show for because the cat was the only one present, but I let loose a series of sighs before falling face first on the bed.

I was out before Merlin stopped preening over his toilet paper ... and the dreams chased me in daylight the same way they did in darkness.

I WOKE TWO HOURS LATER, the sound of wolf howls echoing in my brain. My breath came in raspy gasps and my heart pounded at a fantastic rate. The dream had been a continuation of the one I'd had the evening before, a race through a pack of snapping jaws and extended claws, and I woke only when we reached the woods. I thought we were safe, but then another line of wolves emerged.

I couldn't remember what happened after that. I always woke at that part of the dream. Was it a dream, though? I was starting to have my doubts. For years I could dismiss the dreams as ways for my subconscious to fill in the blanks of my childhood. I was trapped in the foster care system for years and every shrink they sent me to had come to the same conclusion. I didn't tell them the paranormal elements of my dreams, of course. Inherently I knew that would be a mistake. The rest of it, however, I volunteered because it seemed to be expected of me. They all said the same thing: I had abandonment issues. I was afraid of the unknown. They didn't seem to understand that it wasn't fear driving me, it was genuine emotional distress.

What happened to me as a child?

Why was I left in front of the fire station?

Was anyone out there looking for me?

I asked those questions of myself and others for years. I never came up with acceptable answers.

Because I recognized that further sleep was out of the question, I climbed out of bed. I wasn't surprised to find Merlin sleeping on the mountain of his triumph — toilet paper stretched from one end of the room to the other — and left him to what I hoped were happier dreams as I moved to the front porch.

The cabin was a work in progress. I'd done a decent amount of home improvement, which seemed strange because I wasn't prepared to call Hawthorne Hollow home. It wasn't that I didn't like the area — the trees and fields called to me in a way I didn't understand — but I wasn't the stationary sort. I'd been moving my entire adult life (and I wanted to be moving throughout the entirety of my teenage years) and the idea of settling somewhere for the long haul was alien.

Still, the cabin felt like home. Moving with a cat would be difficult anyway, and even though Merlin drove me crazy there was no way I would be one of those jerks who left a pet behind. Merlin was family now, which meant I would probably have to get him used to riding on the motorcycle. I made a mental note to research my options on that front and slid into the rocking chair on the front porch, sighing when the breeze picked up and ruffled my hair.

In Detroit, the great outdoors was a foreign concept. The monster hunting I did with Spells Angels was of the urban variety in the city. There was the occasional water monster to take on thanks to the proximity of the Great Lakes and a variety of absolutely filthy rivers — seriously, I once took down a garbage hag in the Clinton River that smelled so foul it still haunted my dreams — but the majority of the creatures I fought enjoyed hiding in the abandoned buildings that threatened to take over the city.

We're talking vampires, shifters, wraiths and the occasional zombie. Bad witches were like discarded cigarette butts in the city, but they were easy to take out. The variety of creatures I'd crossed paths with since arriving in Hawthorne Hollow was mind boggling. It was also educational, and I loved a learning experience.

I absently rocked in the chair, my eyes drifting to the tree line. The woods didn't frighten me. I'd watched my fair share of horror movies — *Friday the 13th* was a particular favorite — but they didn't fill me with fear. Instead, I found them entertaining. I would love to take on a masked supernatural killer who murdered people by zipping them up in sleeping bags and beating them against a tree. What? That's fun.

I understood there was more lurking in the woods of northern Lower Michigan than a hockey-mask-wearing killer, though. There was a lot more. I was eager to learn, even if I wasn't exactly at the top of Rooster's list of favorite employees. That didn't change the fact that I was restless. The problem was, I couldn't decide if I was restless because I was anxious to move on or because I was running from something.

Slowly, I got to my feet at the snapping of a branch in the woods to the east. I was getting used to the idea of critters living in the woods. It wasn't unheard of to see raccoons, muskrats, deer, coyotes and even bears in this area. Okay, I hadn't actually seen a bear yet, but I was looking forward to the opportunity. This particular noise, however, set my teeth on edge.

I have a sixth sense. Some would argue that it's a seventh or eighth sense. I can "feel" when danger is close, although that wasn't what worried me now. That didn't mean the uneasiness rolling through me was normal. I couldn't shake the feeling that there was something in the woods watching me, and I very much doubted it was an animal. The raccoons showed their faces without hesitation almost every day, consistently climbed into the garbage can at the back of the property, making plenty of racket so I would know they were there.

This wasn't a raccoon. I was sure of that.

"Tim?" I called out to the resident ghost who haunted the area. He was something of a pervert. We'd had more than one discussion about him peeping into the windows of the cabin. I'd splurged on curtains to keep him out — though he could obviously float through the walls if he was so inclined — but he at least tried to pretend he was anchored by the manners of the living. I wasn't so sure that was true, but there had been no issues in at least a week.

"Tim?" I tried again and then shook my head as I narrowed my eyes. He wasn't the type to hide in the woods and spy. He was less likely to catch a gander of a naked woman if he kept his distance. Besides, he would have to exert a lot of effort to make enough noise for me to hear him from forty feet away.

No, this was something else.

I'd just about made up my mind to investigate when the familiar rumble of a motorcycle engine caught my attention. I didn't have to turn toward the driveway to know who was coming. I recognized the specific hum of Gunner's bike. I should've expected a visit given what had happened at The Cauldron.

My stomach did a slow, deliberate roll. Gunner's effect on me wasn't something I could explain. It's not as if I hadn't dated in Detroit. In fact, I dated regularly. Well, kind of. In truth, I dated someone for two weeks and then found a reason to break up with him. I didn't bond easily ... although all the natural defense mechanisms I'd built up over my life to protect my heart seemed to have fallen by the wayside where Gunner was concerned.

I didn't understand it. Oddly enough, I wasn't fighting his pull as much as I should either. I enjoyed having him around, which frustrated me on an entirely different level.

"Hey." His smile reflected genuine amusement as he killed the engine of his bike and yanked off his helmet. His hair fluttered past his shoulders as he looked me up and down. "Nice bedhead."

Crap! I'd forgotten about my nap. I was the type who slept hard, drooled and snored if I was exhausted enough. Merlin didn't seem to mind, but I had a feeling Gunner would be another story. If we made it that far, I mean.

Oh, who was I kidding? We were definitely going to make it that far. It wasn't a question of if. It was a question of when. We were like magnets. There was no keeping us apart.

"I took a nap," I offered, resisting the urge to order my hair. That would only make him laugh ... and give him power. I honestly didn't care how I looked. Er, well, at least most of the time. Sometimes the way he looked at me made me care, which only irritated me more.

"I figured." He smoothly slid off the bike, his motion liquid. He was tall and moved like a cat. "You don't look all that rested."

"I've been having weird dreams." The admission was out of my mouth before I thought better of it. Before, I wouldn't have even considered sharing the dream details with anyone. With him, things simply slid out of my mouth before I could stop myself.

He furrowed his brow. "What sort of dreams?" He climbed the steps and took the open chair next to me even though I'd forgotten my manners and didn't offer it. "Are we talking nightmares?"

I opened my mouth to answer — a snarky response on the tip of my tongue — but I couldn't force myself to sink to that level. He looked legitimately concerned. "I have dreams sometimes, about when I was a kid," I admitted. "I can't decide if they're memories or something I'm making up in my head to fill in the gaps."

He pursed his lips. "Do they feel real?" he asked.

"In the moment, yeah. I just don't know that they are real."

"Tell me about them."

I'd never told anyone about the dreams. Not really. Okay, sure, there had been the occasional blabber-filled night, but they always followed alcohol-fueled outings so the person I'd confided in almost always forgot. This would be different.

"Tell me," he prodded, his voice soft. "I want to know what's going on with you."

And that was the sad truth. He did. He wanted to understand. I was a difficult woman who wanted to keep people out, but he was determined to get in. If anyone had a shot of getting past my defenses, it was him.

I hated that he had this effect on me.

I let loose a sigh. There was no getting around this. "I've had the dream more than once." I launched into the tale, keeping it as clinical as possible.

Gunner listened, never once interrupting, and when I finished, he seemed thoughtful.

"You're sure she wasn't your mother?"

I nodded without hesitation. "I had to call her mother in public so people wouldn't question why we were together, but she definitely wasn't my mother."

"Do you remember your mother?"

"No."

"What about your father?"

"I don't ever remember having parents. Maybe they took one look at me after my birth, decided I was a waste of space and abandoned me."

Immediately, he started shaking his head. "I don't think that's right. Somebody obviously took care of you for the first few years of your life. I think it's far more likely that your parents were killed and you were cared for by others of your ... kind."

I arched an eyebrow at his obvious discomfort. "My kind?"

He didn't back down. "You're not a normal witch. You clearly have witch in your bloodline. There's something else there, too. The fact that you have elemental magic at your disposal — why did you keep that secret, by the way? — could be a hint."

"I didn't realize it was elemental magic," I said. That was mostly true. I was street smart more than book smart. It wasn't that I was uneducated as much as I preferred rushing headlong into a problem and learning by doing rather than sitting back and waiting for answers to come to me. "I told you. Most of the magic I do just happens. I don't really plan it out."

"Which is why you're terrifying." Gunner's grin was friendly. "I wouldn't offer a monster a free pass out of town again if I were you, though. Rooster doesn't like it."

I'd figured that out. "Yeah, well ... ." I trailed off, my eyes holding his for an extended beat. Finally, I asked the obvious question. "Not that I'm not happy to see you, but what's going on? Why are you out here?"

"Well, I thought it was time we talked about our date."

My heart skipped a beat. "What date? We haven't gone on a date."

"No, but we agreed to go on one."

I vaguely remembered. Okay, I remembered every moment of that conversation, but when he didn't follow up on the initial inquiry I'd tried to convince myself he'd changed his mind. It would be easier for me if he was the one who pulled the plug on whatever this was. "I thought maybe you'd changed your mind."

"No." His smile widened. "I wanted to give you a bit of time to settle. You've had more than enough time now, so we should pin down a date."

That was very ... organized ... of him. "Oh, well, I'm not sure what my schedule is like." I averted my gaze. "Maybe we should play it by ear."

He didn't immediately speak, which I took as a bad sign, but after a few moments of quiet he cleared his throat, essentially forcing my attention to him.

"What?" I was feeling defensive as I gripped my hands together.

His expression softened when he registered my reaction. "I didn't say anything."

"You're thinking it."

"I'm thinking a lot of things."

"Like what?"

"Like ... I think we should go on our date now."

"What?" My voice came out squeakier than I expected. "You can't be serious."

"Oh, I'm serious." He chuckled at my discomfort. "If I wait for you to be ready for this, we'll still be dancing around each other a month from now. That's not what I want. I'm pretty sure it's not what you want either."

He wasn't wrong. Still, I couldn't wrap my head around what I was allowing to happen. "Maybe ... maybe we shouldn't do this." I hated the dark look that crossed his handsome features, but that didn't stop me from barreling forward. "This could be a mistake. What if we hate each other? Then we'll have to keep working together and it'll be awkward."

"We won't hate each other. That's not what you're worried about."

There was a challenge in his smile, almost a dare. "Oh, yeah? What am I worried about?"

"That you're going to become so attached to me you'll never want to leave."

His ego was clearly out of control. "Listen here ... ."

He was on his feet. "I'll give you an hour to get ready. As much as I like the bedhead look, I'm taking you to a nice restaurant. It's not in Hawthorne Hollow, which I think is best for both of us. The restaurant I have in mind isn't formal, but you should probably steer clear of leather ... which you can keep for our second date."

Flirty energy flowed from him and practically smacked me in the face. "I need the leather to hold back the wind on my bike," I pointed out.

"This is a date," he reminded me. "I have a truck. I'll be picking you up."

I hadn't thought of that. "Oh, well ... ."

NO CRONES ABOUT IT

He cut me off with a wave of his hand. He obviously wasn't going to allow me the opportunity to talk myself out of this. "I'll see you in an hour. If you're not here, I'm simply going to track you down. Running will get you nowhere."

I'd already figured that out. The time for running was over. It was time to put up or shut up ... and shutting up is never an option for me.

FOUR

*a*s far as dates go, it was a pretty good one.

After I got over my initial nerves, the conversation eased and I found myself laughing harder than I could ever remember.

Gunner was a gifted storyteller, and the tales he told about his youth in Hawthorne Hollow — including his father's insistence on arresting him along with the other kids raising hell in the town — had me shaking with delight.

The restaurant he picked wasn't formal, but it wasn't a diner. We both settled on prime rib and potatoes, which we inhaled as if we hadn't eaten in weeks it was so good, and when we were finished he suggested a walk along the lake. Given the way the moon reflected off the water and the wind tousled our hair, I had a feeling he suggested the walk because of the romantic ambiance ... but I wasn't exactly complaining.

"That was awesome," I enthused, laughing as he sat on the beach and turned his attention to his shoes. "What are you doing?"

"You can't walk the beach with shoes on," he explained. "You need to be barefoot."

"I think you're making that up."

"And I think you're afraid to walk on the beach with me. Chicken?"

My lips curved down. "You don't have to dare me to get me to do something. Sometimes it's okay to just ask."

His eyes were hard to read when they locked with mine. "Fair enough," he said after a beat. "The thing is, you tend to talk yourself out of things if I don't push you a bit. If I dare you, you always come through.

"I think I get it, by the way," he continued. "You don't want to get attached to anyone. In your position I probably wouldn't do it any differently. That doesn't seem like the healthy way to go, though. It's okay to get attached."

I held his gaze for what felt like a really long time and then sighed as I sank to the sand. Even though it was a date, I opted for simple black trousers and a peasant top. I wasn't the skirt sort. I couldn't remember the last time I wore a skirt, in fact. If Gunner was bothered by my outfit, he didn't show it. Instead, the relief on his face when he showed up on the porch and I opened the door — clearly ready and without an excuse on the tip of my tongue — was palpable.

"I haven't even decided if I'm staying here over the long haul," I reminded him. "This was supposed to be a temporary assignment."

"Do you want it to be a temporary assignment?"

That was the question. "I don't know." I searched for an answer that would satisfy the both of us. It wasn't easy. "I never considered myself the country sort, but ... I like this place. I would be lying if I said I didn't."

His grin was back. "Do you like it because I'm here?"

I wanted to throttle him ... and then maybe kiss him. It was a fine line. "I like you." I couldn't lie. I hated those demure girls who played games with people's emotions. I didn't know a lot about myself growing up — it always seemed like a long, hard slog to get any insight about myself — but I did know that. "I don't know if I'll be good for you."

He was clearly surprised by my response. "I don't understand."

"You said it yourself. I'm a live wire who acts before I think. It's possible Rooster will give me the boot at some point. You're clearly never leaving Hawthorne Hollow, so what does that mean? Aren't you afraid that we'll grow attached to one another and then something will tear us apart?"

He worked his jaw, his mind busy. Before speaking again, he licked his lips and tilted his head. "I get why you're afraid," he started, his voice soft. "I like to pretend that I had some horrible upbringing because my father is difficult. What you went through is ten times worse.

"I don't know anything about the foster care system, but the things you've told me make it seem awful," he continued, holding up his hand when I indicated I was about to lodge a protest. "That wasn't meant to be a blanket statement."

I couldn't stop myself from arguing. "Most of the people in the foster care system are saints. They're good people trying to help. It's only a few who make things difficult, taint the system. I had both good and bad foster parents growing up. I don't want you to think I'm scarred by them."

"Aren't you?" Gunner shot me a challenging gaze. "You are without a doubt the most frustrating person I've ever crossed paths with. You speak before you think. You pick fights at the drop of a hat. And your ego, honey, well ... it's a thing to behold."

I narrowed my eyes. The date had taken a turn I wasn't expecting. "You're the last one who should talk about ego."

"I know. Your ego is actually bigger than mine. That's a Hawthorne Hollow miracle."

I didn't want to laugh. It would only encourage him. I couldn't stop myself, though. "I'm just saying that most foster parents are good. I don't want to give you the wrong impression."

"Duly noted." He reached over and snagged my hand, causing my heart to skip a beat. His proximity always had this effect on me. I couldn't explain it. "It makes sense for you not to trust. I can't help but feel you're missing out on the best things in life because of it."

He edged closer to me. Not so much that he was invading my personal space, but near enough that I could feel the warmth radiating off his body.

"You deserve to find a place to call home," he prodded. "I think deep down you want that. It's probably difficult for you to admit, more difficult than it should be, but it's true. This could be your home if you just open yourself up to it."

What he said made sense, but I wasn't always rational. "What if I find I can't live in the country? I mean ... I like going to the movies in the middle of the night. You can't do that here."

He snorted. "Is that the hill you're going to die on? Movies?"

"It's just a symptom of the bigger problem here," I admitted. "What if I'm not geared for country life?"

"You won't know unless you give it a try. You'll always have questions if you leave without giving this your best effort."

"And what if I do that and still want to leave? I don't want to hurt you."

"I'm a big boy. I don't want you to leave. I can say that without hesitation. If, in the end, you can't stay here, I won't fight you. I wouldn't ask you to sacrifice your happiness for mine. It's way too soon to tell if you'll like it here ... but I think you actually do like it and you're fighting the notion of staying simply because you're stubborn."

I shot him a challenging gaze. "You're stubborn, too. That might be another potential powder keg. Have you considered that?"

"I've considered it all." His eyes were sincere. "I'm attracted to you – like you wouldn't believe. My skin sometimes feels as if it's humming when you're around. I want a chance to see if we can make something out of this. I would rather try and fail than not try at all."

And we were back to him daring me to stay. "I'm willing to give it a try. I just ... don't want to disappoint you."

"If you go into this assuming you'll disappoint me, the odds of it becoming a self-fulfilling prophecy are huge. Open your heart. Give it your best shot. I think you'll be surprised by what happens if you simply give in to your urges."

"Are we talking about sexual urges?"

"Eventually." His full smile was back. "Right now, I'm fine with this."

"And what is this?"

"A walk on the beach. I want you to tell me more about your dreams."

I was taken aback. "That doesn't sound very romantic."

"Not everything between us has to be romantic." He was sober. "I want to help you. If these dreams are memories, there might be a clue in them. Whether you want to admit it or not, you need answers. I want to help you find them."

I hesitated, but only for a moment. "It's a long story."

"Then I guess it's good we have a big beach and nothing but time on our hands."

I TOLD HIM ALL OF IT. Everything I could remember. He listened, held my hand as we splashed our feet in the frigid water, and offered the occasional comment.

"None of the dreams have identifiable characteristics," he noted. "I mean ... it's always the same woman. That's good. The memory is from twenty-three years ago. If she's still alive, she probably wouldn't look the same ... and it doesn't sound like you picked up a name.

"The thing is, you're not actively remembering these scenarios," he continued. "They're coming at you in dreams. I can't help but think that's on purpose."

"How so?"

"I think you're not supposed to remember. I think someone spelled you not to remember. At five, you were old enough to form memories and impressions of what was happening around you. The fact that you have no memories, only dreams, indicates that your subconscious is trying to fight what was done to you."

I had never considered that. "I ... ."

"If you want to try to break the spell, I know a few people," he offered, squeezing my hand. "Think about it. There's a very real chance that you're better off not knowing."

He had a point, but still ... . "I'll think about it." For once — and I could rarely say this — I was tired of talking about myself. "Are you looking forward to Raisin's play?"

He laughed as he tucked a strand of hair behind my ear. "Hit your limit of talking about serious stuff, eh? I understand that. When you're ready to talk again, just let me know."

I sighed. He had a sweet nature that was often buried under a thick layer of sarcasm — something we had in common — but he managed to be tough, too. It was an interesting blend of masculinity and emotional grounding that made him all the more appealing.

"I thought maybe you would want to talk about something else," I hedged.

"I'm fine talking about anything. Getting you to open your mouth for anything other than snarky comments is sometimes difficult."

I wanted to argue with his assessment but couldn't. "Yeah, well ... ."

He laughed again, his gregarious chuckle bouncing against the waves. "You are ... something." His fingers were gentle as they brushed against my cheek, and my breath clogged in my throat at the way he looked at me. It was obvious what was about to happen. The outside world had ceased to exist. It was only the two of us now.

"Do you feel that?" His eyes never moved from mine as he shifted my fingers to his wrist. I could feel the steady beat of his heart, and it seemed fast. In fact, the rhythm matched mine. "You do weird things to me," he offered. "I haven't been this nervous about kissing someone since I was twelve and doing it for the first time."

I was understandably dubious. "Twelve?"

His grin was back, sly. "I was advanced for my age."

"It doesn't count if you kiss your sister."

He extended a warning finger. "Just for the record, incest jokes are never funny."

"Good to know." I exhaled a long breath. "I ... ." I had no idea what I was going to say. It didn't matter. We leaned toward each other at the same moment, our lips inches apart ... and then movement to the left caught our attention and we both jerked our heads in that direction.

We might've been on a date but we were trained to recognize potential danger. What we found on the beach was something else entirely.

"Hey!" Gunner took a step away from me. He grasped what was happening before I could wrap my head around it.

In the city it was nothing to run into muggers. It was something you simply became accustomed to. Pickpockets were one breed of criminal. Muggers were another. Overt thieves were something else. I hadn't expected to have to worry about my bag while we were in the middle of nowhere ... and I was regretting that now.

The man who stood next to the spot where we'd discarded our shoes and coats jerked his head up in surprise. He clearly wasn't expecting us to look in his direction. As a shifter, Gunner had superior hearing. I realized it was his reaction to the sound that caused me to look.

The thief had my wallet open and was pulling out bills when he heard Gunner call to him. He stood there, frozen, and then he dropped the wallet and turned on his heel and booked into the night. The reaction was so comical — almost like a scene plucked from a sitcom — I had to swallow the absurd urge to laugh. Gunner had a different reaction.

"Wait here," he ordered, putting his head down as he broke into a run. "I'll be right back."

"Gunner, wait!"

He was already disappearing into the night before I regained my senses. While I was disappointed about losing the moment we were sharing seconds earlier I was more worried about him giving chase. If the man was desperate enough to sneak up on us given the circumstances, he might be desperate enough to go after Gunner. It wasn't that I didn't think he could take care of himself — especially against a non-paranormal who looked a little worse for wear — it was more that I didn't want him to waste his time. There was very little cash in the wallet. If that man needed it so desperately, I would willingly let him have it.

"Well, that was exciting," a voice called out, causing me to freeze.

When I slowly turned, I found Flint standing near the shoreline, his gaze on me. "Twice in one day," I noted. "That's ... convenient." I was mostly bothered by the fact that he'd managed to sneak up on me — much like the man who took my wallet — without me noticing. Either my senses were diluted or I was allowing Gunner to get to me. I had a feeling it was the latter.

"It's just a lucky coincidence," Flint called out. "We were checking out the lake access when we saw you."

"And you just happened to run into me in a different town?" I wasn't much for coincidences. I also didn't believe Flint was the sort of man who traveled alone. He wasn't strong enough to protect himself, which meant ... . I tilted my head to the side and smirked when I felt another mind join the fray. "Mr. Frost," I announced. "Why am I not surprised that you're here, too?"

A quick flutter of surprise washed over Drake before he moved into my sightline. He shuttered his emotions quickly, masking his reaction faster than most, and offered me a quirky grin. "I wasn't sure you were aware I was here."

"I'm aware of more than you can imagine." I craned my neck and looked in the direction Gunner had fled. There was no sign of him. That meant things were about to become interesting between the three of us ... and I couldn't help but wonder if that was purposeful. What were the odds of two different factions showing up at the same time in the middle of nowhere? They couldn't be good.

"Did you need something specific?" I asked, slanting my chin in Drake's direction. Flint might've been the one in charge, but Drake was clearly stronger.

"What makes you think we want something?" Flint challenged. "I told you it was a coincidence."

"I don't believe in coincidences. This feels just a little too ... out of the blue."

"Are you afraid of us?" Flint's expression was wolfish. "You don't have to be. We're perfectly nice men. There's no need to be fearful."

"You've got that wrong," Gunner announced, detaching from the trees between the two men. Somehow he'd doubled back without making a sound. That probably meant he'd been listening in the trees, trying to get a feel for our new friends. I wasn't particularly worried about taking them myself if it became necessary. Still, I was glad to have backup in the form of another wolf. Gunner would be able to suss out their intentions faster.

"We've got what wrong?" Flint asked, his eyes moving to Gunner. There was a challenge there and it made me nervous.

"You should be fearful of her," Gunner replied. "There's no way she's fearful of you."

"You sound sure of yourself."

"You have no idea." Gunner's eyes landed on me. "I take it these are the friends you made this afternoon."

"I wouldn't call them friends, but ... yeah."

"What a fortuitous meeting of the minds," he drawled, folding his arms over his chest. "I think we have some things to discuss, gentlemen, and there's no time like the present."

FIVE

I was familiar with male posturing, but the testosterone fog I found myself mired in was off the charts.

I took a moment to glance between faces and considered crossing between the men to position myself next to Gunner should a fight break out, but then realized it was a bad move. We were balanced this way. If Drake and Flint decided to attack, we could easily take them out ... as long as they were alone.

With that in mind, I shifted to study the tree line near Drake. His full attention was on me, as if he didn't even notice Gunner, and the way he stared made me uncomfortable.

"We're not doing anything," Flint announced after a few moments of silence. "Whatever you're thinking ... ." He trailed off and I didn't miss the disapproving look Drake shot him.

"If that were true you wouldn't feel the need to say it," Gunner noted. His expression was hard to read as he studied Flint. I didn't sense he was about to strike, but I couldn't rule it out. "I find it interesting that you ended up here of all places. I mean ... this place is off the beaten track."

"Not so far off the beaten track," Drake countered. "There's a restaurant right down there." He gestured toward the direction we'd walked from. "I hear the food is divine."

I didn't comment. Odds were he knew we'd eaten there. The notion that they were simply out here to enjoy the view was laughable. Besides, this was shifter business. It made sense to defer to Gunner. He had more knowledge than I did, which was something I was loath to admit in mixed company.

"I'm familiar with your father," Gunner noted, his gaze returning to Flint. "I think we probably met a time or two when we were kids."

"Perhaps," Flint confirmed. "What's your name?"

"Gunner Stratton."

"I know of a Graham Stratton. He's the chief of police."

"He's my father." Gunner was calm. "We share the same name, but I go by Gunner these days."

"Ah." Amusement lit Flint's dark eyes. "Then we have met. It's been a long time."

"Yup."

I noticed Gunner didn't bother with the handy lie that it had been too long. That was probably for the best because nobody would believe it anyway.

I cleared my throat to break the tension. "Well, as fun as it's been running into you guys … again … we should probably be going." I pinned Gunner with a pointed look. "Are you ready?"

He looked torn, as if he believed a fight might be warranted. Ultimately, though, he nodded. "We should get our shoes. We'll be out of your way in a moment, gentlemen." He held out his hand. A clear message was being sent with the move and I took it without hesitation. I wanted the message sent as much as he did.

We were halfway back to our belongings when Flint called out to us.

"I didn't realize you were already spoken for, *witch*."

I didn't slow my pace, but the words ratcheted up my ire. He was trying to throw me off, make me understand that they were aware of who and what I was. Well, they were in for a surprise.

Gunner apparently agreed.

"She speaks for herself," Gunner offered, never looking over his shoulder. "If you plan to test her – if that's what this was tonight – you'll wish you'd kept walking."

"Are you blaming us for this?" Drake asked. "If so, you should know that we had nothing to do with it."

"For your sake, I certainly hope so."

WE MADE THE DRIVE BACK TO the cabin in relative silence. It wasn't an uncomfortable atmosphere, but it was hardly the heightened sexual display we'd been experiencing before we were so rudely interrupted.

"I take it you didn't catch our friend," I supplied as he pulled into my drive-way. "He must've been faster than he looked."

Gunner quirked an eyebrow as he put his truck in park. "I probably could've caught him, but I sensed trouble once I followed him into the forest. I felt an overwhelming urge to check on you, and because money is replace-able and you're not, I went with my gut."

It was a simple statement and yet it warmed me all over. Still, I couldn't let him turn all alpha. "You know I can take care of myself, right?"

He chuckled. "I have no doubt."

"I can take care of you, too, if necessary."

"I have no doubt about that either." He hopped out of the vehicle, leaving me flummoxed. I thought it was an odd way to end a potential argument until I realized that wasn't what he was doing. He pulled open the passenger-side door and held out his hand. "Hopefully you'll get to where you believe we can take care of each other."

I remained in my seat, unsure what to do. I couldn't remember a man ever opening a door for me. I realized now that he had tried when we reached the restaurant, but I'd been too fast for him. I really should've seen this coming.

"Scout?" Laughter laced his husky voice.

I exhaled heavily and then took his hand. "You really didn't have to open the door for me." I hit the ground with a thud, my chest bumping against his in the process. He didn't back up.

"That's what people do on dates."

"I've never been on a date where someone opened the door for me."

"Oh?" He cocked his head to the side, considering. "Perhaps you've been going out with the wrong men."

"Perhaps."

"It's a good thing we're rectifying that."

My cheeks burned at his mocking gaze. "You know what your problem is?" I asked when I'd regained at least a modicum of moxie. "You're far too charming. No one should be allowed to have as much charm as you."

He laughed. "I think that's the nicest thing you've ever said to me."

We were close enough that I could feel his breath on my cheek. This seemed to be the moment of truth and yet my nerves were getting the better of me. "What do you think about our new friends?"

A wisp of agitation washed over his features, but he didn't pull away. "They're intrigued by you. They obviously saw you take down the siren. I doubt they came to town specifically for you, but now that they've seen what you can do … they want you."

41

I lifted my chin so we were staring directly into each other's eyes. "They can't have me."

"I certainly hope not." His smile spread. "They're curious ... and maybe a little leery. I think they wanted to throw you by using the word 'witch.' Seeing you with me makes them understand that you're not exactly hiding who you are ... or what you can do."

It was an interesting take and I'd pretty much come to the same conclusion. "They followed us. There's no other explanation for what they were doing there."

"I agree. But I can't decide if they were following me and got lucky in finding you or they were following you and had their eyes opened to reality when they stumbled across me."

Absently, I raised my hand and pressed it to his chest. He was solid muscle and I could feel his heart beating, thick and strong. "They make me nervous. They've managed to sneak up on me twice. I wrote the first time off because I was busy with the siren and it was a new experience for me. I can't write off the second time."

He chuckled. "Are you sure? I seem to remember we were about to engage in a new experience at the exact moment our friendly neighborhood thief showed up."

Well, he wasn't wrong. "Yeah, but ... ." My breath caught at the way he was looking at me. He was far too pretty – almost criminally so – and I hated the way he made me feel. I also loved it at the same time. It was a weird dichotomy. "You're going to kiss me, aren't you?"

"Oh, yeah. Nothing in the world could stop me this time. I don't care if ten robbers show up, I'm definitely kissing you."

That was both a relief and cause for alarm. "Maybe I don't kiss on the first date."

He continued to stare for a long time and then heaved a sigh. "Well, if that's your stance, I have no choice but to respect it." He took a purposeful step back, leaving me with nothing but disappointment once I could no longer draw on his body heat. "Eventually you'll want to kiss me. I guess I'll just have to wait."

Before I realized what I was doing, I snapped out my hand and grabbed the front of his button-down shirt, hauling him back to the spot he'd occupied only seconds before. "I've given it some thought," I whispered as his eyes went wide. "I definitely kiss on the first date."

His smile turned sloppy. "Good. Then you'd better prepare yourself." Instead of giving me the time I expected, he dipped close and pressed his lips against mine. It was as if he couldn't wait – which was fine because I couldn't wait either – and we collided with an explosion of hormones.

His hands tangled in my hair. I almost fell into him because of the fireworks going off in my head, my equilibrium dissipating in the flare.

It must've gone on for ten minutes ... or maybe ten years. I guess it was possible it went on only ten seconds. I felt changed when we finally separated, both of our chests heaving.

"Well ... that was interesting," he said after a moment.

I could do nothing but laugh. "Yeah."

He sucked in a breath, perhaps steadying himself, and then extended a hand to smooth my hair. "It was a pretty good first date."

"Yeah." That seemed to be the only word I could muster.

"I think we're going to need a second date to make sure it wasn't a fluke."

I pursed my lips. There was that charm on full display again. "I guess I could be persuaded."

"Good. But for now I'm going to walk you to your door and be a gentleman ... and you have no idea how difficult that is for me."

I had some idea, but I decided to play things his way. The trip was just as much fun – if not more – as reaching the destination.

I SLEPT HARD. THIS TIME no cumbersome dreams weighed me down. All I saw this particular evening were flashes of Gunner ... and maybe I heard a few ridiculous moans. I was fairly certain he wasn't a gentleman in the dream, but it was my subconscious assigning motivations, so I could hardly blame him.

I woke with a jolt, a loud pounding dragging me back to reality. I was convinced I'd imagined the sound until I looked over at Merlin and saw the hair on his back standing. The pounding came again, this time echoing throughout the small cabin. Someone was at my front door and they were unbelievably impatient.

"I'm coming," I grumbled, rolling out of bed. I would've preferred hiding my head under the covers and attempting to reclaim the dream, but that seemed out of the question. I double-checked my outfit as I padded over the hardwood floors. I'd changed into simple knit shorts and a T-shirt to sleep. It wasn't an appropriate outfit for an early-morning visitor, but I wasn't exactly feeling gracious.

"What the ... ?" I threw open the door with enough force that I hoped whoever had decided to wake me would run in the other direction. I pulled up short when I realized I was looking at the chief of police, Graham Stratton, Gunner's father. I recovered quickly. "Good morning."

Graham quirked an eyebrow as he looked me up and down. I could pretty much guess what he was thinking … and it wasn't complimentary. "Nice hair," he said finally.

I didn't give him the satisfaction of tackling my bedhead. "That's what happens when you wake me at the crack of dawn."

"It's almost eight," he shot back. "Late night?"

I narrowed my eyes. The question felt like a trap. "Maybe. Why does it matter?"

"We have a situation and I'm trying to pin down your alibi."

That didn't sound good. "Oh, um … seriously?" I had no idea how to respond. This was hardly the first time I'd been questioned by the cops. "I was out with Gunner last night."

Instead of giving me grief, Graham looked relieved. "How late?"

I racked my memory. "I guess it was almost midnight when he dropped me off."

"Was this a date?"

"I don't see how that's any of your business."

"I don't care because of you. I care because I like to keep abreast of my son's activities."

"Does he want you to keep abreast of his activities?"

"Not so much."

"Then … I'm not answering that. You'll have to ask him."

"That's okay. You've already told me all I need to know. Besides, I've seen the way he looks at you. It was only a matter of time."

That was possibly very flattering … or something else. "As enlightening as I find this conversation, do you have a reason for pounding so incessantly on my door this morning?"

His half-smile slipped and he sobered. "I need you to get dressed and follow me downtown."

I was back to being alarmed. "Why?"

"Just … do as I ask. Please."

He didn't strike me as the sort of man who asked politely very often so I nodded. "Can you give me fifteen minutes to shower and change?"

"I'll wait right here."

"Great. I kept my face blank until I shut the door and then let my mind wander. What was going on here?

· · ·

IT DIDN'T TAKE LONG FOR MY question to be answered. I insisted on driving myself downtown. If Graham had a problem with that, he didn't say so. The sight that greeted me in the alley behind the library was straight out of my nightmares, and any thoughts I had of giving Graham grief quickly dissipated.

"Holy ... !" I was agog when I climbed off my bike, absently pocketing my key. Through sheer habit, I remembered to remove the helmet so I could better stare at the body.

I vaguely recognized him. He was the thief from the night before, the man who managed to escape Gunner. He was strung up between two light posts – something that seemingly defied gravity – and the insides of his abdomen were on the outside.

I swallowed hard as I stared at his face, his sightless eyes open and his mouth agape. It looked like he died screaming.

"There's more," Graham noted, ignoring the stares his officers shot in my direction. "You need to go around back."

I slid him a sidelong look and swallowed hard. Something told me I didn't want to see the back of this man, but it was important enough that Graham was playing it coy.

"Okay." I nodded, stiffly, and then walked around the light posts. I gave the body a wide berth ... and then almost fell over when I saw the travesty before me.

His shirt had been ripped, his skin bared, and someone had written a message on his back. If I had to guess, they used a small blow torch to do it. The sight made me sick to my stomach ... and that was before the message sank in.

For you, Scout Randall.

That's all it said, as if it was some sort of tribute. I generally had a strong stomach, but the notion that someone had tortured this man for me, as an offering of some sort, was more than I could bear.

"Oh, my ... ." I turned away and rested my hands on my knees.

"I take it you didn't do this." Graham almost looked relieved. "That's good. I don't think my son would take kindly to me hauling you in. I would do it, don't get me wrong, but it would be a war."

"I'm glad you don't have to fight with your son." I wiped the back of my hand against my mouth, my stomach threatening to revolt. "And no, I didn't do that. Why would I burn my name into a murder victim? It doesn't make any sense."

"I'm not saying this makes sense. I'm just relieved you didn't have anything to do with it."

"I could be lying," I pointed out. "Maybe I'm trying to fool you."

"I don't think you're the type who can fake a reaction like this. Besides, I didn't really think you did it in the first place. Now the tough questions begin. Someone is trying to get your attention. Who?"

That was the question, wasn't it? I wasn't sure I had an answer. "I don't know, but I'm going to handle the retribution myself when we find out."

"We'll just see about that."

"Yeah, we will."

SIX

*G*raham instructed me to take a seat beneath the shade of a large maple tree. I wanted to leave — oh, how I wanted to run — but I didn't think that would go over well, so I did as he instructed. Besides, I felt lightheaded. I was used to blood and gore, absolutely horrible scenes, but this felt worse.

At a certain point — it must've been at least an hour after I sat down — Graham joined me. He had a bottle of water and a look of concern.

"You don't look well."

I shot him a derisive glare. "Thanks. I can tell your son didn't get his charm from you."

He arched an eyebrow. "You might be surprised. But to be fair, the boy has always been magical when it comes to drawing people in."

"Not you, though?"

"What makes you say that?"

I shrugged as I cracked the cap of the water bottle. "You just don't seem to like him all that well." I had no idea what made me say it, but it was easier to focus on Graham and Gunner's tempestuous relationship than the dead body that was seemingly staring at me with accusatory eyes.

"I like him fine. He hasn't always been the most focused kid. That's changed the past year or so ... and I can't say I'm not happy to see it." His eyes were thoughtful as they roamed my face. "He seems to like you."

"And you're basing that on what?" It wasn't as if he'd spent an inordinate

47

amount of time with us — or more than five minutes, for that matter — so I was genuinely curious where he got his insight.

"I know him better than most, no matter what you might happen to believe. He definitely likes you."

"And I'm guessing that means you don't because you want something else for him." Hey, we were telling truths here. It seemed best to get this out of the way.

"I wouldn't say that." He relaxed into an easy smile. "You have a certain way about you. I would be lying if I said your background didn't worry me, but I guess that's not really your fault."

"You mean when I was abandoned at a firehouse in the middle of the night?" I couldn't muster surprise that he'd run me. In his position, I would've done the same. "I don't know. It's always possible I did something worth being abandoned."

"I don't believe that. I'm sorry for what happened to you."

He seemed serious, which caused some of the annoyance that had been building to dissipate. "Thanks, but it's not your fault."

"It might not be anybody's fault. I know you're more powerful than a normal witch. And before you ask, my son isn't the one who told me. I have a special relationship with Rooster, and he mentioned it."

I wasn't surprised. For Rooster to operate the way he did — with a certain amount of impunity — he would need Graham's blessing. "I don't know what I am. The only thing that probably matters from your perspective is that I'm not a shifter. I'm sure you want Gunner to settle with someone from your former pack ... or at least another wolf."

He guffawed, causing me to jerk back. "Oh, please. I learned a long time ago that Gunner is going to do what he wants to do. That includes changing his name, even though it's stupid. If he's set his sights on you, there will be no stopping him." He quieted for a beat before continuing. "You're not so bad. You've got a mouth on you, but as far as I can tell you have the same interests and you're unlikely to try to change him. You might be a good fit."

That was as warm and fuzzy as I'd ever seen Graham. Maybe I'd misjudged him. "Does that mean you'll stop giving Gunner a hard time?"

"Nope. We have our own unique relationship. I'll stay out of your relationship with my son if you stay out of mine."

I'd had worse offers. "Deal." I extended my hand, causing him to chuckle. "Deal."

We lapsed into silence for a few minutes before the calm of the morning was interrupted by Gunner's arrival. He didn't look happy as he muscled his way through the cops lining the scene.

"Speak of the devil." Graham's eyes lit with mirth as his son stalked in our direction. "He's angry."

I was confused. "Why? I didn't kill this guy."

"Not at you. He's angry with me for dragging you down here without giving him a heads-up. I've told him repeatedly that I don't have to run my work past him, but he doesn't seem to agree."

"He'll be fine." I offered up a dismissive wave as Gunner stomped his way to the spot directly in front of me. "Good morning, Sunshine."

He glared. "What's going on?" The question was directed toward Graham. "I heard you brought Scout in for questioning on a murder."

Graham was unflappable. "Who told you that?"

"The entire town is buzzing with it. For the record, she was with me last night."

"I heard. Date night, huh?" Graham's lips twitched as Gunner glowered at him. "I've already had a long discussion with Scout. The problem is, you dropped her off around midnight. This guy didn't show up here until at least two or so. We're still trying to pin down a time of death, so she's not exactly covered."

Gunner worked his jaw. "We were together all night." The lie rolled off his lips, causing me to shift uncomfortably. Graham knew that wasn't true.

"Don't." Graham extended a warning finger, his expression darkening. "This is not the time to lie to law enforcement."

"How do you know I'm lying?"

"Scout was alone this morning when I woke her. And, while you haven't always had impeccable taste in women, you're still a gentleman. You wouldn't have abandoned her in the middle of the night if you were at that point in your relationship yet."

Gunner looked as if he wanted to argue, but he held it together. "She didn't do this. You know that."

"I do know that." Graham nodded in confirmation. "Before you get your panties in a twist, I was fairly certain she had nothing to do with it when I landed on her porch this morning. I still had to question her and you know that. Her name is burned into this guy."

"What?" Confusion slid across Gunner's handsome features.

Graham chuckled. "Did you even bother looking at the body?"

Gunner shifted his gaze to me, held it for a moment, and then he exhaled heavily before focusing on the body. I watched him for a reaction and wasn't

AMANDA M. LEE

disappointed. I recognized exactly when he realized who had been strung up between the poles.

"Oh, geez."

Graham stiffened at his son's reaction. "What was that?"

Gunner didn't immediately answer and I knew better than to fill the silence with lies.

"We saw that guy last night," I volunteered.

Gunner glared as he swiveled, annoyance rolling off him in waves. "What are you doing?"

I waved off the question. There was no reason to start lying now. "We were on the beach and he showed up." I related the story to Graham with cold precision, making sure to keep any emotion out of the retelling. If Graham thought I was upset about what had happened, he might change his mind about my guilt. "I wasn't too worried about the money," I finished. "It was only twenty bucks."

"The money means nothing," Graham agreed. "The fact that you guys were likely the last people to be seen near him is a wrinkle I didn't realize I was going to have to iron. It's bad enough that Scout's name is burned into this guy ... but for you to have actually seen him ... ." He trailed off and I could see his mind working.

"I don't think it's an accident that he showed up here," Gunner said finally. "Someone is trying to send a message."

"To Scout?" Graham appeared intrigued at the prospect. "Why would she be the focal point?"

I briefly wondered if Gunner would admit to our run-in with the wolves. He didn't — hardly surprising — and instead shrugged.

"I don't know," he said finally. "Word might be spreading that she's more powerful than the average witch. That could draw in looky-loos."

Graham looked up at the sun. I could tell he didn't believe the line of bull his son was spouting. To my surprise, he didn't challenge Gunner. "Well, I guess we'll have to keep our eyes open. We don't want Hawthorne Hollow's newest resident to get in over her head, do we?"

Gunner was grim. "Definitely not." He held out his hand to me. "We're going to be looking into this, too. I assume she's free to leave since she's not an official suspect."

Graham didn't look happy at the prospect, but he ultimately nodded. "Take her. Just make sure to watch her back." ·

"Don't worry about that. I'll be all over her."

That was a frightening thought.

. . .

GUNNER AND I SET UP SHOP behind the coffee shop. I slammed a huge mocha latte before asking the obvious question. The caffeine made me more jittery, but I needed the liquid energy.

"It has to be the other wolves, right?"

"That would be my guess, but we don't have proof of that." His expression was hard to read, but when he extended his arm and slipped it around my shoulders I happily gave in to the emotion flowing through me. He wanted to soothe ... and I needed it. "Are you okay otherwise?"

I nodded into his shoulder, taking a moment away from the prying eyes of others to collect myself and draw on his strength. He was already bolstering me, which seemed somehow miraculous. "I'm fine."

He used his finger to nudge up my chin so he could stare into my eyes. Apparently happy with what he found — there was no mental breakdown lurking in the shadows — he nodded. "Okay." He kissed my forehead and then pulled away. Now was not the time for smooching games under a tree. "I already texted Rooster. He's sending the new guy to check out the scene."

I was taken aback. "What new guy?"

"The new Spells Angels recruit."

That wasn't really an explanation. "I didn't know there was a new recruit." Something occurred to me. "Is he here for my position?"

Gunner jerked his head in my direction, surprised. "No. He was always scheduled to come here."

"Oh." That was good. At least I thought so. I wasn't ready to be pushed out.

"We want you here," Gunner insisted. "Don't ... do whatever it is you're doing. I can only take one crisis at a time and I'm assuming that face you're making is because you think we're trying to replace you. No one wants to replace you."

His vehemence was enough to make me smile. "Are you sure you're not speaking only for yourself? I know you don't want me to leave. The others, though ... ." I thought of Marissa's reaction during the showdown with the siren. "Some of the others might not be so keen to keep me."

"Screw Marissa!"

I laughed at his ability to read my mind. "It's not just her. Rooster wasn't exactly happy with me either."

"Rooster wants you here. He told me that. He's impressed with your talent. He simply wants to mold your attitude a bit. Don't let Marissa throw you. She does this to every member of the group."

That made me feel better, if only marginally. "Well, tell me about the new guy."

"He's weird."

We were essentially a gang of monster hunters on motorcycles — most of us with varying degrees of emotional trauma — so that wasn't exactly a defining explanation. "Be more specific."

"I think you should just meet him for yourself."

That sounded ominous.

CRAIG "DOC" DAVIDSON WAS MOST definitely weird. That was easy to ascertain at first glance. His movements were jerky and he had trouble making eye contact. That didn't mean he wasn't brilliant.

"Look at the eyes," he noted, his brown hair swept back from his interesting face. He wore glasses, the sort that made him look like a professor, and his attention was completely focused on the body rather than the cops buzzing around the scene. He was, in a word, fascinating.

He was also weird.

"What about the eyes?" Gunner asked. If he was bothered by the odd way Doc interacted with his environment, he didn't show it.

"They're frozen and open."

I pursed my lips. "Isn't that normal? I mean ... I've seen my fair share of bodies and while that's not always the case, I can't say this is the first time I've seen something similar."

"Yeah, but they were purposely frozen that way."

Gunner and I snared gazes before turning back to the body. Now that Doc mentioned it, there was something off about the eyes.

"The pupils look fixed or something," I said finally. "What would cause that?"

"Magic," Doc replied without hesitation. He hadn't as much as glanced in my direction and I couldn't help but wonder if he was on the spectrum. I was fine with that — and I understood about some of the issues he was grappling with — but it was off-putting when we were dealing with a dead body.

"Magic does that to the eyes?" Gunner asked.

"It's an old spell. I've seen it before." Doc rubbed his palms on the front of his jeans. "He was alive when this was done to him."

My stomach twisted. "I don't understand. What do you mean?"

"He was alive when the message was burned into him. He was alive until the end. Those who did this, they wanted him to feel every cut and burn. It's an ancient spell for torture. I'll have to do more research, but I'm almost positive that's the case."

My head felt light and swirly again. "But ... why?"

"It's a message," Doc replied casually. "They're sending a message to this Scout person. Do we know who that is?"

I tilted my head, struggling hard not to let my frustration take over. "I'm Scout."

"I introduced you when you arrived," Gunner added. "You shook her hand."

Doc didn't appear bothered by the rebuke. "Oh, well, that's convenient."

I almost wanted to laugh. Almost. "I don't know that 'convenient' is the word I would use. It's disturbing is what it is. Why would someone want to send this particular message? I mean ... I don't get it."

"I don't think any of us get it," Gunner said. "The message is too jumbled to make any sense."

"Oh, I wouldn't say that," Doc countered, his forehead wrinkling as he watched the cops lower the body. "The message makes sense to the person sending it. We didn't send it, so we're having trouble understanding. We simply need to put ourselves in the shoes of the sender and then we'll understand."

Gunner looked exasperated. "And how do you suggest we do that?"

Doc shrugged. "That's your job. I'm just here to look at the body and figure out the symbology." For the first time, he turned to me. "How many enemies do you have?"

That was a loaded question. "Enough. I don't know anyone who would hate me enough to do this. Even those wolves we saw ... I don't understand why they would do this. It doesn't make any sense."

"Maybe they're testing you," Gunner suggested. "I mean ... they're clearly infatuated with what you can do. This could be a test of some sort. You used elemental magic in front of them. They might think you're something other than what you really are."

That made sense, but it didn't feel right. "This is a weird test. All they're doing is ticking me off."

"You and me both." Gunner was grim as he watched the medical examiner's staff rush in to cover the body. "We're going to need an inside man on that autopsy."

Doc nodded without hesitation. "I'm on it." He stepped into the street without looking in either direction, causing Gunner to grab the back of his shirt and hold him in place until oncoming traffic passed. "I'll check in with the group later. I've got this."

I watched him go, bewildered. "You were right about him being weird," I said finally.

Gunner's laugh was warm and it chased away some of the cold still permeating my body. "He's definitely weird. He's supposed to be the best at what he does, though."

"So ... why is he here?"

"Is that a dig?"

"No. It's just ... if he's the best I can think of better locations for him. I think he's on the spectrum. I'm worried that he'll wander into the woods and never be seen again because he doesn't look before he leaps."

"Or crosses the street," Gunner groused. "I get what you're saying. Rooster was excited when he heard this guy was joining the group. I think we should give him the benefit of the doubt for now."

That was easier said than done, but it wasn't as if we had many options. "Yeah. I guess. What are we going to do about the wolves?"

"I have no idea. I doubt it'll be long before they show their faces. They'll want to crow about this if they did it ... and watch you for a reaction. We should be expecting them at any time."

That's exactly what I was afraid of.

SEVEN

*M*able's Country Table was the local diner. I'd spent years in Detroit, a city with issues swirling around violence and blight, but not food, so I expected my taste buds to be disappointed when I arrived in Hawthorne Hollow. Thankfully, I'd been wrong.

"I'll have the bacon cheeseburger with extra pickles and onions, and an order of chili fries," I volunteered as Mable took our order.

For her part, the persnickety diner owner appeared amused. "That's quite the refined palate you've got there."

"Add onions and mustard to the fries, too," I instructed.

Gunner leaned back in the booth seat across from me and shook his head. "You're going to kill yourself eating like that." Despite the words, his lips curved. "I'll have the turkey wrap and a side salad with lemon."

I frowned. "That's what you're eating?"

"If you're worried that I'm a healthy eater, don't. I have my share of junk. I try to offset it with a healthy lunch every day. Just one of my quirks."

It was a quirk that I couldn't fathom. "You ate prime rib for dinner last night ... and a baked potato ... and chocolate cheesecake."

Mable shifted from one foot to the other. "You two had dinner together?"

Her daughter, Mindy, was crossing behind her at the moment she asked the question. Mindy snapped her head in our direction, frown lines appearing on her forehead. The young woman had a crush on Gunner — that was evident from the moment I'd met her — and I could tell this conversation wasn't going anywhere pleasant.

"We did," Gunner replied before I could think of the best way to answer. He didn't appear to be interested in – or aware of – Mable's game. "We went over to Ruby's place on the lake. The food was really good."

"I heard the food was good," Mable confirmed. "I wouldn't know from personal experience because I would rather die than eat there – Ruby is a rotten sister, so she's probably a rotten cook – but I'll take your word for it."

Gunner chuckled as Mable's feisty nature made an appearance. "Oh, simmer down. You're still my favorite. We wanted a quiet place to eat where we wouldn't be under the microscope. You must understand that."

I couldn't believe how comfortable he was talking about our date in front of relative strangers. Of course, to be fair, they weren't strangers to him. I was the one who felt distinctly uncomfortable with the conversation.

"I don't blame you." Mable squeezed his shoulder. "You are Hawthorne Hollow's golden boy. You wouldn't have been able to get a word in edgewise over all the crying women if you had your date in the township limits." Her gaze was pointed when it landed on Mindy, who remained rooted to her spot, plates in her hands, and appeared absolutely crushed. "I'm glad you've found someone to tune your fiddle. Maybe that will give the women of this town a reason to move on."

Gunner finally caught on to what Mable was doing and shot her a quelling look. "Do you have to do that?"

She nodded without hesitation. "That girl still doodles your name on the notepads I keep by the phone. It's best she get over it."

If the glare Mindy pointed in my direction was any indication, her idea of moving on was going to involve running me over in the middle of Main Street and leaving me for dead. I swallowed hard and forced my attention back to Gunner. "How many women in this town doodle your name?"

He shrugged, his lips curving into a gorgeous smile. "I'm in demand. That should make you feel good about yourself."

"Yes," Mable agreed, bobbing her head. "You should feel pride in casting a line that managed to catch his attention and so expertly reeling him in. I wasn't certain it was possible."

The topic was starting to give me heartburn — and that was before I downed the chili fries — so I decided to change the topic. "Does anyone know the guy found behind the library? Is he a local?"

"Fred Burns?" Mable's expression turned decidedly dark. "Yeah, I know Fred. He's been around a long time."

"What can you tell us about him?" I asked.

"Not much. He was quiet, kept to himself, but stepped in if he found any kids bullying the little ones. He seemed to have a real thing about bullying, which makes me believe he was either terrorized as a kid or knew someone who was."

I couldn't contain my surprise. That was a fairly nuanced observation. "Did he try to protect you from being bullied?"

Mable snorted. "Honey, nobody bullies me. I'm guessing nobody bullies you either, so you understand what I'm saying. He wasn't the open sort, but he seemed okay. He wasn't a bad guy or anything, but ... frankly, he was a mess.

"He wasn't from around here and I have no idea how he got here," she continued. "I'd never seen him do drugs or anything, but I got the feeling he liked his pot from a few of our rare conversations. As for other stuff ... I'm not sure."

"I don't think he was a user," Gunner countered. "I mean ... I don't have specific knowledge of that. Whenever I saw him, it was on the street. I don't know where he spent his nights or anything. I never got the feeling he was using any hard drugs."

Mable shrugged. "You'd know better than me. Your father taught you to spot the signs of that stuff."

"We saw him last night on the beach by Ruby's place," Gunner volunteered. "We were out walking and he stole twenty bucks from Scout's wallet. I chased him, but I didn't know it was him because it was dark. He got away."

"Apparently he didn't make it far," Mable noted, tsking as she shook her head. "It's sad. I always hoped he would find a way to better his situation. I hoped he would find the strength to try. It never happened." She took a moment to collect herself. "Anyway, I'll put your order in. Just a suggestion for the future, girl, but you might want to lay off the onions. You've officially caught this one. You want to keep him ... and stinky breath isn't the way to do it."

I was mortified, my cheeks burning, and when I risked a glance at Gunner I found his shoulders shaking with silent laughter. "It's not funny," I hissed.

"It's kind of funny. As for the onions, knock yourself out. I'm a big fan of onions, and I don't care if your breath stinks. It kind of turns me on."

I narrowed my eyes. "You're a sick man."

"Oh, you have no idea."

MY PANTS FELT A LITTLE TOO TIGHT by the time we'd finished lunch.

The food bolstered my energy, sorely needed, and now that I had a few hours to think about Fred's death, my anger was starting to take center stage.

"We need to find the wolves," I insisted as I sucked down my soda. "They have answers."

Gunner held my gaze for a moment and then shrugged. "I don't think you have to worry about them. They'll find you."

"How can you be sure?"

He inclined his chin toward the front door. "Call it a hunch."

The hair on the back of my neck stood on end and my shoulders stiffened as Drake and Flint walked through the door – almost as if they'd sensed we'd been talking about them.

"Well, this can't be a coincidence."

"Actually, in this particular case, I'm not sure we can say that with any degree of certainty," Gunner countered. "I think it's unlikely they didn't know we were here, but this is one of the only decent places to eat in town. What happened last night is much more difficult to swallow."

Oh, well, if he wanted to be pragmatic. "I still think they were looking for us."

"And I think you're probably right." He flashed me a tight smile. "I know you're upset about this, but it would be best if you didn't fly off the handle and threaten them in front of an audience."

Exactly what sort of ninny did he take me for? "I have no intention of killing them here. If I'm going to take them out, you can be darned sure that there won't be any witnesses present."

"At least you've given it some thought."

He had no idea how much thought I'd given it.

Flint put on a big show as he entered, his gaze easily tracking from one end of the restaurant to the other. The last place he looked was at our table, which was obviously by design. "Well, hello again."

I glared at Gunner. "Still think it was an accident?"

He shook his head and leaned back in his seat. "He's obviously putting on a show for your benefit. You still can't kill him here."

"Yeah, yeah, yeah." I decided to ignore Flint and focus on my soda. The obvious slap had the intended effect.

"Hey." He appeared at the edge of the table and snapped his fingers in my face.

That was enough to cause me to see red, but before I could act Gunner lost his cool.

58

"Don't touch her," Gunner warned, slapping Flint's hand away from my face. "You won't like what happens if you do that again."

Flint snorted. "Oh, aren't you cute? I didn't realize things were so serious between you two. Are you declaring her your intended?"

I wasn't sure what to make of the question. Now didn't seem the time to put my ignorance of shifter culture on display, though. I filed my curiosity away to explore at a later date.

"It has nothing to do with that," Gunner replied tightly. "I simply prefer a modicum of respect be shown when dealing with ... well ... anyone. If you can't be courteous, perhaps you should leave."

Flint's gaze was keen. "Are you kicking me out of your town?"

Gunner shifted on his seat, uncomfortable. "I didn't say that."

I glanced at Drake and found him watching the conversation with obvious fascination. He didn't insert himself into the competition. He wisely stayed back.

"Of course you didn't," Flint chortled.

The lines of Gunner's face deepened. "If you keep this up, I will say it. I don't care who your father is. He might've earned his reputation, but you didn't. I won't allow you to harass Scout."

Flint's eyes flooded with fire. "If you want to challenge me, let's do it. There's a street right out front that's begging for a show. I have time right now. It will only take two minutes to kick your ass."

"There's not going to be a challenge," I argued, using my most commanding tone. "Whatever is happening here is ... unnecessary. There's no reason to start fighting.."

"I agree with our pretty friend," Drake offered, speaking for the first time and offering me a flirty wink. "I think a tempered approach is how we should handle things. There's no reason to get territorial."

Gunner looked as if he was going to argue, but he settled back into his spot and grabbed his glass. "It's fortuitous you guys arrived when you did," he said, regrouping. "We were going to track you down later."

"You were?" Flint appeared delighted. "I knew you wouldn't be able to stay away from me, Scout. Some things are destined."

I wanted to punch him in the center of his ego. "I agree." I held his gaze, my own steady. "Like, for example, I think your downfall is destined. It's only a matter of time before you get exactly what's coming to you."

"I have a few things I want to give to you, too," Flint shot back.

Gunner moved to stand, but I kicked him under the table, sending a not-so-subtle message. He managed to maintain control of his temper, but just barely. "We want to talk to you about the body found behind the library," he gritted out. "We don't want to accuse you or anything ... but given what happened last night."

Flint's expression changed in a split second and he adopted an air of innocence. "And what happened last night?"

"I'm more interested in the fact that a body was found," Drake volunteered. "I had no idea anything happened last night. Frankly, I'm shocked."

He was a poor liar and his delivery was flat. "You had no idea anyone died?" I challenged, gesturing toward the street in front of the diner. While Fred's body had been removed more than an hour ago, the police contingency remained to continue their investigation. "That seems rather doubtful."

Drake's smirk was smug. "I'm not saying I didn't realize there was a police situation. I'm simply saying that I had no idea it was a murder. That's very ... troubling."

"Especially because we're considering moving here and we want a safe environment," Flint added. "I hate the idea of relocating into a dangerous area."

"Then you should definitely settle someplace else," Gunner offered. The way he looked at Flint told me he wanted to press the man further. That would be a mistake — a big one — and I sent him a silent message in the hope he would pick up on that fact and back down.

If we tried to corner Flint and Drake now they would simply dig in their heels. It was obvious they were playing coy — and there's nothing I loathe more than game players — but we didn't have enough information or evidence to corner them. We had to play it smart, which was rarely the way I did things, but it was a necessity now. I could only hope Gunner felt the same.

Finally, as if in slow motion, Gunner wiped the corners of his mouth with his napkin and slowly got to his feet. "Well, if you'll excuse us, we have plans for the rest of our afternoon." He extended his hand to me.

I wasn't the sort who needed a man to maintain my dominance, but that's not the message Gunner was sending. He was trying to send a different sort of warning, that we were united and would fight together if it came to it. I was eager to send that same message.

I slipped my hand into his and offered Drake a pointed smile as I stood. "I'm sure we'll see each other again."

"That seems to be the way of things," he agreed. He'd shuttered whatever emotions he was feeling earlier, including the obvious delight coursing through him when it looked as if Gunner was going to fight. Now he simply looked on with interest. "It's a small town. There's nowhere to hide."

"You can say that again." I moved around him, my attention on the exit, and then I slowed my pace when the glass door opened to allow Graham entrance. The expression on his face didn't reflect happiness. "Do I even want to know why you're here?" I groused, thoughts of messing with Flint and Drake forgotten.

"No, but you don't really have a choice in the matter," Graham replied. "I don't either. I want you to know that. This isn't my decision."

Gunner bristled as he stepped in front of me. He must've read the situation the same way I did. Things were about to take a turn. "If you think you're taking her in ... ."

Graham held up his hand to quiet his son. "I didn't say I was taking her in. The prosecutor has made an appearance. It seems he doesn't want to take my word on things. He's demanding a voluntary blood sample from Scout to rule her out as a suspect. There's nothing I can do about it."

Gunner balked. "Absolutely not." He gripped my hand tighter. "She's getting a lawyer. We're going to fight this."

I appreciated his vehemence, but it wasn't necessary. I wasn't guilty, so in my book that meant there was nothing to fear. "It's fine," I offered, earning a growl from Gunner, which I ignored. "I can give you a blood sample."

Surprise was evident on Graham's face. "Just like that? I thought you would put up a fight."

"I'm not guilty. I should have nothing to worry about, right?"

He nodded, slowly. "Pretty much."

"Scout, this isn't a good idea," Gunner persisted. "I just ... you should get a lawyer."

Under different circumstances I might've agreed. But I trusted Graham. It wasn't just because he was Gunner's father. He was a good man. I could sense that.

"It will be fine," I reassured him. "I'm innocent. There's nothing to fear."

"I'll arrange for an appointment at the county lab," Graham offered.

"I'm looking forward to it." That was a gross exaggeration, but I wanted to save face in front of the two wolves watching from behind us. I could feel their amusement.

This so wasn't good.

EIGHT

"*D*on't look at my butt."

I was going for levity as I leaned over the examination table, one of the state's finest phlebotomists jabbing a needle into my posterior, Gunner and Graham standing behind me. I would've preferred being alone, but Graham insisted that it was best he watch the blood draw given my powers of persuasion – something the technician knew nothing about – and that meant Gunner was sticking to his father's side. I had small veins in my arms, something that had been troublesome over the years when I was treated for a variety of ailments, so I figured it was easier to allow the bloodsucker to draw from my hip.

That meant dropping my pants, something that perked Gunner right up. His smile was mischievous as he held my gaze.

"I'll try to refrain," he said after a beat. "This isn't exactly what I had in mind for when I finally got to see you with your clothes off."

Graham cleared his throat. That gave me an excuse to drop my eyes, my cheeks blazing.

"I don't think now is the time to try to charm her, son," Graham drawled.

Gunner seemingly remembered we weren't alone – and that he wanted to throttle his father – so he shot a dark glare toward that corner of the room. "Shush."

Instead of being offended, or picking a fight, Graham merely chuckled. "Your mother used to say that."

Even I knew that was the wrong thing to say. Gunner's mother was a sore spot. She was still alive – although I wasn't sure the sanitarium where she resided sounded like a comfortable place to visit let alone live in – but he hadn't seen her since he was a teenager. Given the fact that she got loaded and tried to kill him in a fire, I couldn't blame him.

"Just stop talking," Gunner ordered.

"I agree." I pinned Graham with a pointed look. He obviously didn't understand how to read his son's moods. Gunner was angry. "Let's talk about something else. What does everyone think of the *Child's Play* remake? I think it's a mistake to cut out Brad Dourif, but obviously they didn't consult me. I mean … I love Mark Hamill as much as the next person, but Brad Dourif *is* Chucky."

Slowly, deliberately, Gunner tracked his eyes to me. "Are you talking about the movie with the murderous doll?"

I nodded, doing my best not to cringe when I felt the needle slide in. I wasn't a baby by any stretch of the imagination, but I didn't like needles. They reminded me of the hours after I was discovered at the fire station, when I was stuck with at least ten of them as they drew blood for DNA comparisons and to make sure I was immunized against every microbe out there. Somehow – and I still wasn't sure how – they seemed to realize I'd never seen the inside of a doctor's office before they got their hands on me. It was traumatizing.

"You like murderous dolls?" Gunner strolled closer, never moving his gaze from my face. He hunkered down so we were eye to eye. "I wouldn't think you'd like horror movies."

I recognized what he was doing. He was trying to take my mind off the needle. He had a giving heart, even if at times he suffered from terminal testosterone.

I sighed and nodded. "I like watching movies about dolls, even bad ones. I knew this girl in foster care – we were only together for a few months – she was terrified of dolls. She refused to let any in our room. I was fine with that because I didn't like them either."

A hint of sadness permeated his chiseled features. "Did you keep in touch with her?"

I shook my head. "We got separated at some point. It's too bad. I really liked her. She was … different … too."

He understood without me having to expound. "Do you know what happened to her?"

"Not really." I shrugged as if it didn't bother me, but I'd thought about her more than once over the years. In a weird way, she was the closest thing I ever had to a sister. We both possessed magic, but we were careful not to talk about it, and for a brief time we talked about running away together. The home we shared wasn't so bad. I ended up staying six months after she was transferred out.

"I heard through the grapevine that she ran away and was living on the streets," I continued. "I don't know if it's true because later I heard a ridiculous story from another girl who said that she'd joined the circus. You know how that goes."

He laughed and gently brushed my hair from my face. It was as if we were the only two people in the room, which would've been nice given the circumstances. "I don't know. I don't think joining the circus is so farfetched. I thought about doing it when I was a kid."

"The circus wouldn't have you," Graham shot back.

Gunner narrowed his eyes but remained focused on me. "What do you want to do after this?"

The question caught me off guard. "I don't know. It's going to be hard to top this as a bonding exercise."

"Yeah. We could go for a picnic."

Graham shifted from one foot to the other and muttered something under his breath. It sounded a lot like "give me a break," but I couldn't be sure.

"That sounds nice, but I think I need some time to myself." I straightened when the technician announced he had what he needed and quickly pulled up my pants. "Nothing personal, but ... it's been a long morning."

Gunner didn't look happy with my response. "Are you going to head back to the cabin and blame yourself for what happened to Fred?"

I shook my head. "No. Why would you think that?"

"Because I can tell you're upset."

"Who wouldn't be?"

"Fair enough." He grunted as he straightened and eyed his father. "You and I are going to have a discussion about what went down here. Just so you know."

Graham rolled his eyes. "That's fine. I'm doing my job. I don't regret it."

"You might when I'm done with you."

I FOUND MYSELF LOOKING OVER my shoulder to make sure Gunner wasn't following me as I left the lab. It wasn't that I didn't trust him. In truth, in a short amount of time I'd learned to trust him a great deal. I still wasn't sure how it happened because I was careful when extending my heart, but he was already worming his way in.

I found it disconcerting. Er, well, that is when I wasn't reacting like a typical girl and batting my eyelashes like a moron. Seriously, how did that even happen?

I didn't go home. Gunner assumed I was returning to the cabin to lick my wounds and regroup. If he'd realized what I really intended there's no way he would've let me go alone. Even though I wouldn't have minded the company, I needed time to sort through the busy threads tangling inside my brain.

The wolves were easy to target as suspects. They'd appeared out of nowhere, seemingly developed an interest in me and then acted like smug slimeballs when accused of having had a hand in what had happened to Fred. That wasn't exactly a defining clue, of course. There were still questions. The biggest for me was how Fred played into this. Was it possible Flint paid him to steal from me? I couldn't rule it out. If I believed the shifters had a hand in Fred's death – and, really, what else could I believe? – it was likely they needed help to track him down. Gunner lost him in the woods, after all. Of course, Gunner willingly abandoned the chase because he wanted to get back to me. That was the distinction. Could Fred have outrun Gunner over the long haul? I had my doubts.

I needed information, a direction to point myself in. It made sense for the shifters to be involved. In fact, they were at the top of my suspect list. Which one, though? Could it be all of them? It was possible, but Cyrus only showed a passing interest in me. Flint was another story. He was full of posturing and braggadocio, but I wasn't sure he had it in him to torture Fred ... at least with his own bare hands. He was bloodthirsty enough, liked the idea of being in charge and others being afraid of him, but I could sense fear beneath his tough exterior.

Drake was another story. He was clearly subservient when it came to Cyrus and Flint. He followed orders, was probably paid handsomely, and perhaps was rewarded for loyalty. He felt smarter than the other two, though. I sensed a keen mind in his head ... and he was capable of shuttering. Flint's mind wasn't an open book – and I wasn't always good at reading new people because it was a gift I never spent much time honing – but his surface thoughts were readable. Drake, on the other hand, was an enigma.

That made him all the more dangerous.

Sure, it was possible he was a good guy following a paycheck, but I didn't trust him. It was obvious Gunner didn't either. Gunner had strong instincts, so I tended to believe almost everything he inferred about a particular situation … unless I had reason to believe otherwise, which I didn't in this case.

The only thing I could think to do was go back to the scene of the crime. Not where the body was discovered, but where I had my first (and ultimately last) glimpse of Fred. The beach by the restaurant. It only made sense to start there.

I parked my bike at the restaurant. I left my helmet on the seat and cut through the end of the lot. I wasn't even aware there was a walking path on the other side of the wall until Gunner led me through it the previous evening. At the time, I remembered wondering how many women he'd taken for walks on the beach. I forced the notion out of my head. What did it matter? We were trying to look forward. It's not as if I was under the misconception that he'd been a monk until meeting me.

Thinking about the date caused me to blush, which was absolutely ridiculous. We had fun – until Fred showed up to take twenty bucks and then bolted, leaving us with two unwanted visitors and an abrupt ending to our date – and I was eager to have another go at it. That wouldn't be possible until we fixed this mess, and that likely wouldn't be easy.

I exhaled heavily and headed to the beach. It wasn't difficult to find the spot where we'd discarded our shoes and coats the previous evening, and once there I took a moment to study the footprints.

I was hardly an expert tracker … especially when it came to the wilderness. Still, it wasn't difficult to pick out several different tracks. I recognized my boots first. Even though I have big feet for a woman, the tracks were much smaller than the other four sets. Gunner's tracks were next. His boot prints were always directly next to mine, so his were easy to decipher. Fred's prints ran toward the woods, which made them easy to follow … and that's exactly what I did.

I trailed my fingers out, whispering a spell as I walked. The sun felt nice on my face, but I couldn't enjoy the weather. There were more important things to dwell on, like Fred … and whatever happened to him. He may have been a thief, but nobody deserved that. If he was killed as a message to me – which Graham and Gunner both believed, even though they expressed that belief in different ways – I would always be haunted.

Thanks to the spell, Fred's prints sparkled a bright purple. To a normal person passing by, they would look no different. Another paranormal was unlikely to be able to see the glow even if looking for it. I wasn't worried about being discovered.

Once under the blanket of the trees I increased the power fueling the spell.

Fred's footprints were distinct, and I followed. I wasn't worried about losing my way. I could just as easily follow the prints back.

I picked up my pace and jogged, the blood rushing through my ears as I allowed the spell to take over. My mind was a blank, the trees a blur as I moved. I ran for a long time. My strained calves told me a decent amount of time had passed when I reached the end of the line.

I had no idea where I was. The building to my right – a sagging two-story barn – was past its prime. I bent at the waist to catch my breath, my nostrils flaring when a distinct scent assailed my olfactory senses.

Blood.

I jerked up my head and glanced around, my heart continuing to pound, but this time for a different reason. The drumbeat eventually settled, leaving me with nothing but the faint rustle of leaves and a light wind brushing against my cheeks.

And the blood. I could definitely smell it.

I swiveled in a circle as I searched for the source. I had no idea who the blood belonged to, if it was even human, but it was too much of a coincidence to ignore. Fred was definitely here. Did he leave? Probably not of his own volition. My senses told me he'd met his end here and then was transported to the spot behind the library.

I needed more than that. I needed evidence.

"Well, well, well." A voice sparked from the spot to my left. I recognized it.

My gaze was sour when I slowly turned to find Flint standing amidst the foliage. He wasn't exposed – or open to attack – if I wished to unleash my magic on him. It was as if he'd purposely put a tree between us.

"This must be my lucky day," I drawled, raising a hand and freezing Drake in his tracks with a small burst of magic. It wasn't that I sensed him as much as I understood that Flint wasn't brave enough to risk meeting me in the woods without backup. "I just keep running into you guys over and over."

Flint's eyes went wide when he realized his friend wasn't moving. "What did you do to him?" He peered around the tree, concern settling into lines at the corners of his eyes. "Is he ... dead?"

I laughed at the suggestion. "No. He could be. Is that what you want?"

"No." Slowly, Flint shook his head and stepped away from the tree. I could almost smell his fear, but the realization that his buddy hadn't been frozen for all eternity seemed to embolden him. "What are you doing out here?"

"I was just about to ask you the same thing."

"I asked first."

Flint laughed, delighted. "You're feisty." He wiggled his hips in a sexually inappropriate way. "Have I mentioned I love feisty women?"

I didn't change my expression. "Did I mention I would rather rip your tongue out than talk to you for another second?" I smirked at his visible gulp. "You guys are starting to be real pains. I mean ... you have no idea the things I want to do to you. For the record, I felt that way before Fred turned up dead behind the library, but your actions today are really ramping up my animosity."

Flint was back to acting innocent. "What does that have to do with us?"

"Oh, please don't insult my intelligence." I shook my head. "Fred showed up right before you last night. He disappeared into the woods, drawing Gunner away. I'm guessing that was the plan all along so you guys could get me alone."

I slid my eyes to Drake and found him still as stone. He was completely frozen, except for his eyes, which roamed back and forth as he desperately tried to break free.

"You're going to give yourself an aneurysm," I warned. "You can't break the spell. I'll release you as soon as I'm done talking to your buddy here. Not a moment before. I don't particularly trust people who try to sneak up on me in the middle of the woods."

"That's not what we were doing," Flint protested, outrage on full display. "We just happened to be walking and stumbled across your path."

What a load of crap. "In opposite directions?"

"I ... ." He trailed off. I clearly had him.

"It doesn't matter what you say," I offered. "I won't believe you. This game you're playing of showing up everywhere I go and acting as if it's a coincidence, it's getting old."

"What makes you think we even care about you?" Flint shot back, causing Drake to emit a muffled groan.

Hmm. That was interesting. "If you're not interested in me, that means you're chasing Gunner." That was easy enough to deduce ... and it sort of made sense. "Of course, you could be messing with both of us. It hardly matters."

I decided to take the conversation by the horns, so to speak. "I'm sick of seeing you guys around," I continued. "I mean ... so sick. I'm done dealing with it. I have other things to worry about ... including solving Fred's murder. And, make no mistake, I will solve his murder."

I took several steps back, waiting until I was behind Drake to release the spell. I was feeling a bit mean so I added some extra oomph, causing him to pitch forward and hit the ground face first. It took everything I had not to laugh. Flint didn't even bother trying to swallow his mirth.

"Oh, that's hilarious." He slapped his hand against his thigh as he belted out a hearty guffaw.

For his part, Drake was clearly furious. He rolled until he was facing me, steadfastly refusing to wipe the dirt from his cheek. "I hardly think that was necessary."

I hunkered down so we were eye to eye. "Don't try sneaking up on me again. I can do much worse."

"We weren't going to hurt you," Flint shot back. "We were just ... curious. You're obviously more than a witch."

"I am," I agreed, rolling my neck and standing. "I'm more than you boys can handle. Don't make the mistake of thinking you can take me. Better men have tried ... and failed."

"We're not afraid of you," Flint challenged. "I think you're all talk."

"You would be wrong, but go ahead and test me again. You'll be getting the business end of the spell next time. I have a specific one in mind for you. I can't wait to unleash it."

Flint's face drained of color. "I ... we weren't doing anything!"

He always went back to proclaiming his innocence, but he was a terrible liar.

"Stay away from me," I warned, heading back in the direction I'd come from. "If anyone else dies in Hawthorne Hollow, I'll be coming after you. You've been warned."

"Don't you need evidence to accuse us of something like that?" Drake challenged.

"I have evidence."

"How could you?"

"As your friend said, I'm not a normal witch. Be careful. You've pushed me about as far as I'm going to let you." With those words, I strolled into the trees. I didn't look back. It was cooler not to look back.

NINE

I was feeling okay when I returned to my cabin. A show of power as means to boost my mood wasn't always a good thing. In this particular case, though, it made me feel better.

Flint was big on false bravado, but he couldn't hide his fear. As for Drake, I sensed more anger from him than fear. He was the real power, so I found his response interesting.

I knew the blood I'd scented in the clearing would have to be checked a second time, but it wasn't going to happen with witnesses present so I put it out of my mind ... at least for now. It might make more sense to send another member of the team out because Drake and Flint were apparently obsessed with following me. It was logical ... and yet I hated ceding control.

I was surprised to find Gunner sitting on the front porch when I pulled into the driveway. I probably shouldn't have been — he had an unerring ability to show up when he felt I might need a sounding board — but the fact that he'd let himself into the cabin to collect Merlin to keep him company grated.

"Hey." His smile was hard and flat as I yanked off my helmet. "I expected to find you hiding under the covers."

The statement only served to further agitate me. "I don't hide under the covers."

"Perhaps that was a poor choice of words."

"Perhaps," I agreed, stomping up the steps. Merlin, who appeared to be in ecstasy thanks to Gunner's clever fingers stroking him, gave me an odd look. "Traitor," I muttered, earning a full-fledged smile from Gunner. "Don't you think it's rude to let yourself into someone's home without being invited?"

Gunner shrugged. "I was worried."

"My bike clearly wasn't here."

"No, but I wanted to make sure your things still were."

That's when the true root of his fear hit me. "You thought I was going to run."

"I assumed that you would be upset because you're a suspect in a murder," he clarified. "Anyone would be. There's no shame in it."

"This is hardly the first time I've been a suspect in a murder. It goes with the territory. I wasn't upset about that."

He pursed his lips. "You've been a suspect in a murder before?"

"We don't always work with the cops in Detroit," I reminded him. "We often have to work around them. That means we're noticed at scenes and sometimes our curiosity isn't exactly welcome."

"Ah." He nodded in understanding. "We have that here occasionally when the state police claim an investigation instead of my father."

"I've never been charged with anything, if that's what you're worried about. Well ... I guess I was charged with a mischief offense a time or two when I was a teenager. Nothing serious."

He laughed. "We all have mischief offenses on our record. It comes with the territory."

I cocked an eyebrow. "Your father arrested you?"

"More than once."

That made sense given the things Graham said to me. I let out a sigh as I slipped into the chair next to Gunner, the anger I'd been hoarding at his invasion of my property seeping out. I had bigger things to worry about. "If you're going to yell about me going out ... don't. I'm not in the mood."

He slanted an unreadable look in my direction. "Why would I yell?"

"Because you have a loud voice and you're bossy."

"I hate to break it to you, but you're bossy, too."

"Yes, but I'm bossy in a demure way."

His warm chuckle washed over me, alleviating some of the tension I was feeling. "You're definitely demure. That's the first word I thought of when I met you."

We both knew that wasn't true. Our first meeting didn't exactly go smoothly. Yet, despite that, sparks flew that day. That's how we ended up here. "I went back to the beach."

71

Gunner shifted in his chair and I didn't miss the glint of agitation in his eyes before he clawed back his emotions. "Did you find anything?"

I was instantly suspicious. I expected him to be angry that I didn't invite him along for the ride. "You're really not going to yell?"

"Nope."

"That doesn't seem like ... you."

"I'm pretty sure that yelling is the quickest way to alienate you," he replied. "It's possible that's what you're looking for because part of you wants a way out of this. I'm not giving you that opportunity."

"You make me sound like a coward."

"In this particular instance, you are." His teeth gleamed as he smiled at my frown. "I don't blame you. Your background makes it difficult for you to trust. I'm hoping you'll get over that. Either way, you're an adult. I'm not your boss. If you feel the need to investigate something, that's certainly your prerogative."

I hated that he sounded so reasonable. It made me want to match his tone, unheard of for me. "I needed to think, too," I admitted. "It's been a busy morning."

"And you blame yourself for what happened to Fred."

"I don't blame myself. I ... okay, I blame myself a little." It was hard to admit. I maintained a crusty external shell for a reason. Being vulnerable gave me a sick feeling in my stomach.

"I'm glad you could admit that to me." He shifted so he was looking directly into my eyes, the kitten cradled against his chest. For some reason, it only made him more appealing. I mean ... who doesn't find a strong, masculine guy carting around a kitten hot? It was infuriating.

"Apparently I admit all sorts of things to you that I wouldn't to others under the same circumstances," I grumbled, causing his grin to widen. "It's not because you're special or anything. It's because ... well ... it's just because."

"Uh-huh." He didn't look convinced, which only made me feel more of an idiot. "I really am glad you feel you can confide in me." He was serious. "You need someone to talk to. I like listening because I find you fascinating."

"I find myself fascinating, too. We have that in common."

He barked out a laugh. "See. How is that not fascinating?"

"My narcissism?"

"I like to think of it as self-assuredness. And, frankly, there's nothing sexier than a woman who doesn't need constant reassurance." He stared at me for a full minute before sobering. "If you need reassurance, however, I want to be the person who helps you with that, too. You don't have to be one thing. It's okay to be many things.

"And I understand that you feel you need to be strong at all times," he continued, his voice soft. "You were on your own for a long time. You were abandoned and you have no idea why. You have insecurities whether you want to admit it or not. I'll be here for all of that."

Ugh. He really was charming. It made following my head all the more difficult. "Have you considered that I might not be good at this?" I challenged, opting to lay all my cards on the table. "I don't doubt you'd be good for me. What are the odds I'll be good for you?"

He didn't back down. "Let me worry about that."

"But … ."

"No." He shook his head, firm. "You've already been good for me. My father even mentioned it when I picked a fight with him outside of the health department. And, yes, we got into a huge argument. I think demanding a blood sample was out of line."

I should've seen that coming. "You picked a fight with your father? That's just … so unnecessary. I'm not guilty. We have nothing to worry about."

"Yeah, well, I'm willing to place a wager that all the innocent people who still found themselves in prison felt the same way. I would rather not take unnecessary risks."

He had a point. "Well, it's done with now. You didn't need to fight with your father."

"That wasn't really my point. I probably wouldn't have admitted having a fight with my father if I had my druthers. You don't need to know about that. What he said to me at the time is germane to this conversation."

"And what was that?"

"He said he was glad to see me putting someone ahead of myself. Ever since my mother … well, you know the story."

I nodded to encourage him to continue.

"Ever since that happened, I've had a tendency to put myself above everyone."

I didn't believe that. "I've seen you with your sister. That's not true."

"Fine. I care about my sister. As for other people … I'm like you. I prefer it when it's easy to walk away. That's not what I feel here." He moved his finger between us, causing Merlin to bat at it. "I care enough about you to see where this goes. I need you to do the same."

"I … do." I struggled with my answer. "I've always been a runner when my emotions get involved. I can't help it."

"And that's exactly why I broke into your cabin. I wanted to make sure you didn't run, because if you had it would've been easier to track you down the sooner I started. Once I saw your stuff — and Merlin — I knew you were still around. If you promise not to run without telling me, I promise not to invade your personal space again. Deal?"

I ran my tongue over my teeth to buy time. "I could just curse the property to keep you out," I warned. "I'm more than capable of doing that."

"You could, but you won't. That would put a damper on our end-of-date kisses, and nobody wants that."

I had to bite the inside of my cheek to keep from laughing. "Fine. I promise not to run."

"Thank you. I promise not to let myself into your cabin again without an invitation."

"Great."

"Good."

We lapsed into amiable silence. After a few minutes, he reached over and linked his fingers with mine. It was a perfectly sweet moment ... which completely threw me for a loop.

"This is weird," I said finally, causing him to chuckle.

"Not a hand-holder, huh? You'll get used to it."

"I just ... it's weird." I craned my neck and glanced around. "You don't think anyone is watching us, do you?"

"Why would someone be watching us?"

"I have a Peeping Tim ghost."

"Who only cares if you're naked. If you want to get naked, I'll work up the energy to care. Otherwise ... shush."

"Maybe you should shush."

"I'm trying to shush and enjoy the moment. You keep talking."

"I ... ." I forced myself to be quiet and focus on the woods. After another few minutes — which were honestly pure torture for me — I decided to change the subject. "I ran into Drake and Flint again."

Gunner narrowed his eyes. "Are you kidding me? They were back out at the beach?"

"Well ... ." I told him the story, making sure to leave nothing out. I included the spell I used to follow Fred's footsteps and took glee in the details about freezing Drake before allowing him to fall face-first into the dirt. "It's possible they were out there because they wanted to make sure they didn't leave evidence behind when they killed Fred. It's also possible they were following me. I was in the zone and didn't pay attention to my surroundings."

Gunner stretched his legs, keeping a firm grip on my hand, and rolled his eyes to the overhang. I couldn't read his mind, but I could tell he was bothered. "Well, that's just ... I want to kill them."

And here was the alpha male reaction I expected before. "I took care of myself."

"It's not as if I believe you can't take care of yourself," he shot back, his temper on full display. "When I express worry for your safety, it's not because I think you're inept. Stop jumping to that conclusion. I'm well aware that you're the baddest witch on the block. From here on out, that goes without saying."

For some odd reason that made me feel better. "Fair enough."

"I don't like that they can seemingly find you wherever you are. I just ... have they ever touched you?"

I wasn't expecting the question. "No. I wouldn't let them touch me. I'm not an idiot. Besides, I don't find either of them remotely attractive." Once I said it, I realized that wasn't exactly true. "Okay, I might let Drake touch me if I wasn't convinced he was a sociopath. I find him mildly hot."

Gunner glared. "He is not hot."

"Oh, he's hot."

"He is not. I'm ten times hotter than him."

His reaction made me smirk. It was the first smile I'd managed since Graham woke me with his pounding on the cabin door. "I believe you're the hottest guy in town," I offered. "From now on, if I comment on the looks of another man, can it be assumed that I find you hotter? It might save us some time."

Instead of laughing, as I hoped, he continued to glower. "Sure ... as long as it can be assumed that I find you more attractive than every other woman I cross paths with. You won't mind me commenting on it, right?"

I balked. "That's different."

"No, it's not."

"Yes, it is."

"Why?"

"Because ... because I said so."

This time he did laugh, hearty and raucous, before shaking his head. "See. Fascinating." He jabbed a finger in my direction, causing Merlin to protest the interruption in petting. "I think we should just refrain from commenting on the hotness of others. That seems like a surefire way to get into an unnecessary fight."

"Only if you're against making up."

Intrigue sparked in his eyes. "Good point. Can we table this discussion until after this investigation is behind us? I would rather focus on that."

"Sure. That's the smart way to go."

"Great." He went back to stroking Merlin. "Do you think they were out there checking the scene or following you? I'm not thrilled with either possibility, but one of them makes me extremely antsy."

I had no doubt which option bothered him more. I was having the same issue. "I don't know." I searched my memory. "It's possible that they were just out there to make sure there was nothing to tie them to Fred. That makes more sense than them being able to follow me for miles without me noticing."

He nodded, thoughtful. "You said they approached you from separate directions. They couldn't possibly have known that you would show up out there. That seems to indicate they took advantage of you showing up."

"So ... you don't think they followed me?"

"I don't know. I'm bothered by the fact that they appeared on the same beach with us last night. I don't think that was a coincidence. They had to be following you."

"Or you."

His forehead wrinkled. "Me? Why would they be following me?"

"You're pack," I reminded him.

"Not really. I'm technically part of a pack, but I have very little to do with the politics and haven't been active for a very long time."

"It doesn't matter." I'd been giving this a lot of thought. "You're considered one of the big wolves in town. By all accounts, Cyrus used to have power here. He wanted his own pack, so he split. He's back now for a specific reason. I don't think that reason means you're all going to have a peaceful meeting of the minds.

"Think about it," I continued, warming to the topic. "It makes more sense for you to be on their radar. Sure, they saw me take out a siren — and that probably intrigued them — but not enough to follow me in this manner. You're of much more interest to them."

"I guess." He still didn't look convinced. "Whether I was their initial target or not, you've officially piqued their interest. Perhaps seeing you with me set them off. It's possible they want to get you out of the picture because they think you're my bodyguard or something."

The notion made me smile. "That might be fun."

He rolled his eyes. "If anyone is guarding anyone's body, it's going to be me guarding you."

"I didn't agree to that."

"No." He squeezed my hand. "How about we guard each other?"

I could get behind that. "Sure." I rubbed my forehead, considering. "Drake is Flint's bodyguard, right? I sense the real power from him."

"Yeah, well, I've been thinking about that, too. There's no way that guy came from out of nowhere to climb so high in Cyrus's ranks without anyone knowing who he is. Something is going on there."

"Like what?"

"I don't know but I have every intention of finding out. I think ... I think I know him."

The admission caught me off guard. "You said you didn't."

"I don't recognize him," he clarified. "But there's something familiar about him. I simply can't place him."

Well, that was interesting. "Is there a way we can find out?"

"I think we need to talk to the group."

I figured he would say that. "Can we do it in an hour? I'm not quite ready to face a bunch of questions."

He nodded. "Of course. Will you be quiet during that hour?"

"You're the one talking."

"We'll both be quiet."

It sounded like an interesting experiment. I had no idea if I could pull it off.

TEN

*J*was more centered when we parked in the lot at The Cauldron. The hour of quiet time did me good.

"I told you I could do it," I boasted as I yanked off my helmet. "You should have more faith in me."

His expression was derisive. "First, I have endless faith in you. It's not difficult, because you're a doer who almost always follows through."

I beamed at him.

"Second, you did not do it. You talked throughout the entire hour."

I balked. "I did not."

"You did so."

"I did not."

"Really?" His tone was withering. "I seem to remember talking about a potential new kickstand because you're not a fan of the one you have now and a certain conversation about getting a different bike seat so I could sit behind you. I don't see that happening — and it's not because I'm a toxic male, as you hinted. But I'm willing to give it a try as long as we're not in public."

Huh. Now that he mentioned it, I vaguely remembered that conversation. "Well, I was mostly quiet."

His face split into a wide grin. "Yes. You were quiet for almost an hour."

"I don't have to take this abuse." I was still grumbling when he caught up to me outside the door. I was about to continue complaining when he swooped in and planted a firm kiss against my lips, tugging me close as he wrapped his arms around my waist. All notion of arguing flew out of my mind.

When we finally separated, I was gasping. "What were you thinking?" I suddenly remembered where we were. "Do you want the others to figure out that we're ... you know?"

Amusement lit his handsome features. "If you can't say it, perhaps we shouldn't be doing it. Dating isn't a dirty word, Scout."

"I didn't say it was."

"Also, if you don't think they're aware that something is going on with us, you're nowhere near as observant as I thought. They know."

That was impossible. "Marissa suspects, but she doesn't know anything. I think we should keep it that way until we're sure it's going to work. What if we wake up a week from now and decide we don't like each other?"

"Do you think that's going to happen?"

I shrugged. "Maybe you have stinky feet or something. Maybe you have a hairy back. I don't like hairy backs."

"You've seen me with my shirt off. If I remember correctly, you liked what you saw."

My mouth dropped open. I had indeed seen him with his shirt off when he helped fix my roof. I had most certainly liked what I saw. That didn't mean he needed to comment on it. "You're full of yourself."

"Maybe, but you still liked what you saw."

"I ... cannot continue this conversation. I guarantee those people inside don't know anything is going on. I would prefer keeping it that way until we're more settled." What I didn't say was that I believed it would be easier if we didn't have added pressure weighing us down. We had enough going on without adding rampant speculation from those closest to us.

"Fine." He held up his hands in mock surrender. "I won't say a word even though Rooster and I spend every night gossiping about girls. I'll refrain for you."

I snorted as I pushed past him. "You have the oddest sense of humor."

"Just wait until we start spending the night together. Then you'll see the true lengths I'm willing to go to make you laugh."

I slowed my pace. "You realize you just insinuated I'm going to laugh when you get naked, right?"

His smile dimmed. "Wait ... that's not what I meant." Suddenly, he was very serious. "When you see me naked you'll swear you hear angels weeping."

"That could also be taken negatively. Are they crying because they feel sorry for you?"

He glared. "No. I ... we're revisiting this conversation later."

"I'm looking forward to it." That was true. Whether he'd meant to or not, I was much more relaxed than I had been two hours earlier.

Perhaps this whole relationship thing was going to work out after all. I was already reaping some massive rewards.

THE ENTIRE GROUP LOOKED TO BE GATHERED in the bar. Whistler stood behind the bar drying glasses while Bonnie rested at a booth with Doc, seemingly entranced by whatever he was doing on his computer.

Rooster sat on a stool, sipping a beer and watching the interaction, and Marissa was by herself at a table in the back. She appeared to be painting her fingernails a wild blue color.

"What's your favorite color?" I asked Gunner on a whim.

If he was surprised by the question, he didn't show it. "I'm a big fan of black, but some people argue that's not a color so I'd have to say blue."

That figured. "Marissa is painting her fingernails for you."

Gunner shifted to look in the woman's direction and frowned. "How do you know that?"

"It's a girl thing."

"Does that mean you're going to paint your fingernails for me?"

"I don't ever paint my fingernails. It's too much work and I've never seen the point."

"What about your toenails?"

"Does it matter?"

"Actually, it might. If you have ugly feet I'm out of here."

I choked on my laughter at his deadpan delivery. He really was something. "Occasionally I might paint my toenails, but only during sandal season – and I rarely show them off."

"That sounds like a challenge."

"Yeah, well ... ."

The sound of someone clearing his throat drew my attention to the bar. Rooster and Whistler were watching us with overt interest. I straightened quickly, smoothing my T-shirt. "Hello, gentlemen. How are you this fine afternoon?"

Rooster cocked an eyebrow, his lips twitching. "I'm fine, Scout. How are you?"

"I'm fine as well."

"We're all fine," Gunner offered, pushing past me and shaking his head.

"Well, some of us are finer than others. Scout, for example, is a suspect in a murder."

"I heard about that." Rooster shook his head. "Graham stopped by to give me a heads-up. He assures me that you're not really a suspect, but I figure if he was worried enough to tip me off he doesn't feel he has complete control of the situation."

That wasn't what I wanted to hear. "I'm innocent," I reminded him. "There's no evidence they can find, because I didn't do it."

"Fair point. Of course, the fact that someone burned your name into the body suggests that we have a faction determined to get your attention. That seems to indicate that they wouldn't be above framing you."

I hadn't even considered that. "Oh, um ... ."

"Let's not go there," Gunner supplied, nodding in thanks to Whistler when the grinning bartender slid a beer in his direction. "We have a few things to discuss with you guys. It's probably best that we get them out of the way now."

I didn't miss the way Marissa jerked up her head and the suspicious look that flitted across her face. It was clear she thought we were about to drop a different sort of bomb, which made me distinctly itchy.

"Scout has had a busy day," Gunner volunteered. "Not only did my father wake her and take her to a tortured body, she's also had two run-ins with Flint and Drake."

Rooster couldn't contain his surprise. "Two? How?"

"The first was at Mable's Country Table. We were having lunch when they came in. It was clear they were putting on a show. At first I thought it was for Scout's benefit, but she brought up an interesting point and now I'm not so sure."

"What was the point?" Whistler asked.

"She thinks they might've been looking for me last night when they appeared on the beach. Scout was with me, so it's possible they think she's part of my security detail. They might be trying to test her in an effort to throw me off."

Marissa was shrill when she interjected herself into the conversation. "And what were you two doing at the beach?"

"They were on a date," Bonnie answered before I could conjure an acceptable lie. "Gunner took her to Ruby's place for a nice meal and a walk on the beach."

I openly gaped. "How ... ?" I turned to Gunner. "Did you tell them?"

He snickered and shook his head. "No, but you just did."

"But ... how did she know?"

"There are only so many 'date' restaurants in the area," Bonnie replied, using the appropriate air quotes. "Besides, the way you two look at each other is right out of a porno. It was only a matter of time. Don't be ridiculous."

My cheeks burned even though I wasn't convinced anyone other than Marissa was watching me. "I ... ."

Gunner rubbed his forehead and chuckled into his beer at my discomfort. "I told you."

"Oh, stuff it." I was feeling petulant when I slipped into a chair near the booth where Doc and Bonnie worked. "What are you guys doing?"

"Well, it's quite fascinating," Bonnie enthused, inclining her head toward Doc. "He put together an algorithm — no, really, I watched him do it — and he's been searching for crimes similar to what happened to Fred. He found one."

"He did?" I was officially intrigued. "Where?"

"Detroit."

I stilled, something sizzling in the depths of my memory. "Wait ... in Detroit?" I racked my brain as I tried to clamp onto the elusive thought. "I think I remember this."

Gunner shifted on his stool. "You didn't mention it before."

"I wasn't really trying to tie something that happened in Detroit to here. Now that Bonnie brings it up, I do remember a body being found with a message burned into it. It was about two years ago, right?"

Bonnie enthusiastically bobbed her head. "Yes. Was it your case?"

"No. I'm not even sure we worked it because, if I remember correctly, there were no discernible paranormal ties. I kind of half remember us talking about how weird it was, but I'm pretty sure we didn't take it on."

"Do you remember who the message on the body was directed at?" Whistler asked.

"No, but I have a way of finding out." I thought about my friend Mike Foley. He was a former detective with the Detroit Police Department. He was one of the few ties I still had to the area, and he was well aware of the paranormal angle that most of the cops chose to ignore because they were more comfortable remaining in the dark.

Gunner scowled when he realized who I was talking about. "Not that guy. I don't like him."

"I think you're just saying that because he clearly has a crush on Scout," Bonnie teased. "Don't worry. I'm sure she likes you better."

Even though I was uncomfortable with our relationship being talked about openly — especially because nothing was defined and the only thing I could say with any degree of certainty was that we practically erupted in a volcano of tongues and gasps whenever we were in proximity to one another — I couldn't stop myself from smirking.

"I told you," I taunted, repeating his earlier words.

He scowled. "Just contact your buddy. If this has happened before — and near you — there might be information there we can use."

I hadn't considered that. The notion of two people being tortured in that manner because of me caused my stomach to do an uneasy roll. When I risked a glance at Gunner, I found him watching me with heavy eyes.

"I'll message him," I promised, forcing a smile I didn't completely feel. "I'm sure the cases will turn out to be different."

"I doubt it," Doc piped in. "I think it's probable the two cases are tied together. Whether that means you're tied to the first case remains to be seen. But it would make more sense if you were the cause. That would explain a lot."

I didn't immediately respond. I didn't have to. Gunner did it for me.

"We'll take it one step at a time," he insisted. "We need more information before we can figure any of this out. Let's not get ahead of ourselves."

GUNNER INSISTED ON DRIVING ME home. Mike wasn't in the office when I messaged, so I didn't expect to hear back from him for at least twelve hours. He was off duty, which meant he wasn't checking his email. It was probably for the best, because I needed some sleep.

"Well, thanks for the escort home," I offered lamely when Gunner walked me to my door. "It wasn't really necessary."

"I felt it was." He watched me intently as I inserted my key into the lock. "I don't think you should be here alone tonight. And before you jump into your usual routine, it's not because you're a weak female. You're obviously thinking ... and I want to be nearby if you have a nightmare."

I hadn't even considered that. The nightmares were close to the surface these days. I was exhausted, but if I was afraid to fall asleep that wouldn't bode well for the following day. I would need my faculties firing on all cylinders to figure this out. Still, I didn't think having an over-nighter so early in our relationship was a good idea.

"I don't think we're there yet," I said softly.

"We're not. I have no intention of trying anything. I think it's a good idea if we're together in case ... well, in case of a lot of things. I want to be close if you hear back from Mike, even though I think he's a tool."

The derisive comment had me laughing. "I think the fact that you're jealous of him is amusing."

"I'm not jealous."

"You sound jealous."

"Yeah, well, I'm not." He gently brushed my hair from my face. "If you have nightmares, I want to know it. If Flint and Drake try to attack you when they believe you'll be vulnerable, I want to be here.

"And, yes, I know you can take care of yourself," he continued. "But I want to be part of whatever fiery attack you throw at them. I think I'll find it funny and I'm always up for a few laughs."

That reminded me of our earlier conversation. "Are you going to get naked to incur those laughs?"

He extended a warning finger. "Don't push it."

I exhaled heavily as I rubbed my forehead. I would be lying if I said the idea of him spending the night — no romance expected — didn't appeal. It still felt odd. "Are you sure? I really don't want to jump in with both feet just yet."

"I don't want that either. Sleep only. I promise."

That was all I needed to hear. "Okay."

He double-checked the lock on the front door while I checked Merlin's food and water dish. I changed into comfortable sleep shorts and a T-shirt in the bathroom. I considered leaving my bra on because I thought it might alleviate some tension, but that wouldn't be comfortable. Ultimately, I tossed it in the hamper.

Gunner was already in the bed when I joined him. He was shirtless, which almost made me drool. Seriously, he was unbelievably cut ... and hairless. That seemed to indicate he waxed or shaved his chest, something that seemed out of the realm of normal for a guy like him, but I opted to save that discussion for another time.

"No funny business," I warned as I rolled in beside him. I lifted the blankets enough to assure myself that he was wearing boxer shorts. "I mean it."

"I left my clown nose at home."

I laughed. I rolled onto my back, my eyes riveted on the ceiling. "I'm so tired, but I don't know if I'll be able to sleep."

"You will." He killed the lights and rolled next to me, wrapping his arm around my waist and tugging so I was on my side, my cheek on his shoulder.

It was a new sleeping arrangement for me, something I couldn't ever remember trying. That didn't mean it was uncomfortable.

"Shut your mind," he ordered, his lips brushing against my forehead. "You need the downtime. You're too wound up."

I couldn't argue with that. "Okay." My voice was shaky whisper. "I hope they don't attack tonight. I'm not in the mood for a big battle."

"If they're smart they'll stay away."

That was the question. Exactly how smart were they? I didn't have time to debate it. My mind shut down relatively quickly and I slipped into slumber. I would think about it tomorrow ... after a good night's sleep. That's all I wanted. Somehow I knew Gunner's determination to remain by my side would ensure that outcome. It was a nice feeling, and something to mentally explore the next morning.

ELEVEN

I woke feeling rested. As with every morning, I stretched before getting out of bed ... and that's when I remembered I wasn't alone. Slowly, so as not to wake him, I turned to study Gunner's face. It was serene in sleep, his chin stubbled and somehow adding to his appeal. He looked relaxed, as if he belonged in the bed ... and then, slowly, he opened one eye.

"If you stare any harder I'm going to develop a complex," he muttered, causing me to smirk.

"You're kind of pretty. I couldn't help myself."

"You're kind of pretty, too." He ran his tongue over his teeth, his eyes busy as they roamed my face. "How did you sleep?"

"Good." I meant it. "No bad dreams."

"Perhaps that's because I was here. Maybe I'm the answer to the question."

It takes me a while to wake up in the morning and today was no exception. "What question?"

"The one about what it is, exactly, you need to chase away the dreams."

"Maybe you are the answer." I rolled to face him, ignoring the way my hair tufted out. He'd seen me after a hard sleep before. If my hair hadn't scared him previously, it wasn't about to now. "And maybe I shouldn't be running from the dreams."

He arched an eyebrow and rubbed his cheek before moving his hand to my arm. It was a companionable move, nothing sexy about it, but my cheeks burned at the contact. "Are you saying you want to explore your dreams?" he asked. "I don't think that's a bad idea. I might put it off until we're out of this mess, but after that … ."

"How do I explore dreams? They're not real."

"You seem to think yours are real."

"I didn't say that."

"You didn't have to. It's written all over your face. The dreams you're having are troubling enough that you've convinced yourself they're real." He moved closer, his hand rubbing soothing circles on my back. Again, there was nothing sexual about his movement … and yet the air between us still crackled with energy. "If you believe they're real, I'm right there with you."

My stomach coiled at the look in his eyes. I recognized what he had planned. "Don't kiss me," I announced out of the blue.

He chuckled, taken aback. "What makes you think I was going to kiss you?"

"I'm not an idiot. Sure, sometimes I miss obvious signs, but I would have to be blind to miss this one. You can't kiss me."

His lips curved in amusement. "Why not?"

"I haven't brushed my teeth."

"I haven't brushed mine either. Perhaps we should just suffer together."

"No. I need to brush my teeth."

His gaze remained fixed on me for a long beat. "Are you serious?" he asked finally. "If you're embarrassed about your breath, I guarantee I don't care."

"I have to brush my teeth." I was firm. "You should probably know this about me going forward because it's something you'll have to deal with. I'm rather rigid and set in my ways."

"I've noticed."

"It's worse than you think." I warmed to my topic, gathering my thoughts so I could lay them out in a precise manner. "I might have a few obsessive-compulsive things on the personal hygiene front. Prepare yourself."

His hand never moved from my back. "Lay it on me. I want to know all of it."

Well, now he was opening himself up to a tirade. "Okay, first, I have to brush my teeth before kissing anyone. That's just the way I am. You'll have to brush your teeth, too. It's freaky if you don't."

"I don't have a toothbrush here."

"I brought extra when I moved in."

"That's handy." His delight was obvious. "What else?"

"I need to shower every day and I absolutely have to shave my legs before

87

we ... do anything. Even if I'm completely combusting over you, if I haven't shaved my legs that day we won't be doing anything."

He laughed so hard I thought he was going to choke. "I don't mind a little leg stubble."

"I do. It's a thing I can't get over. It's the same when getting a massage. I can't get a massage unless my legs have been shaved that day."

"Is that all?"

"No, but those are the biggies. Also, if you put the knife back in the butter and there are crumbs on it we'll have to break up."

"I'm glad you warned me." He tightened his grip on me and stared into my eyes. "I'm going to kiss you anyway."

"No way!" I vehemently shook my head. "Brush your teeth!"

"Come on. Just try it."

"No." I was adamant. "You have to do things my way on this. I can't help myself."

"I'll do things your way if you answer one question." He was serious now. "Have you always had this obsession with proper dental hygiene? I mean ... since you showed up in front of the fire station, that is."

The question caught me off guard. "I ... yeah. I don't remember anyone in the foster care system going nuts about it. I think I've always been this way."

"Fair enough." He kissed my forehead and rolled out of bed, heading for the bathroom.

"What are you doing?" I asked.

"I'm finding that toothbrush. Then I'm going to kiss the crap out of you."

"Oh. I ... okay."

He winked. "I thought you might like that."

AFTER WE CLEANED UP – which included a stop by his house so he could change into fresh clothes – we headed back to the restaurant. This time I didn't bother to park in the lot. I knew it was a waste of time. Instead, I recharged the spell I'd set the previous day and followed it from the opposite direction. It didn't take long to find the spot.

"This isn't far from the road," Gunner noted, his hands on his hips. "If Fred was meeting someone here it would make sense for them to come from this direction."

I absently nodded as I circled the area, my mind busy. The blood scent remained, although fainter. There was also the undeniable scent of bleach wafting through the air. "They cleaned up."

He nodded, his nostrils flaring. "They most certainly did." He tilted his head, his eyes closing. "Not all that well. I can still smell the blood."

"Yeah."

When his eyes opened again, they focused on me. "How can you smell it?"

"What do you mean?"

"I'm a shifter. I should, in theory, be able to smell things you can't. Even if you're a super-charged witch, you shouldn't have a super smeller."

That was a lot of information to take in over the course of one sentence. "Super smeller?"

"You know what I mean."

I laughed. I couldn't help myself. "I don't know. I'm not like this with everything. Blood, ... I can always smell it."

He turned thoughtful. "Can you really smell it or do you think you can smell it?"

"I ... don't ... know. I think I can smell it."

"I'm not asking to be difficult. I'm asking because you're extremely powerful. I can't help but wonder if your brain is tricking you into believing you smell something you don't."

"Well ... how would we even test that?"

"Good question. I don't know. I'll file it away to think about later." He circled the clearing and peered inside a bush. "I think it's likely Fred died here."

"Why, though?" That was the part I couldn't wrap my head around. "Why kill him?"

"Maybe they thought he knew too much."

"About what?"

"My guess is they wanted him to steal from you to get our attention. Perhaps they wanted to gauge how you would react."

"Like I would kill some random guy for stealing twenty bucks?"

He shrugged. "I don't know what to tell you. Whether they were following you or me, they clearly wanted to see how one or both of us reacted."

"If they're even guilty. I mean ... we have no proof they were behind this."

"No, but we have a lot of circumstantial evidence. For me, that's more than enough. Isn't it for you?"

"I don't know." Something didn't feel right about this situation. I simply couldn't put my finger on why. "I need to give it some thought."

"Fair enough."

I circled the small clearing, closing my eyes and opening my senses. I wanted to see Fred, get a glimpse of what he'd faced during his last stand. There was nothing. My abilities felt clouded.

"There's something different about Drake," I announced, causing Gunner to slide his eyes in my direction. He was kneeling next to the bush and using a stick to dig in the foliage beneath.

"What do you mean?"

"I mean that he's more powerful than he lets on. Can shifters be more than one thing? You said I was more than one thing ... a witch and something else, although we can't be sure what. Can shifters be more than one thing?"

The question clearly piqued his interest because he became animated. "I don't know ... but I don't see why not. I mean, I don't think you can have a half-wolf and half-vampire because those two creatures are total opposites. A shifter who is also a witch? Absolutely. That might explain why I feel I should know Drake but can't place from where."

"There's just something off." I shifted from one foot to the other and focused my full attention on him. "Why did you ask if my dental hygiene stance was something I came up with myself?"

"Wow. Has that been bothering you this whole time?"

"Maybe a little," I conceded. "I just want to know why."

"Well, I assumed that it was something you carried over with you from childhood." His voice was soft. "From what you've told me, it sounds like you were on the run. Whoever had you, whoever was keeping you safe, likely couldn't risk having to take you to the doctor."

Oddly, that made sense. "It's funny you should mention that. I thought about something similar when I had that needle sticking out of my rear end yesterday. I've always hated needles because I was poked with so many of them right after I was discovered."

"Why were you poked with needles?"

"They said I didn't have any vaccinations or anything. They drew blood looking for a DNA match and pumped me full of every vaccine available ... and then they shoved me into the system."

"I'm sorry." He looked sincere. "I knew you were uncomfortable with the needle. Part of me wondered if it was because you had to drop your pants. Was that thing about having small veins in your arm true?"

"Yeah. I almost died once because I was having an allergic reaction to a bee sting – so, if I'm ever stung, make sure you shove an EpiPen in me. They spent far too much time trying to find a vein in my arm once I reached the hospital. I was almost a lost cause."

He scowled. "Do you carry an EpiPen with you?"

"There's one in the storage bin on my bike."

"Well, that's good to know." He looked annoyed. "You are a lot of work. Has anybody ever told you that?"

"Every foster home that booted me."

He stilled. "I hate it when you say things like that. It makes me look like a jerk for teasing you."

"Why do you think I say those things?"

Even though it was obvious he wanted to remain sour, he laughed. "You really are fascinating." He looked around the clearing. "I think we're done here. There's not much else we can ascertain."

"Where do you suggest we go next?"

"Well, I have an idea. I'm not sure you'll like it."

DUNCAN AND SWAN FUNERAL HOME was exactly as I remembered. The house was majestic, interesting to look at, and shrouded in death.

"Don't get worked up," Gunner chided as we stowed our helmets with our bikes in the parking lot. "Bart didn't try to kill us. That was his sister."

Cecily. How could I forget? The woman was demented. "I don't dislike Bart," I reassured him. "I'm just surprised you chose to come here. I'm not sure I understand."

"Fred's body is here. Bart volunteered to do the funeral for free – given Fred's financial circumstances it was either that or a pauper's grave at the county plot. Once the medical examiner was done, the body was transported here."

That made me like Bart even more, despite his crazy sister. "Well ... that was nice of him. I'm surprised they released the body so fast."

"They only needed it long enough for an autopsy."

"Do you know how he died? Other than the obvious, I mean."

"My father said he couldn't tell me. This was after I jumped all over him for requesting a blood sample from you, so I probably should've seen it coming."

"Odds are Bart will know, right?"

He flicked my ear. "You catch on fast."

BART WAS IN THE FRONT PARLOR when we entered, a serene smile on his face as he folded his hands on a table and greeted us.

"Welcome to Duncan and Swan Funeral Home, where we strive to make the journey from life to the other side as pleasant as possible. How may I ... oh, it's you." His voice turned rugged and he dropped all pretense of being a salesman. "I should've figured you would show up eventually, Gunner. You're here for information on Fred, right?"

Gunner nodded, seemingly amused. "Finish the spiel. I like it. I want to know what to expect on the other side."

"If I knew that I'd be much richer than I am now." Bart turned his eyes to me. This time the smile he mustered was heartfelt. "Hello, Scout. I hear you've been running all over the county with this idiot. I assume that means you're official."

I couldn't swallow my sigh. "The gossip train in this town is unbelievable."

Gunner chuckled and patted my shoulder. "You'll get used to it." He slid into the chair across from Bart, seemingly unbothered by the funeral director's less-than-hospitable greeting. "What can you tell me about Fred?"

"He died hard."

I pressed the heel of my hand to my forehead and turned away from the two men so they couldn't see my expression. That wasn't what I wanted to hear.

"How hard?" Gunner asked.

"He was alive when the message was burned into his back. Somehow – and I'm still not sure how – his eyes were fixed and frozen. I assume a drug was used, but the medical examiner could find no trace of any in his system."

"It might not have been a drug," Gunner countered. "It might have been something else."

"Like ... what you do?"

"We don't do that," Gunner reassured him quickly, "but someone we hunt might do that, though."

"Is there a way to check for it?"

"Not that I know of."

"Then I don't know what to tell you. I've taken thorough photos of the body, but Fred is being cremated tomorrow."

"What will happen to him after?" I asked, finding my voice and turning back. Acting like a coward wasn't going to get me anywhere. I had to pull it together.

"I'm looking at plots in the cemetery. Eventually I'll get him a headstone, although it might take a bit before that happens. I don't have a lot of discretionary funds when it comes to headstones."

"I'll pay for the headstone." The offer was out of my mouth before I'd even considered it. Even after, I realized I was fine with it. It felt right.

"You don't have to pay for it," Gunner argued. "You didn't cause this."

"My name was on his body. You can say what you want, but we both know he wouldn't have died if someone wasn't going after me. I'm paying for it."

Gunner let loose a long sigh. "Fine. I'll help you with the cost, though."

"You don't have to do that."

"I want to. You have a thing about brushing your teeth first thing in the morning. I have a thing about this. It's best not to start an argument."

"Fair enough." I stared at him for a few long seconds, which is how long it took me to realize that conversation in the room had ceased. When I looked to Bart for a clue as to what was going on I found him staring between us, a delighted smile on his face. "What?"

"Nothing." He chuckled. "You guys are just cute. As for Fred, I appreciate the help. I do what I can, but that's not always much ... especially now that I have to funnel money to Cecily. She's been making specific requests at the county jail."

I stilled. I didn't particularly want to talk about Cecily. It felt somehow rude not to ask, though. "How is she?"

"Asking for you to pay her a visit."

I was caught off guard. "Oh, well ... .".

"I told her I would relay the message but could guarantee nothing," Bart offered. "If you wanted to visit, I would be in your debt. Don't force yourself if you're not comfortable. I don't blame you for hating her."

Hate was a strong word. "I need some time to think about it." That seemed to be my mantra of late.

"Take all the time in the world."

TWELVE

"*D*on't give me grief," I warned as we returned to our bikes in the lot.

"Did I say anything?"

"No, but you're thinking it."

"Oh, so now you're a mind reader?"

"I've been known to read a few minds," I grumbled, shaking my head.

He stilled, thoughtful. "Can you really read minds?"

I was only half listening, so I didn't immediately answer. When he cleared his throat to get my attention and repeated the question, I could do nothing but shrug. "Sometimes. It's not easy. I have to concentrate. And some people — Drake, for example — have the ability to shutter. It's never something I've worked toward perfecting."

"Why not?" Gunner didn't bother to hide his distress. "That, honey bunny, would be a great talent to have in our line of work."

I narrowed my eyes. "Did you just call me honey bunny?"

He chuckled. "Yup. That's my new nickname for you."

"Oh no, it isn't."

"Oh, but it is." He didn't back down. "I think it fits you. And I can't wait until everyone in the world hears it."

"You're trying to tick me off."

"I live for little else."

I folded my arms across my chest and pinned him with a dark look. "Don't you dare call me that."

"I'm going to give you a cutesy nickname whether you like it or not. It's either that or baby doll."

I was officially horrified. "I'll kill you."

After holding firm for a bit, his eyes filled with mirth. "You're so easy." He poked my side. "I'm going to try nicknames until I find one that fits. You've been warned. I knew the second that 'honey bunny' came out of my mouth it was the wrong choice."

Well, at least that was something. I rolled my neck to dislodge my irritation and returned to the problem at hand. "You're angry that I volunteered to pay for the headstone. Go ahead and get it out of your system."

"I'm not angry."

"You are. I saw your face."

"No." He shook his head. "You have a big heart. I wasn't surprised you offered to pay for the headstone. You try to hide the fact that you're giving and sweet, but I know better."

I was officially offended. "You take that back."

He laughed as if I'd delivered the funniest line at a comedy festival. "Oh, that was cute, sweetie pie."

"I will kill you."

He didn't stop laughing despite my vitriol. "You really are fascinating. This nickname thing is going to be the source of a lot of amusement. As for paying for Fred's headstone, I'm not annoyed because you're giving money. I'm annoyed because you blame yourself for what happened."

"Who else should I blame?"

"You didn't cause this."

"Would he have been killed — and in such a particularly vile manner — if I wasn't part of the picture?"

"I ... ." He stumbled over his response, which was all the answer I needed.

"I didn't think so." I pressed the heel of my hand to my forehead and forced myself to remain calm. "He's dead because of me. I didn't kill him, but he would still be alive if I wasn't here. You can't argue with that."

"You're going to find out that I can argue with anything. This is no exception."

"Perhaps it's not best for you to argue with it right now."

He sighed, the sound long and drawn out. "Fine. I'm not in the mood to fight." He held up his hands in capitulation. "I don't like that you're blaming yourself for this. It bothers me like you wouldn't believe. But I understand why you're blaming yourself. I think a lot of people would do the same thing in your position."

"I just can't shake the idea that he was tortured."

"I know." He put his hand to my shoulder and tugged me closer so he could offer a hug.

I fought the effort. "What are you doing?"

He arched an eyebrow. "What are you doing?"

"I'm ... not used to hugging people in the middle of a parking lot where anybody can see."

"I guarantee the only one watching is Bart and he's fine with it." He tried bringing me back again, but I fought the effort.

"I don't need to be coddled like a child."

"Trust me, I don't think of you as a child." He brought me back for a third try, and this time I didn't slap him away. Instead, I leaned into him, something I would've declared impossible two weeks ago. "See? It's okay." He stroked the back of my head and sighed.

"This feels weird," I grumbled, even as I buried my face in his shoulder. I needed the moment of quiet so I could clear my mind. Thoughts of what happened to Fred haunted me.

"You'll get used to it," Gunner murmured as he swayed, the movement somehow comforting. "See? This is nice."

"I still feel like an idiot."

"You won't feel that way once you get used to this."

"And what is this?" I was genuinely curious.

"I believe it's called leaning on someone. You may be the strongest person in town, but even you need the occasional shoulder. I'm going to be that shoulder. You're going to do the same for me."

"And who made up these rules?"

His lips quirked. "I don't know. We'll do some research, figure it out."

"Fine." I briefly pressed my eyes shut and let loose a heavy sigh. "Five more minutes of this and then I'm putting my foot down."

"I can live with that."

WE WERE BOTH HUNGRY and needed time to think, so we headed to Mable's Table for lunch. Even though I thought it was impossible to have an appetite given everything going on, my stomach gave a small gurgle of appreciation when we walked through the door and I smelled the grease.

"Now this is what I'm talking about."

Gunner slid me a small smile. "I love that you're not one of those women who is afraid to eat."

"That'll never be me. It's far more likely you're going to have to pry dough-nuts out of my cold, dead hands."

"Ooh. I love doughnuts. I think we're perfect for each other."

I ignored the words because I recognized them for what they were. He was pushing my buttons in an effort to get me to drop my barriers. Sure, in essence I was already comfortable with him, but he wanted all of his bad behavior on display so I would have no cause to complain down the road. I knew his game ... and I applauded it. I was considering doing the same because it was smart to see if either of us hit a wall early, before we were really attached to one another, and it was also fun.

"Breakfast or lunch?" Mable called out as she stood by the menu bins.

"Breakfast," I replied.

"Lunch," Gunner answered.

We slid our eyes to each other.

"You should know that I'm always going to choose breakfast foods," I offered. "It's my favorite meal of the day and we skipped it."

"I gave you a protein bar."

I made a face. "That is not breakfast. That's breakfast." I inclined my head toward the huge stack of pancakes Mindy carried to a corner booth. "There are times I want breakfast for dinner. You'll have to get used to it."

"I'm fine with that." Gunner pointed toward a booth along the far wall and we both slid in across from each other. "I have my own food quirks."

Oh, well, now we were getting somewhere. "And what would those be?"

"For starters, when I'm eating a Reese's Cup I nibble along the outside before attacking the middle."

I snorted. "Everybody does that."

"I don't think everybody does it."

"Everybody with taste buds does." I shook my head. "I like to pour a glass of tomato juice as a snack and dip pickles in it."

Gunner's forehead wrinkled. "That is gross. You'll have to brush your teeth after you do that if you want to kiss me. I'm not a big fan of tomato juice."

He was getting into the spirit of the game. "I can live with that. What else have you got?"

"I like my peanut butter sandwiches toasted."

"Who doesn't?"

"I'm not finished." His eyes narrowed. "I like the bread toasted and I don't like jelly. I like green olives instead."

My stomach shifted at the thought. "That is disgusting."

He grinned. "I aim to please. What about you?"

"When it comes to breakfast, I have to eat my food in a specific order ... and I always get the same thing ... unless I'm feeling sick or rundown and then I get pancakes. Otherwise it's always the same dish."

His eyebrows drew together. "I've eaten breakfast with you several times. Are you saying you've gotten the same thing each time?"

"That's what I'm saying."

"But ... ." He trailed off. "Eggs, hash browns, link sausage and whole grain toast. Tomato juice on the side, but only if it's legitimate tomato juice. You hate V-8."

"It has a horrible aftertaste. Everyone hates V-8."

He shook his head. "I can't believe I've never noticed that. Why don't you branch out? Pancakes are good and you already like them when you're feeling down. French toast is amazing. Omelets are great when they're prepared right and Mable knows exactly what she's doing on that front."

"I'm a creature of habit. Once I find something I like, there's no taking it away from me. I can't help it."

His lips curved into a sly smile. "I guess that bodes well for me, huh? You're not going to let anyone take me away."

I walked right into that one. "Anything else for you?"

He tilted his head, considering. "Just that when I eat a cupcake I pull off the bottom and press it on top of the frosting and make a delicious sandwich."

"Why do you do that?"

"I have no idea."

"Well, I think we're really starting to get to know one another." I turned to the menu, which was a waste of time because I already knew what I was getting. "This is working out well."

He placed his feet on either side of mine under the table. "I agree. You're not weird or a lot of work at all."

"That's a compliment."

"Well, maybe I'll pay you another compliment later. In fact ... ." He trailed off.

I didn't initially worry that something was going on. I figured he got distracted. When the silence dragged, however, I looked to the front of the restaurant, where he was staring.

Graham didn't look happy. In fact, if I had to guess, he would've preferred being anywhere but here ... and staring directly at me.

My heart gave a little jolt and worry burned through the lining of my stomach like acid fog. "You don't think he's here to arrest me, do you?"

"He'd better not be. He won't like what happens if he tries to take you."

There was an edge to his voice that made me nervous. I couldn't help worrying about what he had planned. I had bigger worries than Gunner attacking his father, though. I could actually see my freedom flashing in front of my eyes ... and it wasn't a pretty picture.

"Maybe I should run now," I muttered. "I might be able to beat him to my bike."

"And then what?" Gunner's eyes filled with annoyance. "You won't be able to return to the cabin to get your things ... or Merlin. You'll have to run forever if you leave now."

He had a point, but ... . "I don't think I'll be able to survive prison for the long haul. I'm a bit claustrophobic at times."

He reached across the table and squeezed my hand. "I won't let you go to prison."

That seemed like a promise he couldn't keep, but I let it slide. For now, at least. It was too late to run anyway. "Chief Stratton," I offered with a head bob as he approached. "To what do we owe this lovely surprise this fine morning?"

"It's almost noon," he said dryly, his gaze bouncing between us. "I was just out at your place looking for you. That perverted ghost that hangs around said you guys spent the night together."

I shifted on my seat, decidedly uncomfortable. "Oh, well ... ."

"Not that it's any of your business, but we just slept," Gunner shot back. "You should really mind your own business on stuff like that."

"Tim told me about the sleeping. Apparently there was a crack in the curtains and he thought he would see some action. He was bitterly disappointed."

I pressed my lips together, amused. Gunner looked the exact opposite.

"I'll rip his ghostly head off," he muttered.

Graham chuckled, but the sound was hollow. Rather than drag things out, he turned serious. "I have some news."

"If you're thinking of taking her, you can forget it," Gunner growled.

The look Graham shot his son was withering. "Calm down," he admonished. "Every time I think you're growing up, you prove me wrong. You can't threaten a law enforcement officer because you don't like what he has to say. That's a surefire way to get yourself locked up. Show some maturity."

Gunner's eyes gleamed with irate fire, but he managed to swallow whatever retort was on the tip of his tongue. It looked like a silent battle of wills was going down on the other side of the table. I was too agitated to put up with it.

"What do you want to talk to me about?" I asked, drawing Graham's attention back to me. "Does this have something to do with my blood sample?"

This time when Graham focused on me I didn't miss the sorrow lining his eyes. Whatever he had to tell me was bad. I braced myself for it.

"It does," he confirmed, shifting closer to the table so he could lower his voice and we could still hear. "I have good news and bad news. I have to tell you the good first because otherwise you'll be confused."

"Stop dragging it out," Gunner snapped. "You're making things worse."

"Yeah. I reckon that's true." Graham exhaled heavily. "We found blood and tissue under Fred's fingernails. He put up a fight against whoever killed him ... and your blood doesn't match that tissue."

It took me a moment to absorb what he was saying. Then, it was as if a giant fist relaxed its grip on my heart. I wasn't going to prison. This was good news. "Well ... great. I'm in the clear."

"Sort of," Graham hedged, risking a glance at his son before turning his full attention back to me. "There was an anomaly with your test. The results were so strange we ran them twice just to make sure."

Even though I was no longer afraid of going to prison, something about his tone retightened my stomach. "Are you about to tell me I'm some horrible monster? Is that why I can do some of the things I do?" I tried to keep my voice light, but my heart was heavy.

"You're not a monster," Gunner shot back, shaking his head. "Don't say things like that."

"I agree with my son," Graham volunteered. "That's probably not the best thing to say. As for your question, you're not a monster. At least none of the tests I saw indicate that. It's something else."

"She's not sick, is she?" Gunner barked, his face going pale. "Do we need to get her in to a specialist or something?"

That thought hadn't even occurred to me. "I don't have any knowledge of my medical history so I never have anything to offer doctors when they ask. What do I have?" I was already resigned to some horrible fate. I'm a "glass half empty" sort of girl.

Graham made a face. "You're not sick either. I'm just going to tell the two of you right now that you're likely going to be the biggest downers at any party if you continuously jump to negative conclusions like this."

Well, that was a relief. Still, Graham was on edge. It had to be something we'd yet to consider. "So ... what's the problem?"

"We ran the test twice," he repeated. "We needed to be sure. The thing is, there's no doubt. I'm just going to lay it out for you because I don't know what else to do."

I mutely nodded.

"We ran DNA during the tests and ... you and Fred are related."

All the oxygen in my lungs kicked its way out of my windpipe. That was so not what I was expecting. "I don't understand." My voice was raspy when I found it. "How is that possible?"

"I'm not sure." Graham's eyes flooded with concern. "Are you going to pass out?"

"Don't be ridiculous. I don't pass out." I rubbed my sweaty palms on my jeans. "How were we related?"

"We think he was your uncle," Graham replied. "How that's possible or if it has anything to do with what happened to him, I can't say. You were definitely related. The odds of you two not being from the same bloodline are about a million to one. I'm sorry ... or maybe I'm not. Maybe this is good news for you. Either way, I thought you should know."

I had no idea what to make of it. My rolling stomach had a few complaints to lodge, though. "I think I'm going to be sick." That's all I could say. My mind wasn't working otherwise.

THIRTEEN

$\mathcal{G}$unner must not have liked what he saw. He pushed his father out of the way and hurried to my side of the booth.

"Breathe," he ordered, his tone no-nonsense.

That was easier said than done. I felt as if I was drowning inside my own head.

"Scout, put your head between your legs," he ordered.

Because following his orders seemed better than suffocating, I moved to follow his instructions. Unfortunately, I forgot I was sitting at a table and almost thunked my head against the wooden surface.

"This way," he instructed, shifting my body so I was facing away from the table. "Put your head between your knees."

I lowered myself to what I felt was a ridiculous position, especially in public, but I was rewarded when the clanging in my ears ceased and I no longer felt as if I was going to lose the protein bar I'd scarfed down at Gunner's house.

"That's better," he murmured. "You're okay."

I didn't feel okay, more like an invader trapped in a different body, but I took his word for it.

"How is this possible?" Gunner asked. At first I thought he was talking to me, but then I realized he was directing the question at his father. "How could Fred be her uncle?"

"We're not one-hundred percent sure he's an uncle," Graham cautioned.

When I cocked my head so I could see his features, I didn't miss the pity in his eyes. "He's definitely got a family connection, though. It's possible he was a cousin. But given his age, uncle seems more likely."

"But how is it possible?" Gunner persisted. "She was abandoned twenty-five years ago."

"Twenty-four," I automatically corrected. "I'm not thirty yet."

A hint of amusement flitted through his eyes. "Yes, because that's the important thing right now."

It was to me.

"Keep your head between your knees," he demanded. "You'll feel better in a few minutes."

"I already feel better." That was the truth. And, because I felt a sea of eyes on me, I wanted to put an end to my public torment as soon as possible. "I'm fine."

"You're not fine." His hand felt heavy on my back. "Just sit there and be quiet for a minute. I've got this."

I wanted to argue the point — or maybe pinch him for being such a bossy pain — but I couldn't muster the energy. "We're going to talk about this later," I muttered.

"I'm looking forward to it." He turned his attention back to his father. "What do we know about Fred's background?"

"Not much." Graham scratched his cheek. "I asked myself that after the test results came in. While they were running them a second time, I did some research."

"And?"

"And I don't know what to tell you. Fred showed up in town about fifteen years ago. At least that was the first record of him in our system. He was found sleeping on a bench. That was back when Ben Carson was on the force. Ben tried to move him into a shelter, that one over in Gaylord, but Fred refused. He said he was perfectly fine and not breaking any laws. That was technically true, so there was nothing we could do."

"I'm trying to remember if I had any run-ins with him," Gunner said, his hand rubbing my back. "I can only remember talking to him once or twice. I offered him money once and he turned me down."

"He wasn't panhandling," Graham volunteered. "At least ... not that I ever saw. I never heard reports from locals or tourists that he was begging."

"And yet he was homeless," I pointed out. "He stole from my wallet the other night."

"And then he was killed for it," Graham noted. "I don't have the answers you're looking for. I wish I did. I simply don't. I'm sorry."

He wasn't the only one. I'd never said one word to the man. He died with my name burned into his body and he'd been related to me. I was simply flummoxed. "I think I've lost my appetite," I said finally.

"You need fuel," Gunner countered. "You should eat."

That wasn't going to happen. "I want to go home."

He tilted my chin so he could stare into my eyes for a long beat and then nodded. "Okay. We'll go home. Just give me a few minutes to get takeout — no matter what you say, you need the food — and we'll head out."

I nodded because it was expected and then slowly raised my eyes to Graham. He looked lost ... and sad.

"I'm really sorry," he offered lamely. "I didn't want to upset you. That's the last thing I wanted. When I got the blood results clearing you, I thought you would want to know. As for the rest ... I couldn't very well keep it from you."

No, that would've been worse. "I'm usually not like this," I offered ruefully. "I'm generally much better under pressure."

"Kid, no one can be good under this sort of pressure. I'll keep searching, see if I can come up with something on Fred's background that will be of help. For now, all I can think is that I offered you information that's impossible to follow-up on. Given what you've been through, that's crueler than anything."

"I survived it and I'm fine. I just ... you caught me off guard."

"I did more than that, and I'm sorry. If it's any consolation, I expect my son and I are going to get into it over my bedside manner before the end of the day. That might make you feel better."

It didn't. "I'll be fine. It was a shock, but ... I'm fine." I kept repeating the word even though it was losing all meaning. "You don't have to worry about me."

I wanted that to be true more than I felt it was. This was turning into a long, strange day.

GUNNER ATE HIS LUNCH AT my kitchen table as I made a big show of cleaning the cabin. It wasn't dirty — well, other than the toilet paper Merlin insisted on decorating the space with on a daily basis — but I needed something to do with my hands.

"Eat your breakfast," Gunner pleaded. "You can't go without food."

I'd been through terrible things and never found food to be the answer. I envied the people who could find comfort in chocolate. Sure, I loved candy as much as the next person, but there was no solace to be found inside a Twix wrapper other than satisfying a sweet tooth.

"Stop worrying about me," I shot back. "I'm perfectly fine. You don't have to sit there and ... fret."

Despite the serious nature of the situation, he smiled. "Fret? That's a fascinating word."

"It's the one that best fits our situation." I adjusted my tone so I came off less gruff. "I'm okay," I reassured him. "You have nothing to worry about."

"We both know that's not true. You're reeling. Anybody would be in your position. I want to help you."

How could I tell him that his presence made things worse without hurting his feelings? All the questions I felt silently rolling off him were the same ones taking up lodging in the pit of my stomach. I could not worry about his feelings when I was caught on a roller coaster to nowhere thanks to mine.

"I'm fine." Repeating the same words over and over wasn't going to make things better, but they were all I had.

"Scout ... ." Whatever he was going to say was interrupted by a knock on the door. We exchanged a look. Who was visiting? The only one who stopped at the cabin with any regular frequency was him. "I'll get it."

He abandoned his lunch and hopped to his feet, a muscle working in his jaw. He looked ready for a fight.

On a normal day I would've argued about who should get the door, but I didn't have it in me. I remained rooted to my spot as he strode to the front door. When it opened, I was relieved that nobody seemed to be speaking in raised voices. When he returned, he had Raisin with him. And, as usual, she was a ball of energy.

"I need help learning my lines for the play," she announced.

I kept my face placid by sheer force of will alone. "And you expect us to help you with that?"

She shrugged. "I thought maybe it might be a good idea for all three of us to rehearse. There's a kissing scene and I thought Gunner could play the love interest." Her smile was so mischievous I couldn't help relaxing a bit. Sure, it wasn't much, but she always knew how to make me laugh.

"I'm not kissing you," Gunner warned, ignoring the way she jutted out her lower lip. "Don't even think about pressing the issue. It's not going to happen."

"Because you think Scout will be jealous and stomp me like a bug?"

That was such a teenager response. "Oh, I'll definitely squash you like a bug," I teased. "I won't even feel sorry when I'm finished."

Raisin offered up an exaggerated eye roll. "You're not nearly as mean as you pretend. You would at least feel bad afterward ... and maybe limp a little, too."

A laugh escaped, unbidden, and when I shifted my eyes to Gunner I found him watching me with unveiled interest. "What?"

"Nothing." He shook his head. "I'm glad to see you smile. You can take your mind off ... things ... and delve deep into the world of high school theater. There's no better way to spend an afternoon."

I could think of a few, but there was no way I would deny Raisin. She rarely asked for anything and had been scarce since she saw me take on her father with a show of magic that would've rattled almost anyone. It wasn't that she didn't want anything to happen to her father. He'd earned it as far as she was concerned. That didn't mean she didn't love him. It was an emotion she couldn't exactly put behind her. I understood that better than she realized, but the unconscious step back she took was probably a good thing as she adjusted to her new living arrangements.

"See." Raisin graced me with a cheesy smile. "You should help me. It will do you good."

"What about you?" I asked Gunner. "What are you going to do?"

"I have a few errands to run," he replied coyly, averting his gaze. "Don't worry. I won't go far."

I wasn't worried about that in the least and I knew without asking what errands he planned to run. "Don't attack your father," I warned. "It's not his fault."

"You let me worry about my father. You worry about Raisin. We'll split the worrying for the day. How does that sound?"

It sounded like something I should be worried about. It wasn't as if I had a choice in the matter, though. He was going to do what he was going to do. "Just don't get thrown in jail. I have to pay for Fred's headstone. I'm not sure I have enough to bail you out on top of that."

"I'll be fine. Trust me."

RAISIN'S MODIFIED VERSION OF Little Red Riding Hood was an interesting read. It had been modernized into what felt like a sleek horror movie, a cautionary tale for young girls about the dangers of trusting a bad boy.

"I don't really like this story," I announced an hour into the ordeal. "It's kind of judg-y."

Raisin, the dramatic sort at heart, had been pacing and wildly gesticulating as she delivered some of the most ridiculous lines I'd ever heard. She stopped in her tracks and glared. "What don't you like? It's an absolutely fabulous play in which I get to be the badass and take out the wolf at the end. What could be better than that?"

"Yeah, but ... read between the lines. Basically the script is saying that Little Red Riding Hood would've been fine if she'd dressed like a prim young lady and not crossed to the wrong side of the tracks."

"It's not saying that."

"It most certainly is."

"It is not." Raisin grabbed my copy of the script and started tearing through it. "Show me where it says that."

I wasn't about to be deterred. "Right here." I took the booklet from her and started reading. "What big eyes you have. The better to see you, which wasn't hard to do given what you were wearing. Seriously, this is like a 'how-to' manual on victim blaming."

Raisin furrowed her brow. "I ... ." She looked distinctly unhappy, which made me regret opening my big mouth. She'd been beyond thrilled before I turned into a moron.

"You're going to be great," I reassured her. "We'll simply tweak your performance so it doesn't matter. You're going to bring down the house on opening night."

"Do you really think so?" Raisin's eyes were plaintive when they locked with mine. "I'm afraid I'll screw everything up. My grandmother says I'm being stupid — that I was born to be the center of attention — but now that I've got the part I'm not sure I want to keep it."

I understood what she wasn't saying. "You want to run."

"I ... maybe." She was sheepish. "Would that be so wrong?"

I was the wrong person to tackle that question. "I don't know," I hedged. "In general, I think running is a terrible idea."

"I heard Gunner talking to Rooster the other day. Rooster was teasing him about dating you and Gunner said he was afraid you were going to run. You're not, are you?"

"No." The answer came more easily than I thought. "I mean ... no. I have no intention of leaving right now."

Raisin looked relieved by my answer. "That's good. I think you should stay. I mean ... Gunner would really miss you if you left."

I didn't think Gunner was the only one who would miss me. "I'm not leaving," I reassured her. "I'm happy here." Obviously there were important answers to be found here, too — even if they were going to be difficult to dig out — so I couldn't leave. Things had drastically changed, in more ways than one, and leaving Hawthorne Hollow was out of the question.

"You should be happy. You have Gunner. Although ... why were you guys talking about Chief Stratton? Did something happen? I know you were arrested for Fred's murder, but I thought that was taken care of. You're not still in trouble, are you?"

"I guess that depends on how you define the word trouble. If you're asking if I'm still a suspect, I'm not. There are other things going on."

"Like what?" The question was innocent, but the implications of answering were too great.

"It's a long story."

"Which means you don't want to tell me."

"Which means that I'm still figuring things out," I clarified. "You don't have to worry about me leaving ... and that's not simply because of Gunner, which is obviously what you're thinking. Believe it or not, I would miss you as much as him."

She preened under the compliment. "I'm glad you're staying, but you obviously have other things on your mind. You don't really care about this play."

That was true. The play was inconsequential. Raisin, however, was not. "I'm happy to help."

"It's okay." Raisin plucked the script out of my hand. "You're not into it right now. If you tell me what's bothering you, I might be able to point you in the right direction. I'm not as dumb as the others think."

"Nobody thinks you're dumb," I automatically shot back. "Stop saying things like that ... they're not true. You're a genius in the making."

Raisin's expression was exaggerated. "Okay, that was a bit much."

I couldn't help but agree. "I'm sorry. The core of it is true, though. You're extremely smart. As for me, I don't think there's anything that can be done to help me. I need to remember things from when I was a kid but I don't think I can access those memories. I've been trying for years."

"You should go to Mama Moon."

I stilled. Mama Moon, the local psychic, worked out of a tacky office on the highway. She was a former Spells Angel who lost her way after a tragedy involving a missing boy. She was a bit rough around the edges, but she boasted real power. "What could Mama Moon do for me?" I asked finally.

"She dream walks," Raisin replied. "She can see the past — other people's pasts, too — through this ritual she does. A lot of people pay a lot of money to get her to do it for them."

I wasn't familiar with dream walking, but it sounded intriguing. "Maybe it's worth a shot."

"It definitely couldn't hurt," Raisin agreed. "What do you have to lose?"

FOURTEEN

*M*ama Moon's office was locked when I arrived. There was, however, a sign on the door. It directed those who weren't faint of heart to join the full moon celebration in the field by Grover's Corner. I had to look up Grover's Corner on my phone — apparently it was a small field next to the lake — and it didn't take me long to make up my mind. If I was going to push the issue, it was best to chase answers with gusto. Mama Moon would appreciate it.

At least I hoped that was true.

The country roads leading to the lake weren't well marked. I had to backtrack twice, and by the time I found the field, it was well after dark. I parked my bike a good distance from the light and sound coming from the field so as not to disturb whoever was there and whatever they were doing. I took a moment to observe the festivities from a distance.

They were clearly having a good time.

Music blared from an old-fashioned boom box. It wasn't the sort that utilized cassette tapes — which was a relief because old technology often freaks me out — but played CDs, which seemed somehow surreal. There were at least twenty people in the field, men and women joining in the revelry. A huge bonfire roared in the middle of the clearing and women in long skirts — and men in what looked to be loin cloths — danced around it.

Mama Moon was easy to pick out of the crowd. She sat on a blanket with a man, someone I didn't recognize, and gaily laughed as she watched the antics around the fire. Slowly, as if sensing me watching her, she turned her eyes to me ... and beckoned.

A chill went down my spine at the movement. It was as if she'd been expecting me, which was something I had trouble wrapping my brain around. I swallowed hard, taking advantage of the shadows to smooth my hair, and then headed in her direction. She was laughing and drinking wine when I closed the distance.

"You don't have to lurk in the dark," she chided once I was within hearing distance. "It makes you look like a creeper. Everyone is welcome here."

I felt awkward, out of place. "I wanted to talk to you about something. I saw the sign on your door and decided to come out. I ... um ... this is kind of weird."

She cocked an eyebrow, ignoring the fact that her turban was askew. "You ride a motorcycle and fight monsters. Many might consider that weird."

I made a face as I darted a look to her companion. He didn't appear invested in the conversation. That didn't mean I wanted my business spread all over the clearing for strangers to chime in on. "This was probably a mistake."

"Don't be a pain," she snapped, shaking her head. She held my gaze for a long beat and then leaned closer to her friend. "Darian, I don't suppose you could give me a few minutes with Scout, could you? I think she has something to discuss with me and she's not the sort who enjoys an audience."

Darian didn't look thrilled with the suggestion, but he didn't voice a complaint. "I think I'll grab some more wine. I'll leave this bottle for you."

"You're a dear. Thank you."

I waited until he was gone to launch into my spiel. "So, something has happened."

She wagged a finger to silence me. "Take a breath," she instructed. "Sit down. Rest your mind."

Resting my mind was the last thing I wanted. "Something happened," I repeated.

"Is that something going to change in the next five minutes? No? Then sit down and shut up."

I frowned but did as she ordered, glaring when a rock under the blanket made sitting uncomfortable. There was no way I was going to shift closer to her. I would simply have to put up with the discomfort.

"Have some wine," she suggested, tilting the bottle in my direction. "It's a special brand. Witches brew it in Hemlock Cove, a magical place if you ever get the chance to visit. I think I've told you that before. This particular witch knows exactly what she's doing with wine. It's potent stuff."

"I don't really like wine."

"No? That's too bad." Mama Moon fell silent for a moment and then inclined her chin toward the fire, where the dancers were gearing up for another round. "That's a coven of earth witches. They live in the area, but spread out to various parts of the county. We gather here every full moon and solstice to make our offering to the Goddess."

"That sounds ... neat." Seriously, what else was I supposed to say?

"You try to distance yourself from what you are, but you'll find that's never as easy as you would like. Embracing your true self will smooth those rough edges you always display."

I frowned. "You're kind of rude."

"We have that in common."

That was the truth, so I opted to refrain from lambasting her. I needed her help, after all. It was probably best I didn't insult her before asking a favor.

"Raisin was at my place earlier — I'm helping her practice for a play she's in — and she mentioned you could dream walk." I searched for the right words to explain my predicament without revealing too much of my story. "The man who died ... Fred ... I need to talk to him. Can I do that in a dream?"

The fire cast an eerie glow around the field, and when I risked a look at Mama Moon I found intrigue lurking in the depths of her odd eyes.

"You want to talk to the dead man? May I ask why?"

"You may ask ... but I can't answer. It's sort of a private thing. I need to talk to him. It's really important. I mean ... *really* important."

Mama Moon opened her mouth and then settled, lapsing into silence for a few moments. I had the distinct impression she'd planned to say one thing and then changed her mind. That was probably for the best if she was going to be prickly. Finally, she regained her train of thought. "If you feel you need to talk to him, you have your reasons. You're trying to catch his killer, correct? What was done to him was beyond the pale. Someone deserves to pay for that."

"I agree." Of course, I wanted to talk to him for a few other reasons, too. "Can you help me talk to him?"

"I can try," she replied. "The thing is ... I don't believe Fred was supernatural. The odds of him being on the plane you would need to visit are slim."

"I'm not so sure Fred was completely non-paranormal. If he's not there, there's no harm. I'll pop my head in and climb out. No big deal."

She chuckled. "Visiting the spirit realm is nowhere near as easy as you seem to believe. You will be expending power to do it."

"I'm fine with that. I just ... need to talk to him."

Her gaze was weighted. It was clear she believed something else was going on, but ultimately she opted not to press me. "You're a strong girl. I think you'll be able to master this technique relatively easily. I will guide you."

It was only after I heard her response that I realized how relieved I was to hear it. "Thank you."

"You're welcome." She smiled. "We need to step away from the crowd a bit. You need to concentrate and the dancers might distract you."

"They're not a distraction."

"They haven't gotten naked yet."

Oh, well, that would definitely be a distraction. "Distance is good."

WE PICKED A SPOT HIDDEN beneath the bough of a large willow, the long leaf strands billowing around us. I sat cross-legged on the ground (at Mama Moon's order) and didn't cringe as she did the same across from me.

"Usually I would go into the world with someone and serve as a buffer," she explained. "I don't think that's the right move here. Whatever you're planning ... well ... it's none of my business. I'm going to help you to the line, but then you must cross over yourself."

She sounded ominous. "This line you're talking about ... will I be able to cross back on my own?"

"You shouldn't have difficulty with that. I suspect you can dream walk on your own. You've simply never been trained in the process. It's a useful skill to have."

"Great."

She snickered at my derisive tone. "Close your eyes. Listen to the wind rather than the music. Focus on the darkness rather than the fire. Close everything out ... and listen to your heart."

Her voice became a murmur as I followed her instructions. It was sort of like being hypnotized, something the state workers tried after my initial discovery as a child. It never worked. They could get three layers down and then something inside of me always fought back against them.

This time was different. I was participating voluntarily.

Layer after layer peeled away and I found myself sinking to the ground. It was more a soft slide than a big drop, but I realized I'd gone really deep when I hit the bottom.

I took a moment to glance around, my fight-or-flight senses kicking into overdrive. Mama Moon was long gone — at least I thought she was, because I could no longer sense her — but I wasn't alone.

The forest I found myself in was strange, dark, with trees I didn't recognize. It was only after several moments of study that I realized why they were different. They were upside down.

"Oh, geez," I muttered, shaking my head. "I'm in *Stranger Things*, aren't I?"

The man standing several feet away eyed me with curiosity ... and anger. "Why did you call me here?" his voice rasped, as if he was getting over a winter ailment that refused to completely dissipate.

"I need to talk to you, Fred," I replied simply. "If that is your real name. Is it?" I asked the question on a hunch, but wasn't disappointed in his answer. Technically, he didn't answer, but the furtive way his eyes shifted told me what I needed to know. "It doesn't matter how far Graham digs. He'll never find answers on you because you've hidden them too well."

Fred appeared agitated by the statement. "What do I care about Graham? I've moved beyond him."

"Do you know who I am?"

He blinked several times and then squared his shoulders. "You're the girl with the motorcycle gang. You're a witch. Oh, yeah, I know about the gang. You guys pretend that people not in your inner circle couldn't possibly recognize the truth about your outfit, but I know."

I pursed my lips as I regarded his dingy hair and belligerent expression. He was trying to bait me. That was probably a good tactic, but I was so determined to make this work that I refused to allow him to derail the conversation. "You died because of me," I announced. "I'm sorry about that. I didn't care about the twenty bucks enough to chase you down. You could've had it if you'd only asked."

He frowned. "Twenty bucks? I wasn't stealing money. I was just ... looking. The money was a cover."

Oh, well, that was interesting. "I guess that means you know who I am."

"You're the biker girl."

My voice was soft. "I'm more than that. The medical examiner ran a blood test on me because I was a suspect in your death. It turns out you got a piece of your attacker — good for you — and it wasn't me."

"Of course it wasn't you. What is Graham thinking? Why would he suspect you?"

"My name was burned into your body."

Fred's expression shifted. "Oh, well ... I didn't know that. I knew they were burning something. I'm guessing they wanted you to be a suspect."

"I'm sure you're right. Can you tell me about your attackers?"

He shook his head. "It's dim in my memory. I can't remember. It doesn't matter anyway. I'm better off here."

I glanced around the forest, dubious. "I don't think this is a great place to spend your afterlife."

"Who says I'm spending my afterlife here?" he barked. "You brought me here. This is a place of your making."

Was that true? If so, it was a sobering thought. "I'm ... sorry." It sounded lame. I had nothing else to offer. "I need to know how you're related to me. The medical examiner says you're my uncle. I just ... did you know that when you opened my purse? Were you trying to get my attention?"

He balked. "I have no idea what you're talking about. I've never seen you before. I just happened upon you on the beach. After that, I don't remember anything."

"Then how do you know I didn't kill you?"

"I just do. I think I would remember if you were there. I mean ... come on. It wasn't exactly an easy death."

My stomach twisted at the recollection of his body. "I'm so sorry. I ... so sorry. I didn't mean for anything to happen to you. I didn't even know you. Had I known you were related to me, I would've saved you. I swear it."

"You can't make that promise. You're not omnipotent. Besides, we're not related. Whoever told you that is full of it."

He was a better liar than most, but I recognized the deception in his voice. "You knew who I was." The realization made me sick. "Were you watching me? Is that why you were in Hawthorne Hollow? Wait. That makes no sense. You were here fifteen years before I arrived. There's no record of me ever being here before so ... that can't be it."

"I don't know you," Fred shouted. "How would I know you? It's not possible."

"But you do know me." I took a step in his direction, my hands clenched into fists at my side. "I need answers from you ... and you're going to give them whether you like it or not. You know who I am. You know where I came from. You have to tell me."

"I don't have to do anything."

"Then I'll force you."

The chuckle he let loose was deep and dark. "You'll find you're not nearly as powerful as that big head of yours tries to make you imagine. You can't touch me. I'm already dead."

"Let's find out, shall we." I was determined as I moved in his direction. If he tried to run I would stop him. His eyes went wide when he read my intentions and he took an involuntary step back, stumbling.

Before I could get to him, a bright light flashed to my right and caused me to slow my pace. A fissure appeared in the air, a tear in the fabric of time, something big enough for a person to slide through ... and that's exactly what happened.

I recognized the woman from my dreams, and my mouth went dry. She looked the same. She hadn't aged. Perhaps that was because she died long ago and only truly lived in my memory.

The realization hurt.

"It's you," I muttered, my heart protesting my new reality. "You're here."

"It's not time for this," she barked, grabbing the collar of Fred's shirt and tugging him toward the light. "You shouldn't be here. You shouldn't be doing any of this. I ... this is not what we planned for you. You're doing everything wrong."

"Then perhaps you should've stuck around to teach me what you wanted instead of dumping me in front of a fire station," I shot back. "You did this."

"No. The world did this." She shoved a protesting Fred to the other side of the light and focused on me. "Stop living in the past and look toward the future. You have enemies circling. You cannot focus on us."

"That's easy for you say." I was bitter and I didn't care who knew it. "You know the truth. I'm always left floundering in the dark."

She almost looked rueful, but not apologetic. "That cannot be fixed now. You must focus on the enemy circling you. The rest ... the rest is for later."

"I'm not done with you," I bellowed as she moved toward the light.

"No, but you're done for now. You must go back."

"I'll follow you," I threatened. "I don't care where that portal goes. I'll follow you."

She exhaled heavily, weariness dragging her down. "We can't have that, can we?" She raised her hands, taking a stance that sparked a memory in my head. It was fleeting ... and I could hear wolves howling in the background. "You must go back. It isn't time yet."

"Don't!" The word was barely out of my mouth before she unleashed her magic. I was expecting it, but I didn't move fast enough to block the sparkling wave. The force of the blue blow was great enough that it knocked me backward. I fell again, although this time I was falling up.

. . .

"**NO!**"

I landed back in the field with a hard thud and pounded the ground as I rolled to my back. Mama Moon, who was sitting in the same spot I left her in, was wide-eyed and looked to be awestruck.

"What happened?" she asked, flummoxed.

"Nothing good," I complained, rubbing my forehead. "Son of a ... ." I trailed off when I heard rustling to my right, looking in that direction. To my surprise — and horror — Raisin was detaching from the tree line. She had a thrilled expression on her face.

"That was awesome," she enthused. "You totally need to do it again. That blue light was nifty. Were you in Heaven? I have so many questions."

She wasn't the only one. Unfortunately, the one taking precedence was a doozy. "Did you follow me? Do you have any idea how much trouble we're going to be in?"

"It was totally worth it."

I wished I felt the same.

FIFTEEN

*R*aisin's sudden appearance only served to make things worse ... even though I wasn't certain that was possible.

I didn't know what to do. No one had ever been stupid enough to trust me with an impressionable mind. There was only one solution I could see ... and that was Rooster.

He was furious when he showed up, the ire in his eyes causing me to cringe. He had Raisin's grandmother with him. Irene Morton looked better than the last time I saw her. She had energy, a spring in her step, and a dour expression on her face.

This was obviously going to suck.

"Hey." I felt drained, exhausted, but I had responsibilities. "I wasn't sure what else I should do."

"Well, bringing her to a naked moonlight ritual probably wasn't it," Rooster groused.

I balked. "I didn't bring her here."

"That's true," Mama Moon offered, grinning as she watched Raisin skip in time with the earth witches around the bonfire. Some were dressed, others naked. Raisin didn't seem to notice. She was enjoying the show far too much to complain. "The girl came out of the woods. We didn't know she was here."

"Oh, really?" Rooster didn't look impressed with the excuse. "Given everything that's going on — especially what's going on with Scout — how could

118

you do this without protecting your borders? That doesn't make a heckuva lot of sense."

Rooster held the same position Mama Moon once claimed, so she clearly wasn't in the mood to bow down to him. "Listen here, Rooster ... ."

He held up his hand to cut her off. "I'm not here to tell you your business. You know that's not how I am. But Raisin shouldn't be out here. We have murderous shifters on the loose and a man was tortured to death. Raisin should be at home, where she's safe."

Irene's eyes were shy when they locked with mine. "I don't want to jump all over you," she started.

"It's fine," Rooster soothed. "Scout's strong. She can take it."

I didn't feel strong given what happened in the dream. I managed to stay on my feet, though, which was nothing short of a triumph of will.

"Ruthie is an impressionable young girl," Irene explained. "She looks up to you, wants to be you. I know I was out of it the night Steven ... well, the night he tried to end us all. You saved me and kept Ruthie safe, too. I haven't forgotten."

There was a "but" somewhere in there left unsaid. I was just waiting for her to drop it.

"But ... Ruthie is still a kid, and I want her to have good role models," she continued. "This isn't the sort of place I think she should be hanging out. I'm sorry if that seems rude, but ... I want my granddaughter to be safe."

I felt sick to my stomach, for more reasons than one.

"It's not rude," Rooster countered. "Scout should know better than to bring Raisin to a place like this. I think we're going to have a long talk about her association with Raisin, set some ground rules."

I hated rules more than most, but my reaction to the words was over-the-top. I turned away from Rooster, my stomach heaving and lost what little food I had in me all over the ground. Everything inside of me hurt and I was perilously close to having to sit down. I hated approaching a situation from a position of inferiority, so that was the last thing I wanted to do.

"What the ... ?" Rooster's eyes flashed with fury. "Have you been drinking? Did you seriously bring Raisin out here and get drunk when you should've been watching her?"

"She hasn't been drinking," Mama Moon countered, levering herself from the ground with a terrific groan and then moving to me. Her hand was cool on my blazing forehead, but that didn't mean I wanted her touching me.

"Can that be it for the lecture for right now?" I rasped. "I really need to go home."

"I don't think we're done yet." Rooster tilted his head to the side as he regarded me. "Are you sure you haven't been drinking?"

"I'm not drunk!" I wanted to shake him to get him out of my face. "As for Raisin, I didn't know she was following me. I should've realized that was what she intended to do. She told me about Mama Moon, said she might be able to help me, and she was excited at the prospect.

"If you want to yell at me for being an idiot, yell at me for not realizing that she intended to follow me the entire time," I continued. "I didn't bring her here. I'm not an idiot. I ... oh, geez. I need to sit down."

I didn't spare a glance for Rooster, instead giving in to the sinking sensation bringing me to my knees. I hit the ground hard, and then rolled to my back to keep the world from spinning.

For the first time since he'd arrived Rooster seemed to realize something big was going down. Concern replaced the hostility. "What is going on?" His eyes were accusatory when they turned to Mama Moon. "What did you do to her?"

Mama Moon was having none of it. She immediately started shaking her head. "Don't even. I didn't cause this. The girl showed up looking for help. She wanted information on Fred Burns, a way to contact him. She was very upset."

Rooster's expression was hard to read. "Why was she upset?"

"Because Chief Stratton ran that blood test and found out that she was related to Fred," Raisin announced, appearing at the edge of our small circle and seemingly abandoning the dancing witches. "She's never met anyone she's related to before and now she finds out she's related to a dead guy who had her name burned into his body. It's very upsetting."

I was dumbfounded. "How do you know all that?"

"I heard Gunner talking on the phone earlier." Raisin was calm. "He was yelling at his father. I also heard Scout and Gunner talking, and she said she didn't want to talk about being related to Fred, that she needed time to think. I kind of figured out the rest."

Rooster reached out a hand and rested it on top of Raisin's head. "Did you follow Scout here without her knowledge?"

Raisin nodded, her eyes bright. "Yeah. I've always wanted to see one of Mama Moon's lunar dances and I figured this was my best chance. You're not angry, are you?"

She had the adults in her life dancing on a string. Raisin recognized exactly how to manipulate them. She was good at it.

Rooster sighed. "You know you shouldn't be out here. I yelled at Scout

NO CRONES ABOUT IT

because she brought you with her. It turns out I yelled at her for nothing."

"I told you I didn't bring the kid out here from the start," I growled, throwing an arm over my face. "Now, will you people leave me alone? Take your conversation to the other side of the clearing. I want to die in peace here."

Mama Moon chuckled. "You're not going to die. You're just ... overheated. That occasionally happens when traveling to the spirit realm. Although, your re-entry into this world was nothing short of fantastic. Where did you get the magic that propelled you that way? That's why you feel sick. You moved too fast."

I didn't answer. Instead, I screwed my eyes shut and attempted to tune out the voices surrounding me.

"I don't understand." Rooster crouched down and rested a hand on my forehead, turning alarmed in the blink of an eye. "She's burning up. We need to get her to the hospital."

"There's nothing the hospital can do for her," Mama Moon countered. "She has a magic hangover ... although I still can't figure out why she fired off that much magic to get back when all she had to do was allow herself to float."

"The magic wasn't mine," I barked, irritation bubbling up. Didn't they see I needed quiet? Couldn't they understand that I was trying to absorb everything that happened?

"I don't understand." Mama Moon remained calm. "Did Fred use magic to blast you back?"

"No. It wasn't Fred." The nausea I'd been suffering from before returned with a vengeance. "Fred was there. He was angry I called to him. He wouldn't answer my questions. He claimed he didn't know we were related ... but that's not true. He's a poor liar."

"I still don't understand all of this," Rooster admitted. "How could Fred be a relative?"

"That's what I was trying to find out." I rubbed my forehead. "I asked him if he knew who I was. He kept referring to me in Spells Angels terms, but it was clear he knew who I was beyond that. I don't understand how that works. He's been here for years, long before I was transferred. Do you think he knew I would end up here?"

Rooster shrugged. "I don't know, kid." He snagged the bottle of water Mama Moon had at her side without asking. "You need to drink this. Calm yourself."

I sipped from the water without complaint. I was parched.

"You said you were blown back by someone else's magic," he said, his mind

121

clearly working overtime. "If not Fred, who?"

"The woman from my dreams."

"What?"

"The woman from my dreams," I repeated. "I think Gunner is right. They're memories, not dreams. She ripped a hole in the spirit realm and crawled through it to retrieve Fred. She shoved him through the opening and then yelled at me for forcing issues I wasn't ready to deal with. Then she blasted me with her magic ... and that's how I ended up here."

"That is so cool." Raisin practically glowed with excitement as Irene admonished her. "Do you think she's your mother?"

I tilted my head, focusing on the girl's smooth face so I could anchor myself. "I don't know. I don't think so. My memory is ... hazy. That's why I thought they were dreams. They didn't feel real. It was as if they didn't belong to me."

Rooster frowned. "I need more information. I'm not following."

"And she clearly doesn't have the energy to break things down for you," Mama Moon argued. "The girl needs rest. She expended a lot of energy, so much so that she's probably going to have a hangover tomorrow through no fault of her own.

That sounded absolutely lovely ... or not. "I need to go home."

"You need to rest a few minutes and collect yourself," Rooster countered. "You're in no condition to drive. In fact ... ." He broke off and dug for his phone.

"What are you doing?" I demanded, sobering enough to sense trouble was coming. "Don't call Gunner. I mean it. Gunner doesn't need to be dragged into this. A little sleep and I'll be fine."

"I think you need more than sleep," Rooster countered. "He's the only one I know who can figure out what you need. I'm trying to help you."

"I don't need your help." I was feeling petulant as I squeezed my eyes shut. "I just want to go home. That's all I want."

GUNNER DIDN'T SHOW UP AT the clearing, for which I was profoundly grateful. I heard Rooster talking to him on the phone for a long time. Somehow, I managed to find my footing and flee during the conversation. I was so wobbly I had to pull over twice to be sick on my way back to the cabin.

By the time I reached my driveway, I was a shaking mess. Gunner waited on the porch, his arms folded over his chest. He looked frustrated. I couldn't blame him.

"Don't yell at me," I rasped, pressing my hand to my stomach. "I don't feel well and I can't deal with anything extra tonight. I just ... I'm sick."

Worry clouded his features. "I heard." He descended the stairs, being careful to make no sudden movements. When he was within two feet of me, he stooped to give me a once-over. He shook his head and made a tsking sound. "Why didn't you call me when you decided to go out there? I would've gone with you."

"And what do you think you could've done to change things?"

"I don't know." His expression was bland, but I could feel the turmoil roiling beneath the surface. "You're not alone, no matter what you think. At the very least I could've been there when you went under."

I eyed him a moment, conflicted. "How much do you know?"

"I know what Rooster told me. He seemed a little confused. I filled in a few holes myself. As far as I can tell, you dropped to the spirit world to question Fred. I should've thought of that myself, but ... hindsight, you know. Somehow you were blasted out by someone else in the spirit world and you're sick from the magic. Do I have the gist of it?"

I nodded, morose. "I feel horrible."

"You look horrible."

I narrowed my eyes. "That's an odd way to kick me when I'm down."

Despite the serious situation, a small smile played at the corners of his mouth. "How should I handle the situation?"

"I don't know." Frustration bubbled up. "You could coddle me or something. I feel empty and I need to sleep. I don't want to be yelled at."

He cocked a dubious eyebrow. "You want to be coddled? Why do I think that's a load of hogwash? You never want to be coddled. You hate it."

"Yeah, but ... ."

He waited, refusing to pressure me. The fact that he was giving me what he thought I needed above all else was enough to cause me to break.

I burst into tears. I wasn't sure where they came from. I wasn't much of a crier. I learned early on that crying in front of the other foster kids — many of whom were looking for ways to take advantage of the system — was a surefire way to get beat up. Strength was the only thing respected by the other kids, so I always made sure to swallow my tears. As I aged, that tendency never went away.

It wasn't that I was soulless. I simply want to protect myself. Now, though, I didn't have the strength. I broke down and started swaying as the tears overwhelmed me.

"Oh, hell." Gunner stepped forward and grabbed me before I fell, pressing me to him as he wrapped his arms around me. I buried my face in his chest, letting his strength anchor me.

"It was the woman from my dreams. She was there. She tore Fred away from me and blasted me out of the spirit realm."

His hand stroked the back of my head as he held me. "Do you think she's dead?"

"I don't know."

"Is it possible she came from the world of the living to stop you?"

"I don't know." The questions only made me sob harder. "I just don't understand. I ... how is this happening? How was I related to Fred? Why did they toss me away like garbage?"

"Oh, baby, no." Gunner's arms were around me when my strength fled and he hoisted me into his arms. "You can't think that way, Scout. Not for one second do I believe these people abandoned you because they didn't want you."

"Why else would they do it?"

"They were trying to protect you. Those dreams you mentioned ... you were always on the run. I think you're the reason they were running. They did their best to protect you, but when that failed, they went a different route."

I closed my eyes, too tired to give the idea much thought. "I don't think I can handle this. It's too much."

"You can handle it." He pressed a kiss to my forehead as he navigated the front door. "You need sleep. You're overwhelmed. This is too much for one person to take in a short amount of time ... especially on an empty stomach."

Oh, geez. He would bring that up. "Food isn't always the answer."

"Neither is wallowing." He closed the front door and headed toward the bedroom. "You need sleep. We can't talk rationally until you're rested."

"I don't know that sleep will make a difference. I'll probably be just as messed up tomorrow."

"Yes, but in the morning you can brush your teeth and let me kiss you. That's better than what we're dealing with now."

Only he would think that. "What if I never find answers?"

"You will. You're too determined not to. I'll be with you. You don't have to do this alone."

"Okay." I was out of energy. I couldn't offer up a single word of argument, which was very unlike me. "I'm just going to close my eyes for a little bit."

"That's good. Rest is the best thing for you now."

I really hoped that was true because right now it felt like nothing would ever be the same.

SIXTEEN

$\mathcal{I}$ slept hard, but I didn't wake full of energy. Instead, I felt like a lump of regret. My eyes were swollen and I had to swipe at the crusties gathered in the corners before I could even open them. I wasn't alone. I could feel Gunner resting beside me. I did my best to avoid looking at him, though. I felt like an idiot.

"Hey." He must've sensed me moving because he shifted so he could face me. "How are you?" His fingers were gentle as they pushed my hair out of my face.

I refused to make eye contact. "I'm fine. I'm sorry you felt the need to stay. I ... ." What? Exactly what was I supposed to say? There was nothing I could say that wasn't utter nonsense. I'd fallen apart the previous evening and I was ashamed at the way I crumbled in the face of adversity.

"You're not fine ... and that's okay."

"I really am fine. I feel better." I put on a brave face while staring at the wall. "You don't have to worry about me."

"Scout."

"I'm fine," I repeated. "I think the magical blast knocked me for a loop. That's the best explanation I can come up with." And it was something that got me off the hook for crying like a baby.

"Why won't you look at me?"

Internally, I cringed. "I like looking at you fine." As if to prove it, I flicked my eyes to him. Despite the long night, he looked criminally attractive, which didn't seem fair given how vulnerable I was feeling.

"Scout." His voice was soft, cajoling. "Don't shut me out. I know that you're upset. I get that you can't wrap your head around this. You need to let me help you."

The suggestion rankled. "I'm fine."

His eyes flashed with something I couldn't quite identify. It looked to be a mixture of aggravation and pity. Finally, he shook his head. "You're not. Stop saying that. We're going to talk about this whether you like it or not."

That sounded like cruel and unusual punishment. "Maybe I don't want to talk about it. Have you ever considered that?"

"Nope." He was calm, collected and utterly rational. That only served to irritate me more. "I keep trying to put myself in your position. I wonder what I would be feeling in your shoes ... and I can't come up with an answer because it's so surreal.

"It's hard enough for me to think about what it would be like to grow up in the foster care system, to be shuttled from home to home with nothing to serve as an anchor," he continued. "To not have any memory of where you came from is too much. When you add the magic you have to the equation, I can't imagine the things you must be thinking.

"The thing is, I have to imagine it because you won't confide in me. You won't tell me what you're feeling. What happened with Fred is ... well, it's all kinds of messed up. It's not fair."

The final three words snapped me back to reality. "Life isn't fair," I reminded him. "That's not the way the world works. I need to get over my shock and stop freaking out. That's not going to help anything."

"It hasn't even been twenty-four hours," he noted calmly. "I think you can freak out for a bit longer. In fact, I'll sit here and not say a word while you freak out. It might be cathartic."

That sounded painful. "No."

His forehead wrinkled as he held my gaze. "You can't shut everyone out and internalize everything ... especially not for longer periods of time. I know that's how you've gotten through life so far — and I get it, I really do — but I'm not going to let you shut me out.

"I care about you," he continued, laying himself bare. "I want to help you. I need you to trust me. I'm not so stupid that I think it's going to happen overnight, but I'm determined to see it does happen. So, I think it would be best for both of us if you tried to give voice to what you're feeling."

I worked my jaw, annoyance bubbling up. "I said I don't want to talk about it."

"You're going to talk about it. You need to talk about it."

"I'm fine."

"You've now said that so many times this morning that the words have lost all meaning. I don't believe you. You're pretty far from fine. I'm not going to let this go. We're going to talk."

I didn't like his bossy nature. "You can't make me talk."

"Oh, no?" This time the emotion flitting through the depths of his eyes was something akin to amusement. "Groceries were delivered to your porch five minutes ago. I called in a favor from Bonnie. We have eggs, pancake batter, sausage and that syrup that already has the butter mixed in."

My stomach growled at the mention of food and I wanted to curse it for being a traitor. "What does that have to do with anything?"

"I'm cooking you breakfast," Gunner replied without hesitation. "You're going to take a shower and brush your teeth so there won't be any weird complaints about kissing, and I'm going to tackle breakfast. Once we're done eating, you're going to tell me how you feel."

I had news for him. That was unlikely. "I don't feel anything. I'm fine."

"You're not fine. We're doing things my way this morning. I don't want to hear a word of complaint. Is that understood?"

"You're not the boss of me."

"I'm the one with the sausage."

Despite the serious nature of the conversation — and the fact that I realized what he was really trying to say — I couldn't stop myself from laughing at his unintended double entendre.

He clearly tried to hold it together, but ended up joining in the laughter. "That didn't come out quite right," he admitted.

"Agreed." I rubbed at my eyes. I hated to admit it, but a shower — and then piles of food — sounded good. "I don't know what to say to you about this. I'm genuinely at a loss."

"Then tell me that." He leaned closer and pressed a kiss to my forehead. "Go brush your teeth. I'll handle my teeth in the kitchen while I'm cooking. You need some fuel."

I couldn't argue. "Okay, but I'm not going to simply spill my guts because of your ... sausage."

His grin turned mischievous. "I guess we'll just have to wait to see."
"

. . .

127

I FELT REBORN AFTER TWENTY minutes in the shower. I tilted my chin up, let the hot water beat against my face until all the grime and crusties were gone, and allowed the dregs of the previous day to wash away. By the time I joined Gunner in the kitchen, he'd fed Merlin and was busy working on the pancakes.

He spared me a glance when he heard my bare feet on the kitchen floor and smiled at my jogging pants, oversized T-shirt and wet hair. "You look better. Your skin is glowing."

"I think you're just saying that to make me feel better."

"No. You're beautiful."

His response was so earnest I went warm all over, my cheeks flushing. "I ... um ... ."

His grin widened. "You're cute." He had a spatula clutched in his hand and leaned over to give me a proper kiss. "Don't worry. I brushed my teeth."

I gave in because it felt good to be near him, although I was still reticent to talk about my feelings. By the time we pulled apart, I felt more relaxed. I wasn't expecting his presence to be a calming influence on the ragged edges of my life, but apparently he was magical as well.

"I'm starving," I admitted, shuffling to the coffee pot. "How much longer?"

"Not long. Sit at the table and I'll bring your plate over."

I arched an eyebrow. "Now you're going to wait on me, too? I'm not sure I deserve all this special attention."

"Something tells me you're worth it." He gestured toward the table with the spatula. "Sit ... although there's juice in the refrigerator. You should probably have some of that, too. You need the vitamin C to boost your immune system. In fact, why don't you pour a glass for both of us?"

I was caught off guard by the suggestion. "You don't have to do this. I mean ... you don't have to go all out like this."

"Fifteen bucks' worth of groceries isn't going all out. I could've taken you to Mable's for breakfast, but that would've cut into our private time. It's going to be hard enough to get you to talk here. Just get the juice and don't complain."

I narrowed my eyes. "You're kind of bossy."

"Then that makes us the perfect couple because you're kind of bossy, too."

"Not as bossy as you."

"We'll have a competition later. Get the juice."

Because juice sounded good — and not because I wanted to appease him — I poured two glasses and settled at the table. Merlin finished his breakfast and hopped on the chair to my left. He seemed intrigued by the morning ritual.

It didn't take Gunner long to finish cooking, and when he brought over two plates heaping with food, my stomach almost wept in relief.

"Oh, that smells really good." I leaned over my plate and struggled not to drool. "I didn't know you could cook."

"It's the one useful thing my mother taught me before she tried to kill me."

I stilled. "I'm really sorry for that, by the way. I can't imagine dealing with that."

"No?" He arched an eyebrow and cracked the top of the fresh bottle of syrup. "I think we all have different trauma. I survived what happened to me so it's simply part of my past. To you, it sounds terrible. You've survived other things, and they sound terrible to me."

"I guess." I accepted the syrup from him. "I forgot to ask ... did Raisin make it home okay?"

Gunner smirked. "She did. I believe she's in trouble. Irene grounded her. She's allowed to go to and from her play rehearsals but that's it. Rooster sent out an email warning all of us that Raisin is basically under house arrest for the next week. If we see her, we're supposed to call Irene."

I was horrified at the thought. "He wants us to tattle on her?"

Gunner chuckled, the sound low and warm. "I can ascertain your feelings on the situation. Yes, you're supposed to tattle on her. I don't necessarily think it's a bad idea. We need to make sure that Raisin doesn't follow us on random whims. She could find herself in a lot of trouble if she shows up in the wrong place at the wrong time."

I hadn't really considered that. "Okay, but I feel dirty acting as an informant to 'The Man.' I just want you to know that."

"Somehow I think you'll survive," he said dryly.

We lapsed into amiable silence, the only sound consisting of our silverware clinking against the plates as we shoveled in food. Finally, once the edge was off my hunger, I decided to speak.

"I'm not sure the woman is dead." I didn't even know I was going to volunteer that information until it had already escaped.

Gunner wiped the corners of his mouth and took a sip of his juice before responding. "You're certain the woman from the spirit realm is the same one you've been dreaming about?"

I nodded. "Yeah. She ripped a hole between worlds to get to Fred. That seems to indicate she's still alive."

AMANDA M. LEE

"Or she simply had a greater distance to travel. She might call a different realm home. Did she look different from what you remember?"

That was a good question. "No. She looked the same. I guess that means she has to be dead, right?"

"I don't know. Is it possible you saw what you wanted to see? Maybe you were so surprised to see her you only thought she looked the same."

"I don't think that's true."

"Can you tell it to me? All of it, I mean."

I opened my mouth to deny him and then thought better of it. He was right. I needed to talk things through. He was the person I trusted most in Hawthorne Hollow. Heck, I was starting to think he was the person I trusted most in this world. That was a sobering thought. Either I'd held people at arm's length so long I thought it was normal or he was particularly good at getting around my defenses.

It was probably a mixture of both.

"Fred denied knowing me, but he was lying," I finally volunteered. "He didn't seem excited to see me. He acted more annoyed than anything else."

"I don't know what to say," Gunner said. "Fred was here for years. The fact that he was related to you ... it doesn't make a lot of sense. In hindsight, when I look back at Fred's time here I can't help wondering if he was always waiting for you."

That was jarring to think about ... and then some. "How could he know I would end up here?"

"I don't know. You're powerful, though. Maybe people in your family are equally powerful. It's possible you have powers you don't even realize."

"Like what? The ability to see the future?"

He shrugged and shoveled a huge forkful of pancakes into his mouth. That gave me the opening to spear a sausage link.

"I just wish they wouldn't play games." I bit into the sausage and started enthusiastically chewing, speaking again before I swallowed. "She said it wasn't time for me to get the answers I needed. Do you think that means there will be a time when all the blank spaces in my memory are filled in?"

When he didn't immediately answer, I turned and found him watching me with a wide smile and unveiled delight. It made me feel self-conscious.

"What?" I swallowed the sausage and glanced at my shirt to see if I'd dropped food down the front of it when I wasn't looking.

"You're just a really classy eater," he teased, using his napkin to dab at the corners of my mouth. "I really like the fact that you talk with your mouth full of food."

I scowled. "Oh, don't give me grief."

"I'm not. I'm serious. You're adorable."

I cringed at the word. "I'm not adorable. I'm a badass. You need to remember that."

"You *are* a badass. You're also adorable. I don't think there's a rule about being an adorable badass."

"There should be."

"Perhaps. Eat your breakfast." He inclined his head in the direction of my plate. "You need your energy."

"For what?"

"For the day we're going to spend working around here."

That was news to me. "Why are we doing that? Shouldn't we be tracking down Fred's killer?"

"We don't have any new leads on that right now and you need a break. I figure it's best if we spend the day isolated from others."

"This is just an elaborate way for me to talk about my feelings some more, isn't it?" Oh, I knew what he was doing. Despite the show I was putting on — fake annoyance on full display — I was thrilled with the notion of shutting out the world for twenty-four hours. It sounded absolutely heavenly.

He winked at me, not bothering to deny it. "I just thought we could be productive. I have no hidden agenda."

He wasn't fooling anyone. Still, I was grateful. "Thanks." I stared at my plate so he wouldn't see my embarrassment. "For all of it, I mean. Thank you for all of it."

"You don't have to thank me. There's no place I would rather be." He brushed my hair from my face. "I had stuff to make sandwiches for lunch delivered."

"Bonnie must love being your delivery service."

"I fixed her bike last week and she owes me. Besides, it's not that far out of her way. She was fine with it."

I was glad to hear it. "What are we going to fix today?" I was eager to change the subject.

"I was thinking we would do more work on the roof. We did a haphazard job the first time and we need to get into the nitty-gritty."

"That sounds like a plan."

He held my gaze for a long beat and squeezed my hand. "Once we're up there, it's going to be harder for you to run from my questions. It will be good for both of us."

I stilled. I hadn't thought of that. "Maybe we should pick a different chore."

"Too late."

"I don't know how much sharing I can take. I might be at my limit."

"I guess we'll have to see. I think you're just getting started."

Ugh. I hoped he wasn't right. The day would be endless if that were true.

SEVENTEEN

*G*unner wasn't afraid to work up a sweat. We had that in common.

I was a student of life and took the opportunity to learn various skills at the myriad foster homes I'd been lodged with. Roofing happened to be one of those skills and I needed zero instruction before we buckled down and started hammering.

Within an hour the heat was beating us down. I hadn't yet expanded on my feelings, or delved deeper into what happened, but Gunner seemed comfortable letting me open up on my own timetable.

"It's going to be hot," he announced as he stripped out of his shirt and moved to a different section of the roof. "I don't know how long we'll be able to keep this up without taking a break."

My mouth went dry when I saw his chest gleaming with sweat. He was a ridiculously attractive specimen of a man, which seemed somehow unfair given the circumstances. I hated how "girly" I felt in his presence. It made me feel weak, something I absolutely hated.

"Scout." He snapped his fingers in front of my face, confusion lining his chiseled features. "Where did your head just go?"

I scowled. There was no way I was answering that question. "I was just thinking about the heat," I lied. "I think it's going to knock us down before we finish."

His lips curved. "I believe that's what I just said."

"Oh, well ... ."

"Do you like what you see?" He flexed his muscles, causing my scowl to deepen. "I don't blame you. It's pretty impressive. Before you ask, I work out five times a week. None of this is genetic."

I rolled my eyes. "I'm glad you don't suffer from self-esteem issues. There's nothing worse than a guy who is humble."

"I agree."

I let loose an exaggerated sigh and shifted when I heard the telltale sounds of tires on the gravel that led to the cabin. I shielded my eyes so I could study the vehicle — an older model Ford that had seen better years — but I didn't immediately recognize it. "Do you know who this is?"

He nodded. "Irene. I hope nothing is wrong." He moved toward the ladder we'd leaned against the cabin. "If Raisin has gone missing, I'm going to supply Irene with a pair of handcuffs to keep that kid under house arrest."

Irene, Raisin in tow, was already out of the Ford when I joined Gunner on the ground. Raisin made no attempt to hide her interest in Gunner's bare chest as Irene greeted me with a worried smile.

"I'm glad to see that you're up and about," she offered. I had the distinct impression that she was choosing her words carefully because for some reason she thought I was fragile, which ranked high on my personal annoyance meter. "I was worried about you last night."

"You didn't need to be," I reassured her quickly. "I was perfectly fine. Just a little ... surprised ... at what happened."

"You looked more than surprised."

"You threw up ... a lot," Raisin added, wrinkling her nose. "It was gross."

"Now I'm doubly glad I made you brush your teeth before I allowed you to kiss me," Gunner teased.

Slowly, Raisin's gaze traveled back to Gunner's smooth chest. "How long did you guys kiss for?"

"Not long," I replied, pinning Gunner with a pointed look. The more time we spent together, the bigger the charge he got out of driving me crazy. He knew exactly what buttons to push ... and he wasn't afraid to push them.

"She wanted it to be longer, but I thought we should be productive with our day," Gunner supplied, winking at Raisin. "I hear you caused a bit of trouble last night, Missy. My understanding is that you're grounded."

Now it was Raisin's turn to glower. "I still maintain I'm being punished for nothing." She folded her arms over her chest. "I was just curious. There's nothing wrong with being curious. You told me that, Gunner."

"There is nothing wrong with being curious," he agreed. "You still have to follow rules."

"You don't have to follow rules."

"I'm an adult ... and, yes, I still have rules I have to follow. Don't kid yourself that adults don't have to follow rules."

Raisin stared at him for a long moment and then shifted her eyes to me. "You think rules are stupid, right? They're for other people, not us."

I couldn't stop myself from chuckling. That was such a teenager way of looking at the world. "I can see where you would think I would be your best option for agreement on this, but I'm siding with Gunner. Rules are important."

"Oh, I'm going to write this down," Gunner crowed. "You agreed with me and I didn't even have to browbeat you."

I ignored him. "What you did last night was dangerous. There are dangerous people running around Hawthorne Hollow right now. You could've been hurt."

Raisin didn't look convinced. "What could've possibly happened to me? Mama Moon was there, and nobody messes with her. You were there, too, and you're the biggest of the baddest witches."

"In case you've forgotten, I was also on my knees and puking in the grass," I pointed out. "I wasn't exactly in the best position to help you."

"Yeah." Raisin's eyes lit with keen interest. "What was going on with that? I heard you talking. You were in the spirit realm? How does that work? I want to visit the spirit realm."

"No, you don't," Gunner and I responded in unison.

"You need to stay away from stuff like that," Gunner stressed. "It's dangerous."

Raisin clearly wasn't ready to let it go. She folded her arms across her chest and lifted her chin defiantly. "How come it's not too dangerous for Scout?"

"Because she's an adult," Gunner replied, not missing a beat. "She's allowed to make her own choices, however bad they may be."

"Hey!" I took offense at that remark. "It wasn't a bad choice. I needed to know."

He held up a hand in a placating manner. "I'm sorry. I didn't mean that the way it came out. It's just ... you should've taken me with you."

I wrinkled my nose. "Whatever."

"Yeah, whatever," Raisin echoed, grinning as I shook my head.

Irene cleared her throat to derail what could potentially turn into a ridiculous conversation. Heck, it was already halfway there. "We're actually here for a reason," she started. "I had a long talk with Ruthie last night about what she did — and she swears up and down there was no way you could've known she planned to follow. And I feel that I unfairly jumped on you because I assumed you willingly let her tag along."

"Not willingly." I spared a glance for Raisin, who looked mutinous. "In hindsight, I should've realized what she had planned. I was too caught up in my own stuff to give it the thought it deserved."

"That's not on you." Irene's tone was brisk. "Ruthie knew what she was doing was wrong. I've warned her repeatedly about hanging out with the Bohemian set when they're visiting the lake. She has a mind of her own when it comes to that stuff."

Raisin definitely had a mind of her own. "She wasn't hurt this time. I'll be more careful in the future." It was the only thing I could promise with any degree of certainty. "I apologize for making you worry."

"You didn't do it," Irene countered. "Ruthie did, and she needs to learn consequences. That's why we're here. I thought, perhaps, she should make amends to you as well. She got you in trouble with Rooster. Ruthie, don't you think you owe Scout an apology?"

Raisin looked positively apoplectic at the suggestion. "I didn't hurt her."

"Ruthie." Irene practically growled her frustration.

"Fine." Raisin's eyes filled with something I couldn't quite identify. It wasn't sincerity. "I'm sorry I followed you. I'm sorry you got in trouble — although it wasn't much trouble and Rooster realized his mistake right away, so it was really a 'no harm, no foul' situation — and I'm sorry that I followed you."

Gunner hooked his thumbs in his belt loops and rolled back on his heels, grinning. "Now, if that wasn't an apology for the record books, I don't know what is."

Raisin rolled her eyes but seemed to forget she was mildly agitated with him when she got another look at his bare chest. "What was I saying again?"

Irene was the worldly sort and it was clear she understood exactly what distracted her granddaughter. "I can't wait until these teenager hormones are a thing of the past."

"Oh, hormones stick around long after the teen years fade," Gunner offered. "Just ask Scout. She goes crazy when I take off my shirt."

I wanted to crawl into a hole and die. Actually, I wanted to dig a hole and bury Gunner in it. That sounded much better.

"Anyway, I thought maybe Ruthie could do some chores around your place as penance, Scout," Irene interjected. She clearly didn't want to bear witness to Gunner's heavy-handed attempts at flirting. "It seems fitting that she should make things right with you."

It was an interesting offer, but I couldn't see myself running roughshod over a teenager. That's not how I rolled. "Well, thanks, but I don't know that that's a good idea," I hedged.

"It's a great idea," Raisin countered. "I could help you guys with whatever you're doing on the roof." Her eyes were back on Gunner's chest. "I want to be helpful."

I pressed the tip of my tongue to the back of my teeth and held Gunner's gaze. He looked more amused than concerned. "Now isn't the time," I said finally. "I have a lot going on and I don't necessarily think it's safe for you to be around me right now. Maybe once this is all over with ... ." I left the sentence hanging without extending an official offer.

Gunner sobered as he realized what I was saying. "Scout is right, Raisin." His tone was grave. "You can't be around her right now. There are some things happening – things Scout is in the center of – that aren't safe."

Irene glanced between us and then nodded. "I understand. That makes perfect sense."

"Well, I don't understand," Raisin challenged. "I'll be perfectly fine around Scout. She won't let anything happen to me."

That was true. I would burn the town down to keep her safe. I wouldn't be able to do that if I was incapacitated or dead, though. "You can't hang out with me right now." I kept my tone gentle so as not to hurt her feelings. "It's simply not safe."

Raisin glared. "And here I thought you were going to be on my side."

"That's not fair, Raisin," Gunner chided. "Scout is doing her very best. Your safety is our primary concern. It's not that we don't want to hang with you. It's that we can't because it's too dangerous. It's as simple as that."

Raisin's lower lip jutted out. "You guys suck."

"That's part of being an adult, too," I explained. "Sometimes life sucks. I really am sorry."

Raisin didn't answer. She was too busy being a teenager. Perhaps one day she would understand.

GUNNER AND I ABANDONED THE ROOF at noon. We went inside and ate sandwiches and potato salad, and then moved to the shade of the covered porch to drink iced tea. We hadn't spoken about what happened with Raisin.

"Well, what do you want to do with the rest of our afternoon?" Gunner asked, breaking the oppressive silence when he could no longer take my morose attitude.

"I don't know. What do you want to do?"

"I think we should sit here and pout."

I recognized he was trying to cajole me out of a bad mood, but I had no interest in making things easy on him. "That sounds like a solid plan." I stretched my legs in front of me and pressed the sweating iced tea glass to my forehead. "Do you want to start with the pouting or should I?"

"I think you've already started."

"Then you'd better catch up."

He barked out a laugh. "See. You're completely and totally fascinating."

We lapsed into silence again. This time the silence was interrupted by motorcycle engines. My initial assumption was that a member of the group — perhaps Bonnie coming back to check on us, or maybe Rooster with some information — but the individual rolling up my driveway was an unexpected face.

"Well ... crap." I shifted the iced tea to the table and slowly got to my feet. "What do you think he's doing here?"

Gunner was grim as he regarded Cyrus. "I don't know. Whatever it is, I doubt it's good."

We remained on the porch as Cyrus removed his helmet and took a long, considering look at the property. Finally, the big man's gaze moved to us and I swear I could feel Gunner's hackles rise from two feet away.

"Good morning," Cyrus offered in a friendly manner. "It's a hot one today, huh?"

"It is," I confirmed, licking my lips as I glanced at Gunner for direction. I wasn't sure how I should play this. "Can I help you with something?"

"I'm actually not here to see you," Cyrus replied, ambling toward the porch. He was big enough that I wondered who would win should he decide to challenge Gunner to a fight. Gunner had youth on his side, but Cyrus had sheer bulk. "I asked around in town about your whereabouts because you weren't at your house, Gunner. I was instructed to try here. I guess you spend a lot of time here ... although I can't for the life of me understand why."

The dig on my cabin was obvious, but not haughty enough to pick a fight over. "Who told you he was here?" I asked, genuinely curious. No one in the group would offer that information and I couldn't think of anyone in town who knew me well enough to talk out of turn.

"I believe it was someone at the diner." Cyrus kept his eyes on Gunner. "It's been a long time."

Gunner remained seated — which could've been interpreted as a sign of disrespect — and merely lifted an uninterested shoulder. "It has," he agreed. "I've seen Flint a few times. He's exactly as I remember him."

"As I recall, you two always clashed." Cyrus ran his hand over my porch railing. "I want to invite you to a gathering."

I glanced between the two of them, unsure. It seemed something big was happening, but I had no idea what it was.

"You're having a gathering here?" Gunner lifted a dubious eyebrow. "That's ballsy."

"It's not meant to be antagonistic. It's a pack gathering. Multiple packs, really. It's just a bonfire and food. I'd like you to attend."

"Why?"

"Because I was fond of your mother. She was a good woman."

A good woman who tried to burn her son alive, I thought ... but I kept my opinion to myself.

"My mother was ... something," Gunner replied, shaking his head. "As for your gathering, I'm unsure why you want me there. There's no way I'll join your pack. I can barely muster the energy to care about my former pack, which I'm not really involved with on a day-to-day basis."

"I've heard. You've apparently found another tribe." His eyes shifted to me. "It's an innocent invitation. I promise. You can even bring a date. I'm assuming that would be your friend here. We're fine with that."

"Did you hear that, Scout? They're fine with it." Gunner's tone dripped with sarcasm. "That is one heckuva delightful invitation."

"We're considering moving back to this area," Cyrus offered. "We don't want to rattle cages or step on toes during the process. I want you to know that. This really is a straightforward invitation. We're talking burgers, hot dogs, beer, and stories. That's it."

Gunner furrowed his brow. I could practically see the gears of his brain working, but I kept my opinion to myself. This was Gunner's show.

"I'll think about it," he said finally. "I might have other plans."

"I haven't even told you when it is."

"I'm a busy guy."

Cyrus sighed. "It's tonight ... at Starvation Lake. You know the area, right?"

Gunner nodded. "Like I said, I'll consider it. We might have other plans."

"It's completely up to you. If you don't come, there will be no hard feelings."

He said the words, but I had my doubts. Something really strange was going on here. I couldn't untangle the politics. Gunner had some explaining to do. I knew better than to question him in front of guests.

"Well, if that's all ... ." I lobbed a thin-lipped smile in Cyrus's direction. "I think you can find your way off the property just as easily as you found your way on."

Cyrus nodded. "You're invited even if he doesn't bring you," he offered. "You're of great interest to a few people I've talked with. I would love to spend some time with you."

The feeling was not mutual.

EIGHTEEN

*G*unner wasn't chatty as we locked the cabin and headed to town. It was a sad moment when he put his shirt back on. Of course, we obviously had bigger problems. Still, I felt bereft ... until he offered me a saucy wink that made me feel like a goofy idiot.

"Don't say a word," I warned as I climbed onto my bike.

"I wouldn't dream of it."

It took us ten minutes to get to The Cauldron. I didn't have to ask where we were going. I instinctively knew. Gunner was on edge and whatever had happened — and I was still in the dark on that — was somehow significant.

Rooster, Whistler, Doc and Bonnie were inside when we entered. I had no idea where Marissa was. Of course, I didn't really care.

"I thought you two were taking the day off," Rooster challenged when he caught sight of us, his eyes roaming my face for an extended period. "You look better."

I rolled my neck. "I'm fine. You don't have to worry about me. None of you have to worry about me, for that matter."

"We're a group," Rooster replied easily. "That's what we do. You're going to have to get used to it."

"I told you," Gunner supplied as he moved to one of the stools at the bar. "I could use a drink."

Whistler arched an eyebrow but didn't chastise him. "Beer?"

"Yeah. But make it a short one. I need to run to the lumberyard after this."

That was news to me. "You're going to the lumberyard?" I knew he moon-lighted for a friend, picking up hours there whenever he could fit them in. It seemed out of the blue today, though.

"I have to put some time in. I also want to get some supplies for your cabin."

I balked. "I can do that. It's not your responsibility."

He made a face. "Don't give me grief, okay? If I want to get supplies for your cabin, you'll live."

I wanted to argue, but it was obvious now wasn't the time. "Fine."

Gunner turned his full attention to Rooster. "Cyrus just showed up at Scout's cabin."

Rooster shifted on his stool. "You're kidding. Why? Did he threaten her?"

"He wasn't there for me," I replied. "He was there for Gunner."

"Really?" Rooster's eyebrows migrated up his forehead. "That's interesting. What did he want?"

"To invite me to a gathering," Gunner replied. "He claimed someone in town told him where to find me — which is complete and utter crap — but I didn't call him on the fact that Drake and Flint have been following us. I didn't want to tip my hand and antagonize him ... well, at least not yet."

Oh, well, that made sense. I wondered who was spreading my business. The obvious answer was Flint.

"He's hosting a gathering here?" Rooster was taken aback. "I thought that was against the rules."

"He claims it's not a formal gathering."

"I don't want to be an idiot," I interjected. "I'm confused about what a gath-ering is. It sounded important, but I didn't want to display my ignorance in front of Cyrus ... especially after he extended a special invitation for me should I want to attend without Gunner."

Rooster's expression was hard to read. "So ... which one of you are they watching?"

Gunner shrugged. "I have no idea. He pretended he was there for me, but he was very much aware of Scout. Every time she moved, he watched her. I think ... I think he might be afraid of her."

"He didn't act afraid," I countered.

"He did under the surface. He was prepared to run if you decided to whip out your magic. I don't think you saw it because you don't know him. I defi-nitely saw it."

"I'm assuming that Flint told his father what happened in the woods," Rooster mused. "To Cyrus, Scout would make an impressive addition to his pack. You would, too. Maybe he assumes the two of you come as a unit ... and that's even more impressive to him."

I was still behind. "I don't want to be part of a pack. Besides, I thought only wolves could be pack members."

"Yes and no," Gunner hedged, shifting on his stool. "It used to be that pack politics insisted on blood purity. If a wolf married outside of the pack, he was often shunned. Throughout the years, things shifted a bit ... but only because wolf lines were shrinking."

"They kind of had the China problem," Rooster volunteered. "Male children are coveted in the wolf world. Females? Not so much. So, once a wolf couple had a male heir, many couples stopped adding to their families. I'm sure you can guess how that ended."

"They didn't have enough girls to mate with their precious boys," I surmised, dislike for pack politics rearing up. "What's so great about having a boy anyway? Girls are fun, too."

Gunner shot me a look. "Don't worry. I happen to think girls are just as important as boys. That makes me an anomaly in the pack world, though."

There was no way we were talking about kids. I mean ... geez. We hadn't even seen each other naked yet. I opted to keep the conversation on course. "So, there weren't enough girls and wolves had to start mating outside their lines," I prodded.

Gunner nodded, turning grim. "At first, humans were added to the mix because the pack hierarchy believed they would be easiest to bully. That was mostly true. The problem is, just because someone looks human doesn't mean they are. Before they even realized what was happening there was a lot of inter-mixing."

"Witches, sphinxes and even elementals were added to the mix," Rooster explained. "There was a time that elementals were extremely coveted by packs because, when the two species mated the children were especially strong."

"Huh." I thought about the dream I'd had several nights before. "Were the elementals ever taken against their will?"

"Not that I know of. Why?"

"Just asking." I refused to dwell on that now. "You're saying that wolves will open themselves up to almost anything if it gives their pack power."

Rooster nodded. "It's not pretty, but that's it in a nutshell. You and Gunner would make an intriguing addition to any pack. Graham was high in his pack's hierarchy before stepping away, but Gunner has distanced himself. To others, that might look as if he's prime for the picking."

"Even though I have no interest in pack politics," Gunner groused.

"They don't know that," Rooster pointed out. "As for Scout, she's an enigma. All Flint knows about her is that she took out a siren with elemental magic and she managed to take on him and Drake without breaking a sweat. They're probably panting they're so excited at the prospect of getting her into the pack. It will be the mage situation all over again."

I cocked my head to the side. "What mage situation?"

"That's not really important," Gunner replied, waving off the question.

I still wanted to know. "What mage situation?" I pressed.

Gunner sighed. "Years ago, the son of a bigwig in one of the purist packs — the ones who still believe you should mate only with other wolves — shucked everything and married a mage. She's ridiculously powerful. The pack wasn't happy, but he didn't care. He loved his wife and that's all that mattered.

"They had a daughter," he continued. "The kid was a hybrid ... and great things were expected. Nothing happened for twelve years, but then all hell broke loose. The kid started manifesting powers and the pack wanted to embrace her because ... well, you probably already know where this is going."

I did and I found the entire thing frustrating. "She may have been a girl, but she had power they wanted."

"This particular mage was stronger than most. So was the kid. I'm not aware of all the politics. The pack tried to arrange for the mage and the daughter to join with them for protection. They wanted to control them."

"How did that go over?"

"Not well. The mage — who is even more persnickety than you if the rumors are to be believed — essentially told them to shove it."

A terrible thought occurred to me. "The kid wasn't hurt, was she?"

A slow smile played across Gunner's lips. "No. The mage put on a show of power, took down the enemy by herself, saved all the pack members in the process and then basically did a victory dance over the corpses of her enemies. They never joined the pack."

I was impressed. "Is this the same mage that took down the paranormal college?"

"Yup. She's something."

"I would like to meet her one day."

"You may get your chance. She's still in the state and the kid continues to manifest. Everyone wants the family for their pack, but the mage and the wolf refuse to even consider it."

Hmm. I tucked away the information for a later date. The mage sounded like someone to get to know. I didn't have time now. "I'm not a mage. Why would Cyrus be so desperate to get me?"

"You might not be a mage, but you're all kinds of powerful." Gunner smiled. "I'm a full wolf with a decent pedigree, and you've got magic oozing out of every orifice."

I rolled my eyes. "That was a lovely visual."

My disgust only made his smile widen. "I'm a master with words."

He was ... something. "Basically you're saying that Cyrus wants to schmooze us because he thinks, as a couple, we can help him."

"That's it in a nutshell."

"Well ... he can bite me."

"He can bite both of us," Gunner clarified. "I have no interest in playing his game. That doesn't mean we shouldn't go to the gathering."

His quick shift caught me off guard. "I don't understand. Why would we go?"

"Because they might show their hand," Rooster replied. "We've been conducting research on the group since they arrived. I found a few things that make me uncomfortable."

I wasn't sure I wanted to hear this. "If it's going to make me want to rip their hearts out, maybe you should refrain."

"Information is power," Gunner countered. "We need information. You need to hold it together."

I hated how rational he sounded. "All I'm saying is that they'd better not be torturing puppies or anything. I'll wipe them out without a second's thought if that's the case."

"We'll all be doing that," Bonnie offered.

Rooster grinned before gesturing toward Doc. "Lay it on them, big guy. You did all the groundwork."

Doc remained focused on the screen. It was as if he'd completely tuned us out and we were only shadows in his world.

"Hey, Doc, Rooster wants you to tell Scout and Gunner about the wolves," Bonnie prodded, snapping her fingers in Doc's face. She seemed enamored with him, but in a clinical way, as if he were a friendly science experiment.

"I'm sorry." Doc used his index finger to shove his glasses up his nose. "I was digging deeper on Drake, as you suggested."

Gunner leaned forward, clearly intrigued. "Anything? He's the wild card.

There's something familiar about him, but I can't decide if that's because he reminds me of half the wolves I had the misfortune of crossing paths with as a kid or if I really know him."

"He's indeed a mystery." Doc didn't look at us, instead focusing on his screen. "I've found some records on him. He's something of an adopted son to Cyrus Marsh. The first record I can trace to him was when he was a teenager. He looks to have been about sixteen or so at the time of that record."

"And when was this?" Gunner queried.

"Fifteen years ago."

"Which puts him at about thirty," Gunner mused. "That's right about my age."

"So, it's possible you do know him," I offered. "My guess is, if you feel this strongly about it, you've crossed paths before."

"I agree," Rooster volunteered. "Maybe it was when you were a kid and that's why you're having trouble remembering. People change a lot over the years. You might sense he's familiar and not be able to place him because of that."

"I guess." Gunner rubbed his forehead. "What else have you found on him, Doc?"

"Not a lot. That first record was an arrest record – drunk and disorderly with Flint Marsh."

"Which would indicate that he was friends with Flint as a teenager," I said. "You knew Flint when you were younger because you had to go to a lot of the same pack events, right? Maybe Drake was with him back then and you just don't remember it."

"There's a reason I don't remember that," Gunner countered. "Flint was a loner as a kid because all the other kids hated him. He was the type who would pull the wings off butterflies just to be a jerk. He liked torturing the smaller kids. No one wanted to hang out with him."

"And yet he had a powerful father," Rooster noted. "I'm sure Cyrus forced other people to make their kids hang with Flint."

"I guess." Gunner rubbed his chin. "I don't remember Flint running with anyone. Even as we got older and became interested in girls, the girls wouldn't have anything to do with him."

"It's not as if he's attractive," I pointed out. "He has a decided lack of charm. I'm guessing he was worse as a teenager."

"Yeah, but you heard Rooster. Cyrus was a powerful figure. The parents of the girls our age would've directed their daughters to pay attention to him in an effort to attach themselves to an important family through marriage. I'm not saying I think that's a good thing, but it is normal when it comes to pack politics."

"That's horrible," I muttered, shaking my head. "I hate these people."

"They're people worth hating," Doc agreed. "Cyrus has been arrested three times and charged twice for racketeering. Each time, before the case went to trial, the witnesses against him disappeared and the cases were ultimately dropped."

It didn't take a genius to figure out what Doc was insinuating. "Were any bodies ever found?"

"No."

"Well, great."

"There are a lot of rumors online," Doc continued. "Drugs. Gun running. Human trafficking. Apparently Cyrus has a hand in all of it."

I was appalled. "Human trafficking?"

Doc nodded. "He's a bad guy. Flint is following in his father's footsteps, but from what I can tell he's not respected at all. People are dreading the day he takes over his father's operation."

"That's because Flint is an idiot," Gunner volunteered. "You can say what you want about Cyrus — and he is a total dirtbag — but he's smart. He's managed to evade the law for as long as he has because he knows how to manipulate the system. Flint is the sort of guy who will go to jail the first year he's in charge because his ego is bigger than his brain."

I could see that. "So, what do we do?"

Gunner held my gaze and smiled. "You know what we have to do."

I sighed. I did know. "I guess we're going to a gathering. Do I have to get dressed up?"

He laughed. "No. Just bring your attitude. That's what they want to see. I'll handle the rest."

That sounded too easy. "Is there anything else on Cyrus and Flint we should know before tonight?"

"I'm sending files to your computers," Doc offered. "You might want to go through them before you head in. I don't know that it's necessary, but a little knowledge never hurt anyone."

He wasn't wrong. "That's good. I got a message from Mike. He wants to have a video chat this afternoon. I guess I can do that while Gunner is working at the lumberyard."

Gunner scowled. "Why does he need a video chat?"

I shrugged. "I don't know, but he wouldn't ask if it wasn't necessary."

"He just wants to see you." Gunner slammed the rest of his beer. "I guess I can't blame him."

"He's harmless," I replied. "He's also a good source of information. If he says he has something I need to know, then he means it. It can't hurt to hear him out."

Gunner looked as if he wanted to argue, but he kept his mouth shut. "It definitely can't hurt. We need all the information we can get."

NINETEEN

We took Gunner's truck to the lumberyard because he insisted he had things to pick up. I assumed those things were for my cabin, and I had every intention of paying for the goods when he wasn't looking.

It didn't exactly go that way.

"He said you would try this and I was to ignore you."

Brandon Masters, one of Gunner's oldest friends and the man who owned the lumberyard, was friendly. He also had no intention of budging. The way he folded his arms across his chest and jutted out his chin told me that.

"He's getting stuff for me," I argued. "I should pay for it."

"He wants to pay for it."

"Yeah, but ... it's for me."

Brandon tilted his head to the side and regarded me with an unreadable expression. Finally, he shook his head and sighed. "You're going to be trouble, aren't you?"

I didn't think that was a fair assumption. "There's nothing wrong with wanting to pay my own bills."

"There is when he wants to do it for you."

"Yeah, but ... ." I was feeling frustrated.

"Listen, I get it." He took a reasonable approach that only served to irritate me. "You want to take care of yourself. You're a tough chick who stomps the faces of those who try to take care of her. Gunner told me all about it."

I was taken aback. "Gunner told you all about what?"

Brandon looked around, as if checking to make sure nobody was listening. My heart dropped at the prospect that Gunner was spilling my secrets to a virtual stranger.

"You're a feminist," Brandon offered in a low voice. "You want to take care of yourself and ignore whatever men tell you to do."

I had no idea how to respond. "I don't know if that's exactly how I would describe it," I hedged.

"I do. You want to take care of yourself. Gunner is the sort of guy who wants to take care of you. He can't help himself. You guys are going to have a battle of wills at times.

"The thing is, he's a good guy and he clearly likes you," he continued. "I'm not just saying that because we've been best friends since we were kids. He just wants to help."

I was taken aback. "Well ... I'll give it some thought. I still want to pay for this load. I'll give it thought for the next load."

"No can do. I already agreed to make sure he was the one paying."

I didn't understand. Not a single bit of it. "How did you even know this was going to happen? I've been with him all day."

"And all night from what I understand." He winked at me. He was far too personable to be angry with, but I gave it a good try.

"How did you know I was going to try to pay for the stuff myself?" I pressed. "Someone had to tip you off."

He nodded once. "Gunner did."

"But ... when?"

"About twenty minutes before you showed up. He texted me."

I ran the timeframe through my brain. "That had to be when we were at his house picking up his truck. He said he needed to change his clothes."

"All I know is I promised that I would let him pay. You'll have to take it up with him."

Oh, I intended to.

I FOUND HIM IN THE BACK barn cutting boards. He looked intent, as if he was keeping track of things in his mind. I took a moment to watch him work, marveling as he silently did math and marked boards before leaning them against the wall to organize them.

After a few minutes, he must've sensed my presence, because he looked up ... and smiled. "Where have you been?"

"Trying to pay for all of this — whatever *this* is — with your buddy. He says that you texted him before we arrived that I would try that and he shouldn't allow it."

"He has a big mouth."

"He does," I agreed, regarding him with a mixture of frustration and fondness. "You can't just take over my life when you feel like it."

He arched an eyebrow and ran his forearm across his sweaty forehead. "And why is that?"

"Because ... because ... ."

"I'm going to keep cutting while you think of an answer."

"I have an answer." The statement came out shriller than I would've liked. "I know exactly what I'm saying. I'm a grown-up and I'm supposed to pay for certain things myself. Supplies to improve my cabin are exactly the sort of thing I should pay for."

"You'll live." He was blasé as he moved back to the stack of boards. "I need to think a second. Now would be a good time for you to call your other boyfriend on the computer and ask about that body you remember."

"We're not done arguing."

"About the supplies, we most definitely are, because I'm not backing down and it's already taken care of. If you would like to argue about something else, it needs to wait until I'm done with the table saw. I might lose a finger or something."

I worked my jaw. He was really full of himself. I mean ... really full of himself. "Fine. I'm going to call him. It's not because you suggested it, it's because I want answers as much as you and we need some direction."

His smile was cheery when he glanced at me. "Whatever you need to tell yourself."

Oh, we were definitely fighting later ... when he wasn't in danger of losing an appendage. "I just can't believe I'm letting you run roughshod over my life like this. I don't even understand how it's happening." I muttered as I collected the tablet from the bag I'd placed on the floor before looking for Brandon.

I sat at a small table at the side of the room and clicked on the Zoom app. Mike was a frequent contact and he picked up on the first ring. Apparently he was expecting me.

"There she is," he announced, his grin so wide it threatened to split his entire face. "How's life in the middle of nowhere?" His brow furrowed as he took in my surroundings. "Are you in a dungeon? Do you need me to come up there and rescue you?"

I didn't miss the way Gunner scowled in the background, all the while continuing to write numbers on the boards with a pencil. This wasn't the first time his nose got out of joint where Mike was concerned — although it was a ridiculous worry — and I got a small measure of joy from his annoyance.

"I'm at a lumberyard, if you can believe that," I replied.

"Are you in desperate need of wood?" he deadpanned, causing me to chuckle.

"Actually, I might be overloaded in that department." I pinned Gunner with a challenging look, practically daring him to argue with me. He remained quiet, but the look he shot me was lit with mirth.

"I don't want to hear about that," Mike announced, his features twisting. "It makes me uncomfortable."

"Join the club." I leaned back in my chair and stretched out my legs. "Did you get the message I sent?"

He bobbed his head. "I did. I didn't even have to look up the case you mentioned because I remember thinking at the time that the body dropped relatively close to where you'd been the previous evening."

I frowned. "How can you remember that?"

"We had to check a few surveillance cameras to make sure you weren't on them. We didn't want you to be a suspect."

I'd completely forgotten about that. "Oh, well ... ."

Gunner abandoned what he was doing and strode in my direction, not stopping until he was behind the table with me ... and directly in Mike's line of sight. "Are you saying that Scout was close to this previous death, too?"

If Mike was surprised by Gunner's sudden appearance, he didn't show it. Instead, his eyes momentarily narrowed and he seemed to be having a silent conversation with himself. After a few seconds, he discarded the conversation and came to terms with ... well ... something. "Hello again, Mr. Stratton. That's your name, right?"

"Gunner."

"Gunner." Mike made a face, as if the name was hard for him to speak. "It's nice to see you again. You're all over the place there."

"Wherever you find Scout, you'll find me." The words could've been a warning under different circumstances, but Gunner had other things on his mind. "Tell me about the body."

"It was a woman," Mike replied, all business. "She was a prostitute Scout had words with earlier in the evening."

Oh, geez. Things were starting to become clearer. "I vaguely remember that," I said. "I ... Ruby. That's what she called herself. She picked a fight with me because she claimed I interrupted a transaction and caused the guy to flee without paying."

"That would be her," Mike agreed. "She was known to have mental health problems and fought with a few people that week. Still, we wanted to make sure you weren't considered a suspect because you obviously had nothing to do with her death."

I agreed that I had nothing to do with her death. My stomach twisted all the same. "You don't think ... there wasn't a message to me written on her body, was there?"

Gunner's hand immediately went to my shoulder so he could give me a light rub. It was as if he recognized that I was struggling and wanted to offer what little comfort he could.

"There was a message on her body," Mike confirmed. "It wasn't to you. It read 'Look to the stars, child.' We couldn't figure out what the message meant."

I jolted at the words. "Are you sure that it was a message about the stars? And are you sure the word 'child' was specifically used?"

He nodded without hesitation. "Yeah. I can send you crime photos if you like."

My mouth was dry, but I nodded. "I think I need to see them."

Gunner slid me a sidelong look, but he didn't offer up a question. This was my show and he appeared perfectly happy to be the sidekick.

It took Mike three minutes to send me the appropriate files, and when I pulled them up I felt sick to my stomach. Somehow, even though it had been only a few years, I'd forgotten what Ruby looked like. Now, seeing her face, I wondered how I could've ever forgotten.

She was the ragged sort, as if life had run her down. She was in her fifties at the time and still turning tricks, so it wasn't hard to determine that life had never been kind to her. She picked fights with me regularly. It was as if she wanted to see how far she could push me. Most of the time I ignored her. The day of her death, though, I was in a particularly foul mood and shouted something back at her. There were witnesses, and I got a few laughs.

Then she died and it wasn't so funny. Somehow, I'd managed to push it out of my head.

"Those crime scenes look largely the same," Gunner noted as he stared at the photos. "I mean ... she was strung up the same way Fred was. I don't think that can be a coincidence."

"I don't either," Mike offered. "Once I heard about your death up there, I ran the two files against one another. There are a lot of similarities."

I wasn't really surprised. That didn't mean I wasn't jarred. "I guess that means we're looking for the same person."

"If you are, you're looking for someone who has dropped at least another five bodies."

"What?" I shifted on my chair. "How is that possible? I think I would've heard about that."

"The deaths were spread out over Michigan. We're talking Davisburg, Clarkston, Monroe, Sterling Heights and the city itself."

My breath clogged in my throat. "What years?"

Instead of immediately answering, Mike fixed me with a pitying look. He was smart, brilliant really, and it was obvious he'd already figured out what had me worried. "I already checked the bodies against your records," he said softly. "You were in a foster home in each city at the time the bodies were discovered."

I bent over as a clanging sound began pounding between my ears.

"Put your head between your knees," Gunner ordered, taking over the situation. It was clear he understood the ramifications of Mike's words without anyone having to explain anything to him. He was stalwart and calm, although I could practically feel the anxiety rolling off him despite his best efforts to hide his fear.

"I'm sorry." Mike looked pained. "I really am. I didn't know if I should tell you, but I figured it might be important."

"It's definitely important," Gunner agreed, his hand heavy on the back of my neck as he rubbed. "What about the messages written on the bodies? What about the victims?"

"I can send all the information. None of the murders have ever been solved, and most of the messages were generic. 'The stars shine bright' was one of them. 'Child of the stars' was another. Um ... I can't quite remember the others."

"I'll read them in the files." Gunner sat in the chair next to me, his hand never moving from my neck. "No one ever realized Scout was the one who tied this all together."

Mike shook his head. "No, and it's probably good for all concerned that it never happened. She might've gone to jail even though the first body dropped when she was eight. There's no way she was the culprit, but ... ."

"With this many bodies the cops might've tried to make the facts fit her no matter what," Gunner surmised. "I get what you're saying. I just ... there were never any suspects?"

"No. She was a foster kid. She wouldn't have been on anybody's radar. The only reason I knew to look was because I had information about two bodies being dropped near her. Plus, well, the most recent one had her name burned into him."

"That was brazen," Gunner agreed. "Clearly someone wants to send a message."

I stirred. "What message? I don't understand how this could be happening."

He looked caught as he held my gaze. "I don't have any proof, but ... I mean, it makes sense to me."

I waited for him to continue, my stomach threatening revolt.

"I'm guessing the people who were killed were guardians of sorts," he started. He looked as if he would rather be anywhere other than trapped in this conversation. I couldn't blame him. "I think they were watching you."

"Watching me? Like, ... spying on me?"

"Or protecting you. Maybe they were with the people who took care of you when you were a kid, the people you've been dreaming about. Maybe they realized they couldn't keep you safe no matter how hard they tried so they relinquished you to the system ... but never really left your life. Maybe they protected you from afar until you were old enough to understand what was going on."

That was preposterous ... mostly. "No way. I've been an adult for a long time. If they were watching me as a form of protection, they would've approached sooner to tell me what was going on."

"We don't know that," he argued. "Something might've happened to change their plans."

"Fred was here fifteen years before I arrived."

"That doesn't mean he didn't know you were coming."

I felt light-headed and rested my head on my knees. "This is too much."

"I know." He brushed his hand over my head. "It's too much and yet it explains a lot. I need everything you have in those files, Mike. We need to start putting all this information together if we're going to figure this out."

Mike didn't put up a lick of argument. "I'll have everything to you within the hour. I ... ." He stilled and then regrouped. "Take care of her, all right? I'm genuinely fond of her."

Gunner nodded without missing a beat, or bristling in the slightest. "That's the plan. I'm fond of her, too."

"She has a way about her."

"She definitely does."

"I'm sitting right here," I groused. "I can hear everything you're saying."

"There's that way," Gunner teased before sobering. "We'll figure this out. I promise you that. Don't let it beat you down. I know it's a lot, but ... we'll find the answers you need.."

That was the one thing I had going for me.

TWENTY

$\mathcal{W}$e sat in the small park next to the police station to go through the case notes. I had no idea why Gunner picked the spot, but I was thankful for the fresh air and sunshine.

"Are you feeling better?" His eyes were speculative as they washed over my features. "It's okay if you're not. This is ... a lot."

It was more than a lot. It was a mountain that I had no idea how to climb. "I'm fine." It was my go-to response. I always whipped it out, whether I was truly fine or not.

"You're not fine." He was calm, his voice even. However, I didn't miss the hint of annoyance lurking in the depths of his eyes. "You're pretty far from fine. I wish you would just accept that it's okay for you to struggle occasionally. The only person who expects you to be superhuman is you."

"That makes me sound self-important."

He shrugged. "I don't know. I'm too egotistical to notice."

That made me laugh, which dislodged some of the distress taking up residence in my chest. "I guess we're quite the pair."

"Yeah, we are." He squeezed my hand. "But we need to go over this."

We broke the cases down into separate files and laid out the information. Besides Ruby, there was Bridget Tapper, a seamstress from Davisburg who was supposedly out on a walk. She had no known enemies and lived alone. There was also Frank Davis, a gas station owner in Sterling Heights. His background information was almost non-existent. Other than being a business owner, there was almost nothing on him. It was the same with the others, two men and a woman. The only thing they had in common was the way they'd died.

"I don't know what to make of any of this," Gunner admitted when we were finished, rubbing his hand over his jaw as he exhaled heavily. "None of these people existed anywhere but on paper ... and even then it was a tenuous existence at best."

That was an interesting way of looking at it. "Fake identities?"

He shrugged. "Or people who knew how to remain off the radar. It seems unlikely that all these identities would have to be faked. Even if they were watching you ... ."

"Why would they be watching me?"

"You know why. You're more powerful than a normal witch. There's something else inside you. I'm guessing you're part elemental, although which one is beyond me."

"Marissa thinks I cast love spells. That's a cupid, right?" I knew a little about elementals. I knew they'd all sprung from the same origins and then split hundreds of years before because the factions started fighting. The earth elementals became witches, the air elementals turned into cupids, the water elementals shifted to sirens and merfolk, and the fire elementals to demons. That information was tackled early in my Spells Angels training. Other than that, I didn't have much information.

"You don't cast love spells. She's just jealous and lashes out." His expression was thoughtful. "Some think witches became the weakest link when the elementals split. I don't agree with that. I think witches opted to broaden their horizons.

"Everyone knows that elemental magic is some of the strongest out there," he continued. "It's possible that you're from a group of witches who never abandoned the elemental magic. That could be why you're so strong."

"There are plenty of witches who still use elemental magic," I argued. "I've seen them, fought a few and joined forces with others. I don't think it's that witches gave up using elemental magic as much as they zeroed in on one skill and embraced it. Like controlling the weather or casting hexes."

"You think they became specialists," he mused. "That's an interesting idea. It would seem to fit. Maybe your coven continued using all the magic at their disposal. Maybe they never forgot the old ways. In that dream you told me about, you were expected to supply the power, right? That seems to indicate that you were even more powerful than those you were living with."

Huh. I'd forgotten that part of the dream. "Yeah. I was the one supplying the power. That could be because she was tired. I don't remember much about the dream, but I do remember that. She was exhausted."

"From keeping you safe?"

That was the question.

We went back to poring over the files. Even though I didn't recognize any of the faces in the photos — as a child, I was much more interested in self-preservation than worrying about near strangers — it was fascinating to read about people who had lived — and ultimately died — on the periphery of my life. I was so caught up in what I was reading I didn't notice that we were no longer alone until Graham cleared his throat from behind me, almost causing me to jump out of my skin.

"I'm sorry," he offered, resting his hand on my shoulder. His eyes were kind as they locked with mine. "I didn't mean to frighten you."

"I'm not afraid," I immediately barked.

"She's fine," Gunner said dryly. "She'll spout that mantra until the day she dies. She could be missing an arm and she would still say it."

He was beginning to bug me. "I say it because it's true."

"Whatever." Gunner shifted his attention to his father. "Do you have anything?"

The question caught me off guard. "Were we expecting him to have something?"

Gunner ignored me and waited for his father to answer.

"I have a few somethings," Graham replied, sliding into the chair next to me and lifting an eyebrow when he saw the crime scene photos we were studying. "What's all this?"

"Oh, um ... ." I hesitated. I didn't want to tell him the truth in case he decided to change his mind about me being complicit in Fred's death and lock me up.

Gunner took the situation out of my hands. "We have some information." He laid all of it out for his father, refusing to meet my accusatory gaze. Instead, he slid his hand under the table and squeezed my knee, offering unspoken reassurance as I fumed. When he was finished, instead of being angry or apoplectic, Graham was intrigued.

"Well, that explains a lot," he mused. "Do you want to know what I think?"

"Only if it means you're not going to lock me up," I answered.

He smirked. "Honey, I'm not going to lock you up. I never thought you were guilty. The prosecutor was the one who insisted on getting the blood sample. And, for the record, he doesn't need to know about any of this. It doesn't involve him."

That was a relief. "Then I want to know what you think."

"I think it was a cult."

"A cult? Like the Jim Jones people who drank the Kool-Aid?"

He snorted. "Not exactly, but kind of. I think these people were true believers. I think they gathered together for a common cause and some of them were willing to die for it. Maybe everyone was willing to die for it and there are more bodies out there we're not aware of."

I didn't like that notion one little bit. "I would rather focus on the dead people we already have rather than add more. What common cause could they all have joined together over?"

He arched an eyebrow and turned to me. "Do you really not see it?"

I was at a loss.

"She doesn't," Gunner volunteered. "She can't see it because it's all snow-balling and is too much. I've tried broaching the subject with her, but she hasn't embraced the idea just yet."

His words frustrated me to no end. "What subject? I have no idea what you're talking about."

Graham held up a hand when Gunner opened his mouth to respond. It was one of the few times Gunner acquiesced to his father's demands without putting up a fight.

"You're the cause," Graham said quietly. "You're the thing they were willing to die to protect."

My heart rate picked up a notch. "No. That can't be right. Why would they die for me?"

"You're either their family — which we've determined is the case with Fred — or you're tied to their group through more than blood. I don't think that's up for debate, but I would love to see if there's any blood evidence left in these other cases so we could test the DNA against Scout's."

My heart stuttered at the prospect. "I don't think that's a good idea. I ... no."

"Okay." Graham patted my hand. "When you're ready, we still might be able to conduct the tests down the road."

What if I was never ready? "I ... just ... ."

"Don't dwell on that," Gunner instructed. "It's not important right now. What is important is figuring out how Cyrus's group plays into this. Scout remembers running from shifters when she was a kid. The woman she was with warned her that not all shifters were bad but the ones they were running from wanted something specific. I'm pretty sure that was Scout."

"And you're sure the dream was a memory?" Graham asked. "Isn't it possible that her subconscious filled in certain blanks and perhaps not every-thing she saw in that dream was real?"

"Anything is possible," Gunner replied. "I believe that was a memory, espe-cially because Scout saw the same woman in the spirit realm when she tried to talk to Fred."

Graham's eyebrows flew up his forehead. "I think I'm missing part of the story. Maybe you should fill me in."

Gunner let loose a drawn-out sigh, but acquiesced. When he was finished, Graham was contemplative.

"Well, that seems to indicate that we're on the right track," he said finally. "All we need to do is put all the pieces together. Do we think Cyrus is a piece?"

"I don't know," Gunner replied. "The fact that he showed up here out of the blue at the same time a body dropped makes me leery. But we can't be sure he was in those other locations when those bodies dropped, so ... I honestly don't know."

"I can make some discreet inquiries," Graham offered. "It can't hurt to run financials. If we can pin him to even one of those locations it would be beneficial."

"If you have the time to help, we could use it."

"Then I'll see what I can dig up. As for that other thing you requested, I have some answers there, too."

I lifted my head, my interest piqued. "What other thing?"

"Fred," Gunner volunteered. "I've been bothered about his standing in town since his body was discovered. The thing is, people assumed he was homeless because he was always sitting on benches and watching everyone. No one ever actually saw him sleeping on the street or panhandling."

He acted as if that was a major clue. "So ... what?"

"So, he had to be sleeping somewhere else," Graham explained. "He didn't own a house and he wasn't renting property. I checked with the clerk's office to be sure. Then I had a thought. I once saw him walking out on the highway that leads to the resort. I couldn't figure out why he was there, but he wasn't breaking the law so I let it go."

I remained confused. "I don't understand."

"There's nothing out there," Gunner argued. "There's no way he could've afforded one of those villas at the resort."

"I agree about the villas. But there is something out there."

I watched Gunner's face recognize the moment he grasped what his father was getting at. "Gertie and Gina."

Graham grinned. "It took you a bit, but you finally caught up. Way to go."

Gunner scowled. "Why can't you ever just be a normal father and not go the passive-aggressive route?"

"What fun would that be?"

I was still behind. "Who are Gertie and Gina" I asked.

Now it was Gunner's turn to grin. "They ... defy explanation. I'm just going to have to take you out there to meet them."

That sounded ominous. "Are they dangerous?"

"Only to the rodent population."

That was a really odd answer.

GINA AND GERTIE Pascal were twins, in their seventies, and they lived in a huge house on the highway. From the outside, it looked run down. On the inside it was quite posh and clean. Er, well, other than the twenty cats running around.

"I guess I see what you mean about the rodent population," I muttered as I sat at their small kitchen table and tried to keep the huge tabby sitting on the table from drinking out of my teacup.

Gunner's grin was contagious. "They like cats."

"We love all God's creatures," Gina supplied as she carried a huge tray of cookies to the table. I could only tell them apart because Gina was wearing all blue and Gertie all green. I filed the information away when we knocked on their door and they joyously welcomed us inside. "We simply have a special affinity for cats."

"Scout loves cats, too," Gunner offered. "She adopted a kitten from the lumberyard."

Gertie beamed at me. "That is lovely. You should get him a friend."

That wasn't going to happen. On his own, Merlin was singlehandedly destroying my cabin one roll of toilet paper at a time. "I'll give it some thought," I lied, sipping my tea. "This is an amazing house."

"It belonged to our parents," Gina explained, joining us at the table. "They used to run a bed and breakfast — we did, too, for a time — and it was a grand house. Unfortunately, once the resort came in, people started staying there, so ... well, you know how that goes."

I felt inexplicably sorry for them. "I'm sorry."

Gina waved off my concern. "The world never stops turning. Things change. We have to change with them."

I wanted to ask how they managed to afford the upkeep on the house — which looked to be lagging — and the care of all the cats without steady money coming in, but I didn't feel that was any of my business. Instead, I let Gunner take over the conversation.

"We're actually here for a reason," Gunner supplied. "Did you know Fred Burns?"

"Of course we knew him." Gertie made a tsking sound with her tongue. "We heard what happened in town. Quite frankly, we were expecting a visit from your father. He hasn't come yet."

Gunner straightened. "Was Fred living here?"

"Of course he was. We gave him a room in exchange for him doing odd jobs around the house. The upkeep is more than we can keep up on. It was more for him as well, but he did his best. He was a good man."

"He had a room here," Gunner repeated. "For how long?"

"It's been more than ten years. I think he was in town a full year before he helped us when we were broken down on the side of the road one day. We invited him back for dinner, offered him a roof for one night and things sort of grew from there."

"No one knew he was living here," Gunner said.

"Well, it wasn't a secret," Gina countered. "He's been part of the family for a long time. We're very upset about his passing ... and the fact that no one is sharing information with us. We no longer have a vehicle — the doctor says we shouldn't drive — so we had no way of getting to town to complain to Graham."

"You have a phone," Gunner pointed out.

"Yes, but as we said, we thought Graham would be out here eventually. It simply didn't happen. We were going to call ... maybe."

Gunner shook his head as he turned his eyes to me. It was obvious what he was thinking. We could've had at least some answers days before if we'd bothered to ask the obvious question about Fred's lodging. That was really on us.

"Well, it doesn't matter now." Gunner forced a smile. "I can guarantee my father will be out here before the end of the day. But we need some information now."

"Of course." Gina was congenial as she rested her hands on the table and smiled primly. "What do you need information about?"

"Fred."

"What about him?"

"Anything you can tell us."

"Oh, well, there's not much to tell. He didn't talk about himself much. He helped us around the house ... and with the cats ... and when the lawn needed mowing. He never volunteered any information. I got the feeling that something terrible happened and he was separated from his family. He never wanted to talk about it and we didn't press."

"There has to be something more," I argued. "Isn't there something you can tell us about where he came from?"

"No, but there might be something in his room. You're welcome to look around if you're so inclined. I'm sure Fred wouldn't mind."

TWENTY-ONE

F red's room was tidy and largely devoid of personality. There was a small twin bed and matching dresser. Next to the bed, a stack of books towered on the nightstand. That was it.

"It's not much of a life," I murmured as I ran my fingers over the aged comforter. "There's nothing of him here."

Gunner squeezed my shoulder and dropped a kiss on my temple as he passed. "We don't know that yet. We've only been in here five minutes. Give it some time."

Time felt like a commodity we didn't have. "We need answers."

"And we'll get them. Have faith."

I didn't snap back, even though I had something snarky on the tip of my tongue. Instead, I focused on the books. "He liked murder mysteries."

"So do you. I've seen your e-reader."

"I doubt that was a genetic trait."

"No." His eyes were thoughtful as they held mine. "Is that what you're really looking for? Do you want to see something of yourself in him? Will that make you feel better?"

"I ... ."

"It's okay," he prodded. "I get it. My father drives me nuts — as you've seen several times already — but it's a comfort to know we drink our coffee the same way ... and only like strawberry jelly on our toast ... and have the same hairline, which means I'll never go bald. That's only one of the reasons I'm a keeper, by the way."

I couldn't stop myself from smiling at his enthusiasm. "I hadn't really thought about the hair. You're right. I'm sold."

He laughed and moved back to the dresser. "You're looking for hints of yourself in the others because you want to belong," he surmised. "There's nothing wrong with that. The thing is, you don't need blood to belong. You already belong to a group ... though you might not want to claim some of its members."

I easily grasped his reference. "I don't want to claim Marissa."

"That goes without saying."

"The rest of you aren't so bad."

"I'm the bomb."

I choked on my laughter. "I don't think I can date someone who refers to himself in that manner."

"Well, suck it up. I'm the bomb and I don't care who knows it."

"I guess I will have to suck it up." I paged through the books. I had no idea what I was looking for but thought there was a possibility of a stray sheet of paper ... a letter ... or something other than prose on pages. I was disappointed.

"I found something," Gunner announced, drawing my attention back to the dresser. He'd been searching through Fred's clothes and seemed to be having as fruitless a time as me. When I turned my attention to him, though, he was holding up what looked to be a necklace.

Something sparked in the back of my memory as the light glinted off the delicate chain and pendant. I recognized it.

"It looks like it belongs to a woman," Gunner noted, his eyes never moving in my direction. "I wonder if he had a wife or daughter. The charm thing is weird. It's ... odd."

My hands were shaking when I reached for it. "That's not a charm."

He glanced at me. "I don't know the technical term for it, but I was close enough for you to understand what I was talking about."

"It's a locket." My breath barely came out in a whisper.

"Locket?" Gunner glanced back at the item in his hand. "How can you be sure? It doesn't look like a locket."

"It used to be mine."

His mouth dropped open. "I ... are you sure?"

I nodded. I felt numb, as if disconnected from the scene transpiring in the room. It was as if I was watching from outside myself. "I only owned three things." It was coming back to me in bits and pieces. "A blanket ... a small tin full of money in case I was separated and needed food ... and that locket."

Gunner wordlessly handed it over and the second my fingers touched the cool metal it was as if I'd been transported back. For a brief moment, a split-second really, I thought I remembered everything. Then the cloudy veil descended again and the memories dissolved into a hodgepodge of sights, sounds and screams. "I can't believe he had it."

Gunner was clearly at a loss. "Do you remember when you last saw it?"

"I ... no. I don't even know why I remember it. It's probably because I just had that dream. I remembered the locket in the dream."

"Well ... it's still something. Can you open it?"

"Maybe." I flipped the locket over and stared at the back. There was an etching there, but it was long faded. "There were stars on the back. I remember that. I guess they're gone now."

"Or hidden by magic," Gunner noted. "We can figure out the stars later. If you can open it, there might be answers inside."

That seemed far-fetched, but I was willing to try. "Yes. I'll open the locket and somehow I'll magically remember everything."

"You don't know. That could happen. There could be a spell on the locket or something. Maybe it's been waiting for you to find it again and to provide the answers you've been looking for."

I shot him a dubious look.

"Or maybe there's nothing inside," he conceded with a weak grin. "That's entirely possible, too. I don't want to get your hopes up or anything, but ... this is the first truly tangible lead we've had on your childhood since ... well ... ever. I mean, I know you probably had other leads throughout the years, but this is the first one I've been present for, which makes it special."

"There's that ego again." I fumbled with the hasp on the locket. "Hmm. I remember there being a trick."

"Let me try." He tried to take the necklace from me but I clutched it against my chest. "Or you could hold onto it and try again when you're alone later." He studied my face. "That's what you want to do."

"I don't care if I'm alone." That was true. "I just ... don't want to let it go yet. I can't explain it. Something inside is telling me to hold onto it. I'm sorry." I made a concerted effort to hand it to him but he didn't take it.

"That's yours." He was firm. "You hold onto it. I'll be here when you're ready to talk about it."

For some reason, relief coursed through me. "Thanks, but ... I don't mind if you touch it. Don't be ridiculous."

He closed my fist over the necklace. "You finally have a piece of your past. It makes sense that you're feeling territorial. It's okay."

"It won't even open."

"Maybe you'll remember the trick. Until then, we'll treat it like the one ring. I can't carry it, but I can carry you."

I was flummoxed for a moment, and then I remembered the *Lord of the Rings* and smiled. "That was really geeky."

"You're going to learn that I might be a hunk on the outside, but I'm a total geek on the inside. I love books ... and movies ... and music. I love comic books, too. You'll have to learn to deal with it."

"Okay." I slipped the locket into my pocket and forced a smile. "We should finish searching and then get out of here. We still have to get ready for the wolf gathering tonight ... and dinner couldn't hurt."

"Dinner definitely couldn't hurt," he agreed, tipping up my chin to stare into my eyes. "I still stand by what I've said about twenty times now. We'll figure this out. The locket might not seem like much of a lead right now, but I think it'll be more helpful than we realize."

"I hope so. I just feel ... shaky. It's weird."

"Maybe it really is like the one ring. Maybe it's magical ... but somehow directly at you. If so, I'm sure we'll be able to untangle this mess eventually. You're not alone. We'll do it together."

For once I was happy for the backup. I'd never had a situation in which I thought I was in over my head. I was officially there. "Thanks. I was serious about dinner, though. I'm starving."

"Dinner it is. Are you okay with the diner?"

"Sure. Comfort food sounds divine."

THE DINER WAS PACKED. I shouldn't have been surprised. Other than a few sandwich shops and a pizza place, it was the only location in town that served full meals. Still, the room hummed with activity.

As if sensing the noise was too much, Gunner placed our order at the front counter and we took takeout containers to the park outside. We settled there, silent, and ate in companionable silence. I was about halfway through my fried chicken meal when I found the courage to speak.

"I really am sorry about the locket thing. I don't know what came over me. I'm not usually like that with material possessions."

His gaze was speculative. "It's okay. My guess is you haven't had anything to call your own in a very long time."

"That's not true. I have my bike."

He smiled. "There is that. Was that the first big purchase you ever made?"

"Yup." I bobbed my head. "I saw her in a window in Detroit and knew I had to have her. At that time, I had a different bike. I rebuilt her from parts myself. I couldn't afford anything new. I saved up a long time to buy my first new bike and I'm probably irrationally attached to her."

"We're all attached to our bikes. That goes with the territory. As for the locket ... that's yours. You don't have anything else from your childhood?"

I shook my head. "No. I don't know what happened to the blanket. I just remember loving it because it was mine. I didn't have toys or anything."

Gunner looked pained. "Now I kind of want to buy you a toy. What's your poison? I'm guessing Barbie Dolls are out of the picture."

"Yeah. Dolls are not my thing."

"Action figures?"

"Not really."

"What about Lincoln Logs? I used to love building things with the old set my father kept from when he was a kid. None of the other kids had them — and they used to make fun of me for playing with them — but I didn't care."

"I honestly never cared about toys. I mean ... there was a stuffed dog I wanted not long after I was in foster care. I saw it in a store and I remember feeling something I couldn't quite identify inside. I know now that I was coveting the stupid thing, but I didn't know it then."

"I know I'm going to regret asking this, but did your foster parents buy you the dog?"

I shook my head. "They didn't have extra money. It was fine. I just remember the dog looked kind of like a wolf and I liked it. That was the only toy I ever really wanted."

"Well, I still don't like it." He shifted in his chair. "You can come over to my house and play Lincoln Logs with me."

He winked at me, his smile easy, and then let his eyes track to the sidewalk in front of the park. The smile slipped almost instantly. "Son of a ... ."

I followed his gaze, frowning when I caught sight of Drake. He was alone this time, at least as far as I could tell, and he was completely fixated on us. I couldn't help wondering how long he'd been standing there, staring.

"Good evening," he called out, offering a half-wave. "It looks like you're enjoying your dinner."

"We are," Gunner agreed. "It's a private meal, though."

Drake ignored his warning tone and crossed over to us. "That looks good, but there will be food at the gathering tonight. I was under the impression you were attending."

"We haven't decided yet," Gunner countered, taking me by surprise. He clearly wanted to keep Drake on his toes. "It depends on if we want to do something else or not. There's talk of going to bed early, but we'll see."

I kept my face placid, but just barely. Gunner's insistence on playing Testosterone King in front of an audience — especially a wolf audience — was mildly entertaining. It was often annoying, too. I didn't want him getting too comfortable with the "free love" thing, although I enjoyed watching Drake's obvious discomfort.

"You should come," he insisted. "You'll miss out if you don't. Cyrus puts on the best gatherings."

"Have you been to other gatherings?" I asked, legitimately curious. I popped a fry into my mouth and regarded him. "I mean ... have you been a member of different packs?"

Drake shrugged, noncommittal. "I'm a wanderer at heart. I'm sure you understand something about that. I've found my place with Cyrus's pack, but that doesn't mean I don't want to travel. I'm guessing Hawthorne Hollow, while nice, doesn't sate your wanderlust either."

"Actually, I'm pretty comfortable here," I countered. "I like the town ... when innocent men aren't being strung up and branded with my name, that is. Are you still maintaining you don't know anything about that?"

Gunner arched an eyebrow at my direct question, but said nothing. Obviously he was ceding the floor to me.

"Of course we didn't have anything to do with that." Drake's response was smooth. "Why would we? I think you're being overly suspicious ... and I don't have to guess why." His gaze was heavy when it landed on Gunner. "You really shouldn't fill her head with nonsense. It's unnecessary and she's going to get the wrong idea about us."

"I think she's fully capable of formulating her own opinions," Gunner countered. "You'll find that there's very little she can't decide for herself ... other than whether or not she wants to play with Lincoln Logs. That's the only thing she's hesitant about."

I wanted to kill him. Instead, I kept my gaze trained on Drake. "Your arrival in town is suspect. The other thing that's suspect is your interest in me. Right from the start, you guys have been on me. Why is that?"

"You mean that day at the lake? That was a coincidence."

I didn't believe that for a second. "No, I think you were there for a specific reason. I also think you were on the beach outside the restaurant that night for a reason ... and in the woods the following day ... and again later. You might think you're smooth — or maybe you don't care — but nobody is falling for your act."

Drake's expression didn't change, but his shoulders slouched a bit. "I don't think I like what you're insinuating."

"And I don't think I care."

"You want to watch how much attitude you sling around," he warned. "That won't go over well in wolf circles. Well ... in circles with real wolves who aren't neutered, I mean." The derisive look he shot in Gunner's direction was enough to make me bare my teeth. "Not everyone will find that mouth of yours entertaining."

"I guess it's good I have more than a mouth, huh?" On a whim, I sent out a bolt of magic. It was visible as it escaped from my fingertips, a green lash that barreled toward Drake, gaining speed as it moved.

He saw it at the last second. Perhaps he wasn't expecting it, which is how he overlooked it at the start. It didn't matter, though. The magic was on him before he could react, smacking into his chest with enough force that he was thrown off the sidewalk and slammed into the road.

For his part, Gunner continued eating his fish and chips rather than reacting. He seemed blasé, although I could feel the mirth rolling off him.

"What the ... ?" Drake sputtered as he struggled to a sitting position in the middle of the street. Thankfully, Hawthorne Hollow is a small town and there was very little traffic. "Why did you do that?" He was incensed.

"Why not?"

"Because ... because ... ."

Gunner nipped a fry from my takeout container and dunked it in ketchup. "We'll see you at the gathering tonight. I can't wait to tell this story, by the way."

"You wouldn't dare."

Gunner's eyes were narrowed to slits. "Try me."

The testosterone show was officially back on. Something told me it was going to be worse at the gathering.

Ah, well, at least I had something to look forward to.

TWENTY-TWO

J wasn't sure what to wear to a gathering. Ultimately, I settled on jeans and a simple black shirt. I liked the vee in the neck that made it appear I had more cleavage than I really did. Apparently Gunner agreed, because when he met me on the porch at our designated pickup time his eyes took an appreciative roam before locking with mine.

"Is this okay?" Oddly, I felt nervous, an emotion to which I rarely fell victim.

"You look perfect." He smiled and then shook his head. "I'll have to beat the other wolves off with a really big stick."

"I don't think you have to worry about that."

"I know. You can take care of yourself." He rolled his eyes when he said the words. "You don't have to keep repeating yourself."

"Oh, not that. I mean ... I *can* take care of myself. But that's not what I was talking about. There's a curse on my jeans."

He furrowed his brow. "I don't understand."

"I know how my butt looks in these jeans. That's why I bought them."

His smile turned sly. "You do look really good in the jeans."

"You're not the first to think so. I've received several errant grabs." His expression fell and I had to bite the inside of my cheek to keep from laughing. "The thing is, I don't believe I should have to change my wardrobe because a few people can't keep their hands to themselves. With that in mind, I cast a curse on the jeans. Anyone who does a little reaching and

172

grabbing without being invited gets a nasty shock ... and a little something else."

He tilted his head to the side, considering. "What's the 'something else'?"

"You'll only find out if your hands wander."

"What if you want my hands to wander?"

"There's a failsafe built in ... but I haven't given you permission for wandering hands, so until that happens watch yourself."

His smile only widened. "Have I mentioned how much I like it when you're stern?"

I shook my head. "You're kind of a pig."

"Well, we're going to be hanging out with a lot of wolves this evening. I know you don't want to hear it, but it would be better if you stick close to my side. I may be a pig ... but I'm a pig you happen to like, which is better than you'll be getting from them. Do you think you can manage that?"

"Yes, but not because you need to protect me. I want to be close in case you need me to protect you."

"I'm fine with that." He held out his hand to me. "It will be a fun experiment, watching the others take you in. I think the protection bit will occur naturally."

Something told me he was right.

IT MADE SENSE FOR US TO ride our bikes. The gathering was in the woods, about three miles as the crow flies from the cabin. It took us almost ten minutes to drive by road, though, and I found my nerves were back when we landed.

"What is this place?" I asked, glancing around as I removed my helmet.

"We used to have gatherings here ourselves," Gunner explained, following suit. It was warm enough that he stripped out of his jacket and stashed it in the storage compartment under his seat. I followed suit because I didn't want to keep track of my coat, but my eyes never left his face.

"There has to be more to the story than that," I prodded.

He sighed and nodded. "I told you about when Cyrus split from the pack, how he took some people with him?"

I had no idea where he was going with this but I nodded. "You told me the basics."

"Well, as part of that split, there was a fight." He turned grim. "Wolves aren't allowed to just abandon their packs. It can lead to death ... and in this case it led to a fight."

"Obviously Cyrus didn't die."

"No, but several others did — on both sides — and it happened right here."

I swallowed hard. "Oh." I glanced around the space, which was open and pleasant. The setting sun cast an ominous red glow over the clearing now that I knew what really happened here. "They couldn't have picked this location by accident."

"Not even a little."

"So ... why?" I was genuinely curious.

"He wants to send a message." Gunner kept his eyes on the curious faces as he slid his arm around my waist. It wasn't a proprietary move as much as a protective one. "He plans to stick around and challenge the other pack, my former pack, for dominance."

"You said you basically had nothing to do with your pack. Will you get involved?"

"I won't have a choice. Cyrus isn't a good man. You've seen that for your-self. While I'm not particularly fond of pack politics, sometimes you really do have to pick the lesser evil."

Sadly, that made sense. "He won't pick a fight with you tonight, will he?"

"He shouldn't. It would be stupid. He will be laying out the hard sell, though ... for both of us."

"Don't worry. I'm never going to join a pack regardless. It's not my thing."

"You've already joined a pack. What do you think our group is?"

"I ... ." It wasn't the first time he'd brought it up, and the more I thought about it the more I realized he was right. "I guess it's a pack of a different sort."

"Without a doubt." He squeezed my hand. "Come on. I'll show you around. Try to ignore all the stares. I guarantee we're the main event here tonight."

THE TOUR DIDN'T TAKE VERY long. In fact, other than the bonfire and the river, there wasn't much to look at.

"This is directly behind my cabin, right?" We took a break from walking around to toss stones into the river and have a quiet conversation without having to worry about other wolves eavesdropping. The rushing water was enough to drown us out.

"About three miles that way," Gunner noted, pointing.

I looked in that direction and nodded. "Right. That's not very far."

"No, especially when there's running involved."

"Can you run faster in your wolf form?"

He nodded. "Yeah. Have you not spent a lot of time around shifters?"

That was an interesting question. "Not as much as you might think. I know this is going to sound weird, but when I first started with Spells Angels I was irrationally afraid of wolf shifters."

His eyebrows drew together. "Just wolf shifters? What about the other shifter varieties?"

"I don't remember thinking about them as much. It was the wolves I feared."

"Why? You're stronger than most shifters."

"I ... ." There was no easy answer to that question. "I'm not sure. I said it was an irrational fear. All I knew is that my palms got sweaty and my heart started pounding when I was near them."

"You weren't that way with me when we first met."

"That's because I cast a spell over myself years ago so I would stop acting like a crazy person. It was getting embarrassing."

Gunner shifted from one foot to the other, his expression hard to read. "Do you think that's a good idea? I mean ... your instincts are usually pretty good. Do you want to shut them off that way?"

"I get what you're saying, but I couldn't operate when I was overcome with fear like that. Besides, I'm pretty sure I know why I reacted that way."

"Why?"

"I told you about the dream. Er, memory. Maybe it's both, I don't know. I've been plagued by similar dreams my entire life. In all of them, wolves are chasing me and they're painted as bad."

He swallowed hard. "Yeah, but ... maybe from your perspective wolves are bad people. You might not be safe dampening your natural instincts this way."

I couldn't hide my surprise. "Are you saying you want me to fear you?"

"Absolutely not." He vehemently shook his head. "I want you to trust me. It's just ... now I'm a little worried. You said that Drake and Flint managed to sneak up on you twice, that your senses let you down. Maybe this is why."

"Or maybe I was amped up because I was fighting a siren and spending time with you."

He flashed a quick grin. "As much as I would like to believe I have that sort of power with you, I'm not sure it's true. I just ... I'm a little concerned."

"You mean you're a worrywart," I countered, smirking despite the serious nature of the discussion. "You don't have to be. I did this years ago. I've been fine ever since. It's not as if I killed my instincts. I simply muted the fear."

"Because the woman in your dream told you to be afraid of shifters." He didn't look thrilled at the prospect. "I wonder why she was so terrified of shifters getting their hands on you."

"I don't know." That was the truth. "She said not all shifters were bad. I have a feeling she planned on eventually teaching me a way to suss out the difference. She never got the chance."

"And you can't remember what happened right before?"

"No."

He was silent for a beat and then cracked a smile. "Maybe one day when you least expect it the memories will come roaring back."

That was a nice thought, but I wasn't sure I should hold out hope. "Maybe."

We went back to our stone tossing. It was a way for us to stand close and still isolate ourselves from the others. After several minutes, I felt a presence move in behind us, and when I turned around I wasn't surprised to find Cyrus watching us with unveiled interest.

"Can we help you?" Gunner drawled. From all outward appearances he seemed calm. But I knew better. He was poised and ready for action. With that in mind, I took to scanning the other wolves in case they decided to move on us while Cyrus served as a distraction.

"I simply came over to offer my thanks," Cyrus replied, an amiable if empty smile on his face. "I wasn't sure you would attend tonight's festivities. I'm glad you saw past your personal bias, the untrue stories I'm sure you've heard, and decided to give us a chance."

Gunner's eyes narrowed. "A chance for what?"

"To change your direction. I mean ... you've always been a smart boy, Gunner. I remember when you were competing against the other kids in your age group at gatherings. You excelled ... and not just on the physical front.

"Given your size, we all expected you to be a tremendous athlete," he continued. "That meant you'd become a solid warrior, even though your father seemed horrified by the thought. Did you ever ask yourself why he didn't want you using the gifts you were given?"

I was confused, out of my depth. It was obvious that Cyrus was trying to drive home a point. To me, the manner in which he chose to do it felt awkward and rude. A quick glimpse at Gunner's face told me he felt the same way.

"It would probably be best if you didn't speak poorly about my father," he warned, choosing his words carefully. "You don't know him."

"Are you sure? I bet I know him better than you. We grew up together."

"That doesn't mean you know him."

"He was always a rule-follower," Cyrus continued, either oblivious to

Gunner's growing annoyance or purposely ignoring it. I was leaning toward the latter. "He didn't understand that rules are made to be broken. That's what I did when I split from the pack. And look at us now." He extended his arms to encompass the individuals milling about the clearing. "We're thriving."

I knew I should keep my mouth shut. This was Gunner's show, after all. I couldn't quite will myself to follow the rules I'd set before leaving the cabin, though. "If you're doing so well, why are you here?" I demanded, curiosity getting the better of me. "You set up shop in mid-Michigan. Why wouldn't you stay there after spending so much time setting up a new home base?"

Cyrus's eyes flashed with something I couldn't identify. It felt like malice. "I missed home. No matter what happened here, this is still my home."

He was a terrible liar. I couldn't understand how he maintained control of his pack when he was so bad at spinning a story. "So ... it had nothing to do with Covenant College falling?" I decided to go for broke. The worst he could do was verbally slap me back. Even if he tried to physically attack, Gunner and I could take him. I had no doubt about that. When you added in the rest of the pack, though, I was less certain. There were a lot of them.

"Covenant College?" Cyrus let loose a hollow laugh. "Why would I care about Covenant College?"

I risked a glance to my left and found Drake loitering by the trees. He seemed agitated, as if my magical showing earlier in the afternoon had left him with serious anger issues, but he kept his distance. The look on his face told me I was on the right track.

"The college was known to be a hotbed of paranormal activity," Gunner replied for me. "There was a wolf pack there — bitten wolves who had superiority complexes — and they tried to take over several times."

"I believe they were swatted back several times," I offered. "A mage was involved each time the wolves suffered a defeat. Were those wolves part of your pack?"

"Why would I care about having a presence on a college campus?"

That wasn't exactly an answer. "Has anyone ever told you that answering a question with a question is a sure sign of guilt? I mean ... you've done it twice now. That seems to indicate that you were involved with the things that happened at Covenant College."

"I agree." Gunner moved slightly closer to me. Whether he realized it or not, it was a warning gesture to the other wolves who were trying to listen to our conversation. He was ready to bare his teeth — and maybe more — if it came to it. "The timing of your arrival here hasn't gone unnoticed, Cyrus. Quite frankly, if you want the shifters in this area to treat you with respect —

and stop laughing behind your back — you'll have to admit the truth instead of telling weak lies."

This time I was certain I saw malice flash in the depths of Cyrus's coal-colored eyes. He was furious, the anger radiating off him. Somehow, he managed to hold it together.

"I'm not lying," he replied after a moment. There was a hint of strain in his voice, but otherwise he put on a calm face. "I'm a truth teller. I always have been. That's why people rallied behind me during the schism years ago."

"I will agree with you there," Gunner offered. "You told the truth. It was a racist truth, but it was the truth."

Now I was behind again. "He's a racist?"

Gunner kept his eyes on Cyrus and nodded. "There's a faction in the wolf world who believe that we shouldn't inter-marry. Remember I told you what happened to our ranks because there were more boys than girls? Well, some people don't care about that. They only want wolves mating with other wolves."

That was interesting. "Even though your population was shrinking?"

"Their solution was to make more bitten werewolves, which are weaker and therefore subservient. They're basically slaves in the hierarchy."

That wasn't what I wanted to hear. "Oh, well ... ."

"It's not that I don't think there should be no breeding beyond the pack," Cyrus countered. "I simply think that the breeding should be carefully monitored ... and only allowed if it benefits the pack."

Slowly, I started to catch on. "Like me," I offered, my stomach twisting. "I would be one of those allowable instances because I have magic at my disposal."

"It's not nearly as simplistic as that," Cyrus countered, pinning me with a dark look. "You would be an allowable instance because you're important to Gunner. We think he's a good fit for our pack. I'm assuming you would be part of the package in that scenario. That means we would allow you to join."

"Oh, well, you would allow me?" I turned my incredulous gaze to Gunner and found him smiling. "Can you believe this?"

"Actually, I can. This is exactly what I thought they were doing here. The thing is, they're much more interested in you than they're letting on. They're pretending that I'm the big catch to inflate my ego — and kudos on that because it would work with a normal wolf — but you're the one they really want. I'm just an added bonus because it will upset my father."

Cyrus shook his head. "That is not true. I've always respected you. I told you, your physical prowess as a kid was expected. When you tested better academically than the others your age, that's when I knew you were special. I've always wanted you."

"But I don't want this," Gunner countered. "I don't want pack life. I never have. That's why I joined the group I'm with. I have very little to do with pack politics. I'm guessing you already know that, which is why you approached me. I seemed an easy bet for turning. Sadly for you, I'm not."

"And I'm never joining a pack," I added. "I don't care about wolf politics."

"You're with Gunner," Cyrus countered. "If this relationship continues, you'll have to join a pack. Those are the rules."

"Those aren't the rules we live by any longer," Gunner countered. "Scout has a choice in her life. I respect that. Either way, we're not going to play your games."

"Well, that's disappointing."

"That's reality."

TWENTY-THREE

Cyrus obviously wasn't happy with Gunner's quick shutdown of his offer. He retreated to his spot near the bonfire, offered up a series of stories to make random observers believe things were going his way, but didn't refrain from casting dark looks in our direction during the next two hours.

"How long do you want to stay?" I asked as Gunner handed me a bottle of water from one of the coolers.

It was dark now, the only illumination coming from the fire and moon. I was growing antsy.

"Do you want to go?" He turned to me. "I thought you were having a good time watching all the antics."

That was true ... for the first thirty minutes. I found myself fascinated watching the younger wolves compete against one another. I'd never seen anything like it. There was one boy, clearly stronger and faster than the others, and the adults and children alike fawned over him. I wondered if it was like that for Gunner when he was a child — Cyrus said he was in a power position during his youth — but that didn't feel like the sort of question I should ask when there were so many prying ears. Besides, Gunner was never keen to talk about his childhood.

"I'm fine," I reassured him quickly. "We can stay as long as you want."

He studied my face for a long moment and then shook his head. "We don't have to stay. There's nothing else to learn here."

I wasn't sure that was true, at least from his position. He never once grew bored of watching the games. In fact, there were times he seemed exhilarated. "Maybe we should stay a bit longer. You know, just in case."

He worked his jaw. Before he got a chance to respond, a shadowy figure detached from the darkness and invaded our space. I sensed Drake an instant before I could make out his features.

"You should listen to your girlfriend," he offered, his smile sly. "She knows what she's talking about."

"She does," Gunner agreed, not mustering even a word of argument for the "girlfriend" distinction. "She's bored, though. There's nothing worse than a bored woman."

I pursed my lips. That felt like an assault on my gender, but it was obvious Gunner was trying to feel out Drake. I decided to keep quiet ... at least for now.

"Bored? How could she be bored of this? Gatherings are great. They're the heart and soul of our people."

"*Your* people," Gunner corrected. "The heart and soul of our people is a bar."

Now that he mentioned it, that was sort of true. The Cauldron was definitely the heart and soul of the Hawthorne Hollow Spells Angels operation.

"You really don't see yourself as part of a pack, do you?" Drake's expression reflected confusion. "I don't see how you can be born into this world, earn the accolades you did as a kid, and not want to be pack."

That was an interesting sentiment. Drake had let something slip. Did he realize it? More importantly, did Gunner? I shouldn't have worried about that. Gunner was on top of things, per usual.

"I didn't realize you were part of the original pack," he said smoothly. "I don't remember you."

Drake realized too late what he'd said and scrambled to cover. "I just meant that I heard you were quite the competitor. Flint mentioned it a time or two."

"I'm sure he did." Gunner's expression was hard to read, especially in the limited light. I knew him well enough to recognize he was thinking, though, ... and thinking hard. "What did he tell you?"

"He just said that you dominated."

"I liked the games. I didn't really think about it as dominating. I enjoyed competing ... and, of course, I liked winning. Dominating has a negative connotation. That makes it sound as if I held down others for glory."

"Didn't you?" Drake's tone was accusatory. "I mean ... did you even let others participate in your games? It seems to me that only those of a certain birthright were allowed to play."

Well, if I wasn't sure before, I definitely was now. That feeling Gunner had about knowing Drake from somewhere was spot on. Drake's bitterness was clearly personal.

"I don't remember you ever trying to participate in the games," Gunner prodded. "I don't remember you at all. Maybe you should refresh my memory."

Drake gritted his teeth. "I already told you ... I wasn't part of your pack. My family joined Cyrus's pack when I was a teenager."

"And where is your family now?"

"I ... what does it matter to you?" Drake's demeanor turned quickly and he went on the offensive. "Why does my past mean anything to you?"

"It doesn't." Calmly, Gunner slipped his arm around my back and tugged me to his side. "I was just making conversation. I didn't realize it was a sore subject."

"I didn't say it was a sore subject." Now, on top of being annoyed, Drake was also petulant. He'd nearly turned into a pouty teenager in front of my eyes. That was ... interesting.

"I didn't mean to offend you," Gunner offered. "I thought there was something familiar about you. Apparently I was wrong. No harm, no foul."

Drake muttered something under his breath. I was going to ask him about it, but Flint picked that moment to join the party ... and he was the last person anyone wanted to see.

"Well, this looks like a cozy group," he supplied, his grin wide as he moved to stand next to Drake. "Everybody having a good time?"

"We're having a fabulous time," Gunner drawled. "It's an evening for the ages."

Flint clearly wasn't good on picking up sarcasm because he bobbed his head in agreement. "I know, right? This is going to be one of those nights our children talk about in hushed tones twenty years from now."

That was way over the top ... and delusional. "And why would they do that?" I asked.

"This is an important evening. This is the night Gunner decides to join our pack. I mean ... that's a really big deal."

I could think of a few other words for it; none of them were pleasant. "Excuse me?"

Gunner's hand was warm on the center of my back. "What are you talking about?"

Flint's expression faltered. "My father said you were attending because you were interested in joining our pack."

"Your father is confused or misinformed."

Gunner was much more diplomatic than me. I would've called Cyrus out on the delusional nutbag he was. Clearly he had other thoughts on the subject.

"But ... ." Flint slowly tracked his gaze to Drake. "I guess I'm confused."

"You're always confused," Drake groused, shaking his head.

"You're at least confused on this front," Gunner agreed. "There are no plans for me to join your pack."

"But ... ." Flint broke off, licking his lips, and then regrouped. "What about you?"

It took me a moment to realize his gaze was on me. "What about me?"

"You're joining the pack, right?"

I wanted to laugh, maybe throw some pointing and ridicule in for good measure. Instead, I remained placid ... but it wasn't easy. "No. I won't be joining any pack, your father's or otherwise. That's not really of any interest to me."

"But you're with him." He jerked his thumb in Gunner's direction. "You have to be considering joining a pack if you're with him."

Gunner cleared his throat to get Flint's attention. "Not that it's any of your business, but things don't work that way in our pack. Scout doesn't have to do anything she doesn't want to do."

"Besides, that's a long way down the road ... if at all," I added.

"Not all that long in the grand scheme of things." Gunner's smile was tight. "It doesn't matter. She can live her life however she wants. That's the beauty of a free pack. We don't believe in despots."

"That's an inflammatory word," Drake shot back. "You should be careful what you say. You might not be joining this pack, but respect is still required."

"I don't agree there either." Gunner downed his water and then tossed the empty bottle in a nearby trash receptacle. "But it hardly matters. We're on our way out. We won't keep you a moment longer."

"That's probably best for everybody," Drake agreed, his eyes glinting with malice. "It's obvious you don't want to be here."

Gunner prodded me toward the area where we'd parked our bikes. "It looks like you're getting your wish and we're leaving early. We're going to have alone time later. Whatever are we going to do with the extra time?"

My cheeks burned at the unsaid suggestion. "You're just unbelievable sometimes. Has anyone ever told you that?"

"I tell myself that regularly."

I'd almost turned my full attention to what we were going to do for the rest of the evening when we crossed in front of Flint. I should've seen the move coming — seriously, he wasn't bright enough to hide his intentions — but I was distracted by other thoughts.

As if in slow motion, Flint's hand darted out and he reached for my rear end. I saw the motion out of the corner of my eye and opened my mouth to warn him, but it was already too late. The second he made unwanted contact the curse I'd warned Gunner about earlier sparked to life. It was like an explosion, a fireworks display without the holiday.

Flint's hand sparked, fire erupting from his fingertips, and he was blown back a good ten feet before he hit the ground. He looked dazed as he sat there, his eyes glassy and his reflexes clearly off because he didn't realize his hand was still smoking.

"Son of a ... !" Drake hopped to action and raced in his friend's direction, a bottle of water in his hand. He upended the bottle over Flint's smoking fingertips and stared into the confused man's eyes. "Are you okay?"

"I've never been better," Flint replied dreamily. "I just saw heaven and it was glorious."

I pursed my lips as Gunner slid me a sidelong look. It was probably best to keep my mouth shut, so I did.

"That's your curse?" he asked finally. "I was expecting more ... though you got a really good arc on him. I like the way he flew through the air like a football."

"It's not quite all," I said. "There's more."

"Oh, yeah?" He returned his attention to Flint, his eyes going wide when he realized the man's pale demeanor was turning a different color. "Are those ... spots?"

"Cold sores," I corrected.

"So, you're saying he's going to have cold sores all over his face? That is ... awesome."

One look at Cyrus's furious expression — he'd joined Drake in front of Flint when I wasn't looking — told me he didn't feel the same way. "We should probably go," I prodded. "I think we've officially worn out our welcome."

"Yeah, but what a way to go."

GUNNER WAS STILL LAUGHING ABOUT the turn of events when we arrived at my cabin.

"Oh, I would pay real money to see his reaction when he wakes up tomorrow and realizes he's a walking case of herpes. That's going to impact his love life for the foreseeable future."

There was actually more to the spell — a small bit of magic I added when I was feeling particularly mean one day — but I thought it best to allow Gunner to discover it on his own. It might put a damper on the rest of our evening.

"Something tells me it's going to be a loud morning."

"That's what he gets for putting his hands on you." Gunner's expression went momentarily dark. "I hate the idea that you were touched in that manner so many times you had to come up with a spell to combat it. That seems somehow ... wrong."

"It's basically a karma spell," I explained. "I made a few enhancements, of course. The herpes was added after the fact, but I think it adds a certain something."

"It was a stroke of genius," he agreed, walking me toward the porch. "I'm glad I was there to see it."

"Yeah, well ... ." With every step we took toward the cabin, my heart rate accelerated a notch. I sensed something would be different about this night. Of course, my hormones were lodging their opinion on the matter. Heck, I could practically hear them cheering me on. "What do you think will happen now?" I was desperate to buy time. "Will Cyrus try to get you into the fold again?"

Gunner shrugged. "I don't know. The effort he put in tonight was sloppy." He leaned against the porch railing and folded his arms across his chest. "He either thought I was going to jump at the chance to join his pack or was only going through the motions."

"Which is more likely?"

"I don't know." He rolled his neck and looked to the sky. "My father and I have issues. That's obvious to anyone who has ever spent any time with us. We're ... like cats. We can't seem to stop ourselves from fighting."

"I don't think that's true," I countered. "You seem like a normal father and son to me. I don't have much experience in that area, but I saw a lot of parental bonding when I was in the foster care system. I'm talking about kids who were reunited with parents after an extended period and others who lived in the houses because their parents volunteered to take kids in.

"Fathers and sons can't help but butt heads because there comes a point when a son wants to be as powerful as the father and that causes static," I continued. "You keep talking about how bad your relationship is with your father, but I see the opposite."

His eyes were keen as they held mine. "Oh, yeah? What is it you see?"

"I see a man who feels as if he failed his child and almost lost him in the process. Your mother almost killed you. Your father blames himself for allowing the situation to get so out of control. Worse, your father believes you still blame him."

Gunner made a protesting sound. "I don't blame him. My mother was a nutjob. There's no getting around that. He did the best he could."

"Have you ever told him that?"

He balked. "No. We don't talk about feelings. Believe it or not, my father is much like you. He likes to collapse inward and shut out the rest of the world. That's why I can so easily deal with your moods."

He was deflecting. "Your father loves you. He does what he thinks is right for you ... and yet he's always second-guessing himself. He's proud of you. He also wants to be part of your life. That's why he asked me what was going on between us."

"And what did you say?"

"That he would have to ask you."

"Oh, you shouldn't have said that." He turned whiny and pinched the bridge of his nose. "Now he'll know exactly what's going on."

I couldn't hold back my chuckle. "Funnily enough, he said the same thing." His gaze was dark, causing me to heave out a sigh. "Look, I'm not telling you what to do with your life. Your relationship with your father is your own business."

"Maybe I want it to be your business," he countered. "Just because I think you're spouting nonsense doesn't mean I want you to hold back. I value your opinion ... even if it's ludicrous."

This time I smiled for another reason. "That could be the most romantic thing you've ever said to me."

He took a step closer, his arms dropping to his sides, and held my gaze. "I can be more romantic."

And we'd circled back. It happened much quicker than I thought. Still, I'd expected it and was ready this time. "Oh, yeah? You might have to back up those words with some action."

He arched an eyebrow. "Wait ... are you saying what I think you're saying?"

I nodded and gestured toward the cabin. If we were going to do this, I was going to be in charge. That's how I liked things. Of course, that was probably how he liked things, too. Apparently it was going to be a learning experience ... for both of us.

"We should probably go inside," I suggested. "There's a Peeping Tim out here."

"Oh, man." The ghost started complaining from a stand of trees about thirty feet away. "You're not happy unless you're ruining all my fun, are you?"

Gunner ignored the specter and slipped a strand of hair behind my ear. "Are you sure? We don't have to. If you're not ready ... ." He left the sentence hanging.

"I'm ready. Besides, I'll probably explode if we wait any longer."

He snorted. "I like your honesty."

"It's a matter of survival."

"For both of us. I guess we'll have to save each other."

"That's the plan." I slid toward the front door. "By the way, I'm a little nervous. Don't judge me because of it."

His expression softened. "If you want to know the truth, I'm a little nervous, too. The thing is ... your pants aren't going to set me on fire, are they?"

"I guess you'll have to find that out for yourself."

"Oh, hell. There are worse ways to go."

TWENTY-FOUR

J woke in the middle of the night to noises outside the cabin. At first I thought it was my mind playing tricks on me. It sounded like fireworks. When I looked to the window, I found Gunner standing there — naked — and staring through the opening in the curtains.

I was instantly alert.

"What is it?" I bolted to a sitting position, immediately reaching for the shirt I'd discarded the previous evening.

"We have visitors," he said grimly. "It's Flint and Drake ... and maybe a few others."

Ah. That explained the noises. They were revving their bikes in an attempt to frighten us. "Apparently a case of herpes wasn't enough of a learning experience," I muttered, kicking the jeans away from my feet and striding toward the dresser. I grabbed the first pair of stretchy pants I found and tugged them on. "Well, they're going to learn a thing or two about interrupting the best night of sleep I've had in weeks, maybe years."

Gunner looked amused as he put on his pants. "The best night of sleep? Why, you humble me."

"Don't let your ego get out of control. I'm already sorry I mentioned it."

"Oh, don't be sorry. I'm just going to hold it over your head for the rest of our lives."

"Why doesn't that surprise me?" I slipped into a pair of slippers rather than boots because it was faster. "Are you ready?"

188

He stood across from me and stared, making me uncomfortable.

"What?" Frustration bubbled up. "We can't let them keep this up. We have to scare the crap out of them."

"I agree. It's just ... I don't know that fuzzy pajama bottoms and slippers with cat heads will paint the correct picture."

I glanced down at my outfit and found I was indeed dressed in fuzzy sleep pants and animal slippers. "They're lions," I corrected of the slippers. "They're not cats; they're lions. That's way scarier than cat slippers."

"Uh-huh." He didn't look convinced.

"Do you think I should change?"

He shook his head. "No. They'll never be able to live down the shame of being beaten up by a girl in lion slippers. It's an inspired choice."

"Well, then let's do this. The faster we dispatch them, the faster we can get back to sleep."

"The best sleep of your life."

"I don't think that's exactly what I said."

"And yet that's what I heard. How do you explain that?"

That was a very good question.

FLINT AND DRAKE OBVIOUSLY EXPECTED US to confront them. They were standing in the middle of the yard when we exited the cabin. One look at my bedhead and sleep outfit had them uproariously guffawing.

"Oh, did we interrupt something?" Flint challenged, the cold sores still evident on his face. "That's quite the bedtime outfit. I take everything I said back, Gunner. You should definitely trade her in for a different model, because this one is obviously defective."

Instead of being drawn into a verbal slap-fight, Gunner crossed his arms over his bare chest and waited for me to unleash my fury. "You guys are going to be sorry you woke her," he warned. "She's a bear when she doesn't get her full eight hours. If you think the herpes curse was bad, you'll be crying when she's done with you here."

That was a lot of pressure and I wasn't exactly feeling my best. "I wish you hadn't said that," I groused. "Now I have to put on my thinking cap."

He appeared more amused than contrite. "Does it have animals on it, too?"

"It might."

"Then I can't wait to see it."

Drake cleared his throat to get our attention. "Not that this verbal copulation isn't stimulating, but we're here for a reason."

AMANDA M. LEE

"And what reason is that?" Gunner challenged. "If you're here to terrorize her — or me, for that matter — you'll be bitterly disappointed. We don't bow down to bullies."

"We have no interest in you other than the obvious," Flint shot back. "My father realizes what a mistake it was to try to recruit you to a righteous cause. You have no interest in being a prime pack member."

"You say that like it's a bad thing," Gunner noted.

Flint narrowed his eyes. "I'm serious. We don't want you. I'm sure that's hard for your ego to swallow, but it's true. If we never see you again, it will be too soon."

Something told me that Flint was talking out of a southern orifice. His father was obviously still interested. Flint had his nose out of joint because of that interest and enjoyed talking big. That was hardly the concern for tonight, though. "What do you want?" I really was eager to return to bed and the welcome slumber I'd been enjoying before their encroachment on my territory.

"What do I want?" Flint practically screeched. "I want you to fix this." He pointed toward his face. "I can't walk around like this. You did it to me, so it's up to you to fix it."

"Oh, that." I was blasé. "I can't fix that. Once the spell is cast, it's done. It holds until you learn the error of your ways."

Gunner slid me a sidelong look. "Is that true?" he murmured.

"That's crap!" Flint raged. "It's impossible to cast a spell and not be able to reverse it. I'm not a complete and total idiot."

He was doing a good job of convincing me otherwise. "Most witches wouldn't cast a spell they couldn't reverse," I clarified. "There are rules and covens enforce them. The thing is, I'm not much on rules."

"She's not," Gunner agreed.

"This particular curse is designed around the concept that you have to learn something to vanquish it," I explained. "You incurred the curse because you tried to put your hands on me without invitation. To get rid of the curse, you need to volunteer your time at a women's shelter or willingly help a female in need — and not just to get rid of the curse but because you're pure of heart. It usually takes those who have been cursed a decent amount of time to get to the cure."

Flint's mouth dropped open. "You can't be serious."

"Oh, I'm serious. Sorry to be the bearer of bad news but ... you're screwed."

"You should've thought about that before you tried to put your hands on

190

her," Gunner growled. "All you had to do was keep your hands to yourself, not treat her like a piece of meat. There's a lesson in there for you, Flint."

"I am going to kill you." Flint was all snarls and hate as he stepped forward, his hand moving in such a manner that I realized almost instantly he was brandishing a weapon.

My instincts took over and I started chanting, a bolt of magic escaping out of my fingertips and slamming into Flint's chest with the strength of a small freight train.

"*Burn*," I intoned, my voice low.

As if on cue, Flint began screaming as the gun heated in his hand. He wasn't the only one. Even though I could only sense the other figures in the woods — they purposely kept hidden — that didn't mean I couldn't curse them at the same time. Everyone holding a weapon, whether gun or knife, began screaming in unison.

"What is that?" Gunner was breathless as he jerked his head toward the woods.

"A different kind of karma spell," I replied. "If they don't drop their weapons, they'll be sorry."

"You're the one who's going to be sorry," Flint gasped, struggling to hold on to the gun. He tried to raise it, but it was too hot. Finally, he did the only thing he could and dropped his weapon. The second it hit the ground it exploded into a million small projectiles and acted as shrapnel. "Son of a ... !" Flint screamed again as some of the super-heated particles struck him. "What are you doing? I'm going to kill you!"

I cocked my head to the side as the distinctive sound of fleeing feet and crying men assailed my ears. Flint's reinforcements were running in the opposite direction. That left him and Drake, who stood unharmed about five feet from his friend. Apparently he hadn't brought a weapon. Smart boy.

"Aren't you getting tired of this?" I challenged for his benefit. "Why do you guys keep doing this?"

"I didn't make the decision." Drake's countenance was dark. "I told him it was a bad idea, but he didn't listen."

"Oh, shut up," Flint gritted out, cradling his burned hand. "Help me, you idiot. I need to go to the hospital."

"You probably shouldn't do that," I countered. "It's going to be hard to explain what happened."

"Don't tell me what to do!" Flint's eyes flashed with malevolence. "You're going to wish you'd never met me."

"Yeah? I'm already there."

Gunner and I remained rooted to our spots until Drake and Flint disappeared into the darkness. It was only when he was certain that we were alone that Gunner spoke again. "That was a pretty interesting show. I'm impressed."

"Just wait until tomorrow. The spell has a little added something."

"What?"

"It will probably be funnier when you see it for yourself."

"Do all your spells have a little added something?"

"Not all, but a lot of them."

"I can't tell you how excited I am to see how this turns out."

That made two of us.

WE DRAGGED OURSELVES TO THE Cauldron shortly before ten the next morning. We would have preferred spending the day in bed, but after the altercation on the lawn we decided to play a different game inside the cabin. By the time we fell asleep a second time it was nearing four in the morning ... and I slept as hard as I had the first time.

We woke to texts from Rooster. We were being summoned for a meeting. That probably wasn't good.

The bar buzzed with activity when we entered. I didn't miss the appreciative look Whistler shot me as I headed toward a table in the corner.

"Good morning, kids," he drawled, his eyes sparkling when he met Gunner's admonishing gaze. "I heard you had a bit of fun last night."

"What fun?" Marissa demanded. She still looked half asleep and was drinking juice as she slouched morosely in a booth. "Not all of us were out partying last night. Some of us were working. You could've put this meeting off for a few hours."

"I didn't think that was a good idea," Rooster countered. He had a ledger open and had obviously been tallying numbers before our arrival. "I saw Flint this morning. He's spitting mad ... and his father wants to have a sit-down with me."

Uh-oh. That didn't sound good. "Listen, before you say anything ... ."

Gunner put his hand on my shoulder to still me. "Flint earned everything she doled out. She's not apologizing."

Rooster's expression remained placid. "And what did he do?"

"Well, for starters, he tried to grab her rear end at the gathering last night." Gunner launched into the tale, not leaving anything out. When it came time to explain the assault on the cabin, he didn't gloss over the fact that he'd spent the night — even going so far as to describe my outfit to the delighted members of our group.

"Wait ... she was wearing fuzzy lion slippers?" Whistler was obviously tickled. "Why didn't you get a photo of that?"

"I didn't think about it." Gunner shot me a sly smile before hopping onto one of the bar stools. "By the way, I didn't lift a finger. She took all of them out without breaking a sweat ... and the spell was geared to attack those who were armed, so they have nothing to complain about."

"Well, that's a little tidbit that was left out of the telling," Rooster mused, rubbing his chin. "It wasn't Cyrus doing the talking, by the way. It was Drake. He seemed agitated. Said Cyrus was demanding an audience."

"What about Flint?" Gunner asked. "How did he look?"

"Bald."

Gunner shifted on his stool and focused on me. "Bald?"

"Yeah." Rooster smirked at the memory. "All of his hair is gone. We're talking everything on top of his head ... and face, including his eyebrows. I'm betting he's bald as a newborn rat under his clothes."

"Oh, you would be wrong there," I countered, doing my best to tamp down the malicious energy bubbling up. "That's the after effect of the butt-grabbing spell, by the way. The final little surprise, so to speak. The others in the group won't suffer the same symptoms."

"You said I would be wrong about the hair," Rooster noted. "How so?"

"All that hair he's missing from the top of his head — and other places — has been re-directed to his back."

"Oh, gross," Bonnie and Marissa squealed in unison.

Rooster looked amused. "I guess that was a conscious choice on your part."

"It's a karma spell. He now has cold sores and a hairy back. He touched me without being invited and now he's reaping the consequences. There's no woman in the world who will touch him when he looks like that, even those who are paid to do so."

Rooster let loose a hearty guffaw, his shoulders shaking. "Oh, that is just priceless. Do I want to know the after-effects those in the woods face?"

"Probably not. It will lose in the telling. But you won't be able to miss it when you see them."

"Now I can't wait." Rooster rolled his neck and closed his ledger. "That doesn't change the fact that Cyrus is probably spitting mad and will make certain demands."

"He can make all the demands he wants," I said. "I can't remove the spell.

He has to do it for himself. As for the others, the remnants of that spell will wear off in a few days. I can't hurry the process."

"And that's because you built the spells this way?" Rooster asked.

"Yup. It's not a true karma spell if he doesn't learn something."

"I guess that's how I can phrase it with Cyrus. I don't expect him to get violent or anything, but we're having the meeting here regardless ... just to be on the safe side."

"That's smart," Gunner agreed. "Is that the only reason you called us here? If so, I can think of a few things I would rather be doing." He shot me a wolfish grin, which caused Marissa to groan and roll her eyes.

"That's actually not the only reason," Rooster countered. "Doc has come up with some useful information ... including Fred's real name."

"Real name?" I swiveled to focus on the quiet computer guru. "How did you figure that out?"

"I developed a program to access the law enforcement databanks of every state," he replied simply. "It didn't take that long, but sometimes the search results are delayed. That's what happened here because there was a match for Fred's fingerprints in North Dakota. Their system is notoriously slow."

"North Dakota." It didn't mean anything to me. I'd never been there – as far as I knew.

"His real name is George Culpepper. He was fifty-eight years old and he essentially disappeared from his life sixteen years ago. He worked as a postal carrier in North Dakota before then. No criminal record. Postal carriers are automatically fingerprinted, though, so there was a record."

"So ... how did he end up here?" Gunner asked, shooting me a worried look.

"We don't know," Rooster replied. "What we do know is that a quick scan of George Culpepper's finances showed that he once received a personal check from someone we know."

My heart skipped a beat. "Who?"

"Cyrus."

And, finally, things were starting to come together. "That means Cyrus is here for more than just a pack war. He's here for me, too."

"That would be my guess," Rooster agreed. "We need answers. He's scheduled to be here in an hour, so I figured you guys might want to be present for the conversation. I think it's time to put all cards on the table."

I couldn't agree more. Answers were finally within our reach.

TWENTY-FIVE

I was anxious as I paced the aisle between booths at The Cauldron. Learning that Cyrus had financial ties to Fred — er, George — was almost more than I could absorb.

"Tell me again," I instructed Doc.

He was blasé. "It's not as if the information is going to change."

"Tell me again," I gritted out.

"Tell her," Gunner prodded gently. "She needs to hear it."

Doc nodded. "He lived alone in North Dakota. I don't know whether he had friends, but someone named Marsha Thompson filed a missing person report. The police looked, but there were no signs of foul play. He just ... disappeared. They assumed he went out hunting and had a heart attack or something."

"And instead he ended up here, acting as if he was homeless for fifteen years," Bonnie mused. "I wonder how that happened."

"Too bad we can't ask Fred," Marissa suggested. "He died with Scout's name burned into his back, so that's out of the question."

Gunner shot her a quelling look. "Is there a reason you have to be difficult right now?"

Marissa balked at his expression. "I was just stating a fact."

"An unnecessary fact. Scout is dealing with enough right now. She doesn't need you making things worse."

Marissa's eyes went from wide to a squint in a split-second. "Why are you more worried about her than everybody else? We're all in danger here thanks to Scout. She's made us a target for rogue shifters and ... well, Goddess knows what else.

"According to the research you guys came up with, there's a trail of bodies in her wake," she continued. "Have you ever considered that she dropped those bodies and now she's simply putting on an act? I know she was a child, but she was powerful even then. It's possible."

Gunner bristled. "You don't want to go there."

"Why not?" Marissa wasn't backing down. Her eyes flashed as she got to her feet. Her crush on Gunner might've been legendary, but she was obviously more interested in making sure a message wasn't burned into her body rather than kissing up to him. "She's not what she pretends to be. She can do so much more."

"She doesn't pretend to be anything," he shot back. "She is who she is."

"We were told she's a witch."

"And she is."

"She's more than a witch!" Marissa practically screeched, causing my shoulders to jerk. I felt out of place and on display, vulnerable. "She could kill us all and you don't even care."

"You're right," Gunner agreed. "I don't care because that's not who she is. Have you taken a moment to look at her since all this started? She's traumatized by what happened to Fred. She blames herself. She doesn't need to take on that grief, though, because you're more than willing to heap it on her."

"Oh, don't you blame this on me." Marissa's voice went deep and dangerous. "I didn't cause this. Rooster brought her here. Then, even after she displayed magic she has no right to be able to wield, you fell for her. Now she'll never leave."

"I certainly hope not," Gunner agreed. "She belongs here. Why do you think Fred was here? It's obvious that whoever has been watching Scout for most of her life had some knowledge of her ending up here. She's where she belongs."

"You don't know that she's here to do good," Marissa snapped. "If this ... faction or whatever you call them ... managed to track her movements through time, something significant is set to happen here. You're assuming she's fighting on the right side. I maintain she's on the wrong side and we'll be fighting against her."

I hadn't even considered that. The possibility that I would be an enemy that needed to be put down at some point was almost too overwhelming. "Oh, geez." My hand shot out and landed on a nearby table so I could steady myself. I was shaking when I found the strength to lift my gaze and found Gunner watching me.

"Don't listen to her." He was firm. "You're not the enemy. I've seen you work. I've seen your heart. I mean ... not literally or anything, because that would be gross. I've seen the way you think and feel. You're not the enemy. Marissa just wants to make you doubt yourself."

That was very possibly true ... and working. "Maybe ... ." I could get only the one word out before I lost my nerve and averted my gaze to the window.

"You're not leaving," Gunner argued, as if reading my mind. "You're meant to be here. No matter what Marissa says, you're meant to fight on the right side. Don't let her win by being afraid ... and running."

I didn't say anything. I couldn't because I had no idea what I was supposed to say. Marissa decided to fill the void.

"Well, great," she intoned. "Does that mean we're all living our lives according to the whims of Gunner's hormones?"

Bonnie stirred. "If his hormones were directed at you, somehow I think you'd be fine with their judgment. As it is, I've seen Scout in action. She might be a little unorthodox in the way she approaches things, but she's clearly on the right side. You need to lay off."

"I agree." Rooster shifted on his squeaky barstool. I didn't turn in his direction. I couldn't. I was afraid of what I would find staring back at me. "Scout has proven her worth to us several times over. I refuse to be afraid of something that you think might happen, Marissa. If that was the way we operated, you would've been booted from this group the first time you lost it over a television show."

Marissa's mouth dropped open. "That happened, like, once."

"And yet nothing has happened with Scout, but you want her ousted," Gunner groused.

"She killed a siren with elemental magic," Marissa reminded him, haughty. "And that was after she threatened to let it slink away quietly into the night."

I'd almost forgotten about that. How could I? Was she right?

"Oh, shut up," Gunner snapped. "I'm sick of your voice. Leave her alone. She's been through enough."

"Right, poor little Scout. She needs the big strong wolf shifter to protect her. I want to know how the most powerful being we have working for us has managed to turn you into her guard dog."

Gunner snarled in response as movement through the window drew my attention. I recognized the figure parking his bike and removing his helmet.

"Cyrus is here," I volunteered weakly. "We should probably position people outside the front and back doors to make sure we don't have any unwanted guests in case he didn't come alone."

"That's a good idea." Rooster got off the stool and straightened his shoulders. "Marissa, you take the back door. Bonnie, wait in the kitchen until you're sure he's inside and then circle around to the front door. We don't want him to know we're watching the entrances."

Bonnie nodded perfunctorily. "You've got it." She was already on her feet and moving, but paused in front of me before completely disappearing. "I have faith in you," she offered. "Marissa is only acting like this because she's jealous."

"I am not jealous!" Marissa stomped on the floor. "Why would I possibly be jealous?"

Bonnie's lips curved at her reaction. "See. She's a petulant child. Don't let her get to you." She squeezed my wrist as a show of solidarity before hurrying toward the kitchen and disappearing through the swinging doors.

"Gunner and Scout, you should be at the bar when he comes in," Rooster ordered. "Act more interested in each other than him. Doc, stay where you are. I'll take him to the table by the window. Everybody should be able to hear, but don't interrupt the conversation. I've got this. Does everybody understand?"

I had no trouble following his logic. On the flip side, I wasn't naive enough to believe that I would manage to keep my mouth shut for the entire conversation. There was no reason to tell him that and start trouble before it was necessary.

"We've got it," Gunner said, moving to my side. "Make sure you question him as much as you can about Fred. We need answers about Scout's past."

Rooster nodded without hesitation.

CYRUS SWAGGERED THROUGH THE DOOR with enough attitude to suck all the oxygen out of the room. He was clearly feeling full of himself, and he only puffed up further when he noticed us sitting at the bar.

"I didn't realize I was getting the full Spells Angels treatment," he said.

"They're not here for you," Rooster called from the table in the corner. He'd taken his ledger with him to give Cyrus the impression that he'd been tied up with something else — not waiting for him — in the run-up to his arrival. "Ignore them. They're supposed to be working, but they claim they need a break. They're kind of lazy, if you want to know the truth."

I narrowed my eyes, the words causing my temper to flare. Under the bar,

Gunner gripped my knee and gave it a squeeze. I knew Rooster was saying it because he didn't want Cyrus to be suspicious. I still hated having my work ethic called into question.

"I don't doubt they're lazy." Cyrus strolled away from us, as if we were no more than pesky children underfoot. The look he spared for Doc was even more cursory and his gregarious personality was on full display as he approached Rooster. "It's been a long time," he boomed, shaking Rooster's hand with more enthusiasm than necessary. "I wasn't sure if I actually missed Hawthorne Hollow or only thought I did until I crossed the township line. It turns out, I really miss it."

"I can see that." Rooster looked relaxed as he took a seat across from Cyrus. From the outside, they looked like two old friends catching up after a long time apart. It was only if you knew him that you could sense the nervous energy buzzing around Rooster. "I heard you were considering moving back. I'm surprised. I didn't think that was allowed under the negotiations of your pack split."

Thanks to the mirror behind the bar, I didn't miss the way Cyrus's eyes flicked to Gunner's back.

"Rules are made to be broken ... or changed," Cyrus countered. "When I agreed, I thought I was fine leaving Hawthorne Hollow. Now I'm not so sure."

"Does this have anything to do with the razing of Covenant College?"

"Why would you ask that?" Cyrus's eyes felt as if they were boring holes into the back of my head. "We didn't have anything to do with Covenant College, something I've told other members of your group already."

"Really?" Rooster's reaction was blasé. "I was under the impression you were recruiting at one of the fraternity houses. Bitten wolves, not born. At least that's the word I heard circulating."

"You heard wrong."

"I guess so." Rooster sipped from his beer. "Do you know what happened with the college? Even if you didn't have anything to do with the wolves there, that was a big story. People say that mage who took down Kennedy Reagan years ago came back and wiped out the entire college."

"The mage was present," Cyrus replied. "I don't know that she did it on her own. They say one of the lesser gods was there, too, although that's just talk."

I arched an eyebrow, surprised. A god? In Michigan? That didn't make any sense. I wanted to ask what god, but Gunner, perhaps reading my mind, slowly shook his head. Now wasn't the time to go off on a tangent.

"Well, it's still an interesting story." After another sip, Rooster kicked back in his seat and stretched his legs. "I heard you invited Gunner and Scout to your gathering last night and things didn't go well."

Cyrus growled. "That's an understatement. Have you seen my son? He's bald as a cue ball. It's happening all over his body, too."

"Not his back," I called out. "All the hair that's gone missing from his head and ... other places ... is on his back."

Cyrus tilted his head in my direction, sneering. It was clear he was angry. He was too smart to immediately jump in with both feet and threaten me, though. "I understand there was an incident," he hedged. "I think you might've misconstrued something my son inadvertently did."

This time it was Gunner who inserted himself in the conversation. "She didn't misconstrue anything," he snapped. "The curse was designed to take motivation into consideration. He put his hands on her rear end because he's a jerk and now he's reaping the consequences."

Cyrus' eyebrows drew together. "I didn't know he'd touched her."

"That's the only reason the spell kicked in," I offered, twisting on the stool to face him. Rooster wanted us to stay out of the conversation, but I didn't see how that was possible now. "Of course, if you'd taught him at a younger age that he should keep his hands to himself he might've learned some respect for women."

Cyrus shot ice daggers out of his eyes as he glared. "Well, from where I'm sitting, your mother should've taught you to dress appropriately so he wouldn't have been tempted."

Outrage, hot and fast, coursed through me. Before I could decide how to respond, Gunner was on his feet and striding across the room.

"You take that back," he snapped, fury on full display. "It's not Scout's fault that your son is a piece of trash."

Cyrus knew better than to remain in his seat. That would allow Gunner to claim the dominant position. He jumped to his feet, his chest bumping against Gunner's as the two came face to face. "She was dressed like a whore and teasing him. You're upset because you know it's true."

"Don't talk about her like that!"

Rooster, who was stronger than he looked, muscled his way between the two spitting men and gave Gunner an extra shove that caused him to take two steps back. "That will be enough of that," he warned, his tone no-nonsense. "If you two can't play nice, we probably shouldn't play at all."

Cyrus held Gunner's gaze for an extended beat and then shook his head. "I didn't come here to get in a pissing contest with Gunner. I don't care about him."

"That's not how it seemed last night." Gunner's smile was smug. "The full-on recruitment push was evident last night."

"And you said you weren't interested. I'm not going to beg you to join my pack. I don't beg anyone. I thought you would be a good fit. You said you weren't interested. That was that. I'm not here because of you. I'm here because my kid looks like a freak and I want that one to drop the curse." He gestured toward me. "I want to know what it's going to take to get her to release Flint."

I couldn't hide my smile. I felt drunk with power. "What about the others who ended up cursed last night?" I asked.

Cyrus scowled. "As much as I'm not a fan of them smelling like cooked cauliflower — that was a particularly nasty treat, by the way, but also brilliant — I can live with that. You were protecting yourself. What happened with Flint is different."

"Not so different," I countered. "I was protecting myself from him."

"He says differently."

"Well, if he says something, it must be true, huh?"

"He's my son." Cyrus was unruffled. "I'm taking his side on this. There's nothing you can do to change things."

"You're right about that." I allowed a grin to slip through. "There's nothing I can do to change things. It's a karma spell. He has to change his behavior to end it."

Cyrus narrowed his eyes to dangerous slits. "I don't believe you. You're only saying that because you're enjoying torturing him."

"I certainly am enjoying it," I agreed. "He has it coming ... whether you believe it or not. But there's nothing I can do to lift the spell. He has to become a better person to escape the ramifications of his own actions."

"But ... he's not going to do that."

"Then he'll remain bald and continue suffering from herpes of the face. I don't know what to tell you."

Cyrus slammed his fist on the table, the noise loud enough that even Doc jerked from his location across the room. "You will fix this!"

"Your son has to fix this."

"Wait up now," Rooster interjected, his expression unreadable. "Maybe you're acting too hastily, Scout. I mean ... Cyrus might have something worth trading to get you to drop the spell. Have you considered that?"

Slowly, an idea dawned. I recognized what he was getting at ... and it was genius. "You're suggesting a trade," I mused. "That's interesting."

Cyrus was instantly alert. "What sort of trade?"

"The sort where you give me information about your ties to the Children of the Stars and I see what I can do for your low-life cretin of a son," I replied.

"I don't know what you're talking about." He said the words, but the furtive darting of his eyes told me he was lying.

"Then I guess we're done. Your son can look that way for the rest of his life for all I care. I hope you weren't expecting grandchildren." I turned on my heel with every intention of walking out the door, but he stopped me with a panicked yelp.

"Wait! I need your help."

"Then you have to help us," Rooster shot back. "That's your only option if you want to put this behind you."

"But ... that was a long time ago." Cyrus was obviously frustrated as he gripped his hands together. "I don't understand why you're even asking about that."

"You let us worry about that," Gunner challenged. "Just spill it. We'll handle the rest."

"All right. But it's a long story."

"We appear to have plenty of time."

TWENTY-SIX

"*I* need a drink," Cyrus announced as he settled back in his chair. It was obvious he was uncomfortable being the center of attention for something that he didn't arrange.

"Sure." Rooster inclined his head toward Whistler, who nodded in understanding. "Your drink is on the way. How about you tell us what you know regarding the Children of the Stars?"

It was the first time I'd used that term in mixed company, but Rooster had no problem running with it.

"First, that's not what they call themselves," Cyrus hedged. "The only reason I even knew what you were talking about was because of the woman. She always used that term."

I stirred. "What woman?"

"I didn't know her."

"You had to have heard a name."

He shrugged. "I might've heard a name. What is it worth to you?"

I'd had enough of his games. Rather than respond, I tossed out a magical rope and wrapped it around his neck, immediately cutting off his oxygen. He gurgled and reached for the rope, trying to loosen it.

"Scout, that's enough," Rooster warned. He was calm, but I didn't miss the furtive glance he shot Gunner.

Reluctantly, I withdrew the rope. "He needs to stop playing games," I insisted.

"I believe he understands that."

"Yeah, I understand that." There was something wild I couldn't quite identify in Cyrus's eyes. It looked like rage ... but also fear. "Like I said, it was a long time ago. I think her name was Claudette. Before you ask, I never got a last name."

Claudette. I ran the name through my head. Did it fit? I had no idea. I couldn't ever remember calling her anything but "mother," and that was only when we were trying to fool people into believing we were related. Otherwise ... nothing.

"Does that name mean anything to you?" Gunner asked.

I shook my head, not trusting myself to answer should my voice betray me. I was overwhelmed by emotions I thought long forgotten.

"Why would the name mean anything to her?" Cyrus asked, his eyes squinting. "Unless ... are you one of them? Is that why you're so worked up?"

"Leave her alone," Rooster instructed. "That's none of your business. Tell me about the group."

Cyrus continued to stare at me for before he slowly drew up and squared his shoulders. Smugness wafted off him, which shouldn't be happening. We'd made a mistake somewhere and he was feeling powerful. I didn't like that one bit.

"I think we should renegotiate," he started. "You want information only I can provide. I think that's worth something."

Rooster shot back. "And what is that?"

"I'm thinking your little Swiss miss there will make a great fit for my pack."

Gunner immediately started shaking his head. "That's not going to happen. She's not interested."

"Oh, don't start crying like a girl," Cyrus admonished. "You're attached to her. I get it. I even get her appeal, but if I were you I'd be afraid to close my eyes at night in case she strips away all that pretty hair you seem to love so much. She can do it. You've seen it."

"I only touch her when I've been invited," Gunner shot back. "I'm not worried."

"Well, bully for you. I meant what I said. There's room for you in the pack. You don't have to be separated from her."

"I'm not joining your pack." Gunner was firm. "Neither is she. You *are* giving us information. You already agreed."

"That was before I realized what I was agreeing to. I've thought better of it."

I made up my mind on the spot and took a step back. "Fine. We're done here." I swept my hand toward the door. "Have a lovely day."

He obviously wasn't expecting my reaction, because he glanced in that direction and then back to me before speaking again. "I'm not leaving until you take that curse off my son."

"And I'm not doing that without information. We had a deal. I'll return your son to normal — at least as normal as he's capable of looking— and in exchange you'll answer our questions. I'm not adding to the deal. That's not how I work."

"Come on. You have to give me something."

"I really don't."

"She doesn't," Rooster agreed. "You seem to be missing the obvious here, Cyrus. She's the one with the power. You either agree to her terms or leave. Those are your only options."

"But ... ."

"Or Rooster and I could leave," Gunner added. "You and Scout could have a conversation alone. I bet then she would get everything she wants and give you nothing. You've seen what she's capable of. Do you want to risk that?"

Cyrus visibly gulped and his hand, unbidden, returned to his throat, the memory of the magic rope fresh. "I'm not afraid of her," he said finally.

"Then you're dumber than you look," Rooster shook his head. "Of course, that's usually what people say about you."

"No one says that."

"You'd be surprised."

Silence descended over the room, and then Cyrus, resigned, heaved out a sigh. "Fine. What do I care? The information isn't important to me anyway. I didn't even know you were looking for it until a few minutes ago."

"Great. Now talk," I pressed.

"I don't know the woman. I can't identify her. There's nothing else I can tell you about her."

"You can tell me where you met her. You can tell me about the conversation you had. You can tell me about the group. You said they're not called the Children of the Stars. What do they call themselves?"

"The Nexus."

"Seriously? That's the name they gave themselves?"

He reluctantly nodded. "Yeah. I thought it was stupid, too. They didn't really call themselves that, but that's the name that was on all their paperwork."

Now we were finally getting somewhere. "What sort of paperwork?"

"I think it would be best if you started from the beginning," Rooster suggested. "That's the only way both sides will truly understand what's going on."

Cyrus didn't look thrilled with the prospect but he acquiesced. "Fine. You asked for it." He accepted the beer Whistler delivered with a flat smile and leaned back in his chair. He wanted to give the impression that he was in control of the conversation, even though he obviously wasn't.

"It started not long after I moved to Midland," he began, scratching his chin as if searching his memory. "That was a confusing time. I was happy to have my own pack, don't get me wrong, but I wasn't aware of how much work went into it."

Gunner snorted. "It seems to me that should've been the first thing you realized."

"Nobody asked you," Cyrus shot back, his nostrils flaring. After a moment, he reined in his temper and returned to his story. "I wasn't familiar with the area and there was already a wolf who had sort of taken control of the territory. He was powerful, son of a state senator, and I thought it might behoove me to join forces with him."

"Aric Winters," Gunner supplied. "He's married to the mage. Are you telling me you offered him a position in your pack? Are you stupid? Everyone knows that guy wants nothing to do with pack politics."

"I think Cyrus believed he could bully him into seeing things his way," Rooster interjected. "That's how he's always been. Plus, well, a mage. That particular mage has quite the reputation. People say she's the most powerful supernatural being in the state, maybe even in the world."

"They say their kid is even more powerful," Gunner added. "That's why they protect her the way they do. Jerks from every corner of the world try to take the kid so they can tap into her magic ... and the mage sends a stern message every time. I believe the message is often accompanied by fire."

Cyrus scowled. "She is a little fire-happy. No matter. I made overtures and was turned down. This was when the kid was little, barely a toddler. The wife looked ragged, as if she hadn't slept in days, and the kid was running around pointing at everything and screeching 'mine' as the mother tried to corral her."

I smiled despite myself. "I believe all toddlers go through that phase."

"Flint certainly did," he agreed.

"It seems to me he's still going through that phase," Gunner groused, causing Cyrus to frown.

"Get back to the story," Rooster prodded.

"I tried to get the Winters boy on my side, but he refused and it irritated me. I was going to try to grab the kid to shore up my negotiation position when the wife went nuts and blew up our entire convoy. We're talking twenty bikes, fifteen trucks and even a few fifth-wheelers. She went berserk and took out everything we owned."

"Obviously she didn't kill you," I noted.

"She killed the people who crossed onto her property. She didn't even break a sweat when it happened."

"Good for her."

"No, not good for her." He scowled. "Everything we owned was in those vehicles. It was all gone in the blink of an eye."

"Am I supposed to feel sorry for you?"

"No, but it does explain a few things," Gunner noted. "They needed money. He just said everything they owned was destroyed by a mother who didn't take prisoners. He lost men and all his resources. He needed to build capital ... and fast."

Realization dawned. "And that's how you got involved with Nexus."

Cyrus nodded, bitter. "They were offering money for protection services. We needed money. It seemed like a good partnership."

"I'm guessing something happened," Rooster supplied.

"Yeah. Something definitely happened." Cyrus rolled his neck until it cracked and downed more of his beer before continuing. "They were moving to a new location. We didn't know much about their group, other than that they were witches. They seemed to be normal witches, but one night we were hanging around their property — I still can't remember why — and we saw one of their rituals. They called the stars down from the sky. I mean ... they literally called them down."

I stilled. "No, they didn't. They used the stars as camouflage and to fuel their spells. They didn't call them down from the sky."

"It looked that way to me."

"That was an optical illusion."

Rooster slid me a sidelong look. "How do you know that?"

"I've seen it in my dreams."

He nodded and turned back to Cyrus. "I'm guessing they weren't happy when they found you spying."

"That's an understatement. They called it a breach of trust, if you can believe that."

I could. There was more to the story that he wasn't telling. "You weren't hanging by their property because you were bored or curious ... or even lost.

You were scoping it out because you were going to steal from them. You figured if they had enough money to pay you, they had enough to steal."

Cyrus made an incredulous face. "What do you take me for?"

"A thief," Gunner replied without hesitation. "You've always been the sort of guy who wants to take the easy way out. Don't pretend otherwise."

"Well, aren't you just a little ray of sunshine," Cyrus muttered. "What does it matter? We didn't threaten them. We were never a threat. They went after us, and hard."

"Some of this is starting to make sense," Rooster offered, his mind clearly busy. "The reason Doc managed to track down financial ties between George and Cyrus is because the wolves were technically on the payroll of the witches for a time. But they were never truly allies."

"George." Cyrus snorted. "That guy was a nutball. He worked for the government or something — I can't remember exactly what he did — and only visited the other freaks on the weekends. He was from North Dakota but moved somewhere in the state about the time we paired up with the Nexus folks. He was always threatening that if we didn't follow the rules they would make us pay. I hated that guy."

"Is that why you killed him?" I asked, my temper getting the better of me. "Is that why you strung him up in the middle of town and burned my name into his back?"

Cyrus looked taken aback. If he was acting, he'd suddenly gotten much better at it. "What are you even talking about?"

I opened my mouth to unleash a torrent of curses, but Gunner's hand on my shoulder served as a warning to keep it together.

"Don't," he whispered. "Let Rooster handle the next bit."

"Yes, let the adults talk," Cyrus chided.

It took everything I had to keep from wrapping my hands around his neck and squeezing until he could no longer flap his evil lips.

"George Culpepper, the man you knew in Midland and briefly worked for, is also Fred Burns," Rooster volunteered. "That's the man who happened to follow Scout and Gunner to the beach the other night, steal from them, and then disappear until someone strung him up in the middle of town."

Cyrus looked perplexed. "What does that have to do with me?"

"Drake and Flint were also on the beach that night ... and in the woods the next day. They happened to show up at location where we believe Fred was killed."

"But ... no." Even as he said it, Cyrus's demeanor changed. I felt I could hear the gears of his mind working — and they sounded rusty — as he considered the new information. "My boy didn't have anything to do with that," he said finally. "He wouldn't have even remembered George. I don't think he ever met him."

"What about Drake?" Gunner asked. "How does he fit into all of this?"

"Drake? He's nobody. I met him when he was in his early twenties — that was, like, ten years ago. He was packless. He had a few interesting personality quirks, so I decided to bring him on. It turned out to be a good decision because he moved up the ranks quickly."

"I recognize him somehow," Gunner countered. "I don't know who he used to be, but he hasn't always been Drake Frost."

Cyrus shrugged. "I don't really care about any of that. I mean ... it has nothing to do with me. I just want soldiers and he's always been a good soldier. His sister was with him at the start, but she disappeared about five years ago. I don't think the pack life was for her, which was too bad, because Flint had the hots for her and I thought she might make a good match."

My stomach turned. "She probably ran away rather than have to deal with Flint. I think anyone with a brain would've done the same."

"Hey! Flint is a catch."

"No, Flint is the fish that always hops on the line but every fisherman in the free world wants to throw him back because he's undersized and smells foul."

Gunner pressed his lips together and I got the distinct impression that he was trying not to laugh.

"You don't even know what you're talking about," Cyrus argued. "Flint will take over as pack leader when my time is finished. I've been grooming him."

"Then you've been doing a terrible job. He has no leadership qualities and isn't smart enough to lead a pack to anything other than destruction. I'm not saying you're the strongest tonic in the medicine cabinet, but you at least understand the realities of pack life. Flint lives in La-La Land."

"He's also a suspect in a murder," Rooster added. "It's too much of a coincidence to believe that Flint and Drake weren't involved in Fred's death. They might've been too young to know him as George, but they figured things out. They also realized he had ties to Scout. You'll never convince me otherwise."

Cyrus looked genuinely flustered. "What ties to Scout? I don't understand any of this."

"You don't need to understand," Gunner insisted. "You need to provide us with information. Drake is the key. We need to know where you met him and what happened to his sister. I have no idea if Flint or Drake is really in charge when it comes to their very weird relationship, but I'm going to find out ...

and whichever one of them killed George is going to pay. No one deserves to die in that manner."

Cyrus extended a warning finger. "You want to stay away from my boy."

"And you want to stay out of my way," Gunner shot back. "This is non-negotiable. We need information on Drake."

"I don't know that I have information to give. In fact ... ."

At the same moment I registered an unholy roar, which obviously came from a gun, the window shattered. Cyrus pitched forward on the table, a heavy grunt escaping as Gunner threw himself on me and dragged us both to the floor.

"Shots fired!" Rooster roared to Doc and Whistler. "Everybody get your head down!"

TWENTY-SEVEN

"Stay down!" Gunner pressed me to the floor as he craned his neck. Someone fired two more shots into the bar after the initial one took out Cyrus, but it had been quiet for almost a full minute.

"Is everyone okay?" Rooster called out. "Whistler? Doc?"

"I'm fine," Whistler replied from behind the bar. "Doc never looked up from his computer and is still working. He seems to be in the zone." I shifted my eyes in that direction and shook my head when I realized Whistler spoke the truth. Doc continued to calmly tap away on his computer, as if he was unaware we'd just been shot at.

"What about outside?" Rooster asked. "What about Marissa and Bonnie?"

Whistler was grim. "I'll check."

"Call my father first," Gunner instructed. He was still firmly lodged on top of me, which was annoying because it was becoming increasingly difficult to breathe given his sheer size. "We need backup out here, but we can't clear all the pockets in the hills surrounding the bar without help."

"Yeah, yeah, yeah."

I waited another twenty seconds and then elbowed Gunner with everything I had. "I can't breathe."

"Oh, sorry." His smile was weak as he rolled to the side. "Keep your head down." As if to prove he meant business, he pressed his hand to the back of my head and applied pressure. "I just got you. I don't want to lose you."

I rolled my eyes. "Whoever did this ran."

"You can't know that."

"I can. Only an idiot would remain behind. He's gone."

"Yeah, well ... ." Gunner growled but ultimately acquiesced when I slapped his hand away. "If you get your head blown off I'll be really angry."

"I'll try to refrain." I rolled to my knees and focused on Cyrus. I assumed he was dead, but that thought fled when I realized his eyes were open and a pulse point was working in his neck. "Oh, geez." I crawled to him, my hands automatically searching his body for an entry wound. "He's alive," I announced. "We need an ambulance out here, too."

"You're kidding." Gunner moved to my side, draping his body over mine. When I shot him a dirty look, he smiled. "I'm not trying to smother you this time. I swear it. I'm just checking on Cyrus."

"Can't. Breathe," Cyrus wheezed.

I frowned as I moved my hand to his chest, wincing when I felt the moisture on the front of his shirt. It was obviously blood ... and there was a lot of it. "Chest wound," I muttered. "It came in at an angle." I turned my eyes to the window and studied the foliage through the gaping opening. "Whoever it was had a clear view of us from up there." I pointed toward a small bluff partially obscured by a grove of trees. "I wonder how long they were watching us."

"I don't know, but that would be an easy enough location to get to without alerting us," Gunner replied. "It didn't make sense to me that Cyrus came to this meeting without backup. I'm guessing, at the very least, he had Drake with him."

"Why do you say that?"

"Flint was never good with weapons. He couldn't have made that shot. Only someone who was trained could."

I rolled the information around in my head. "Like with the military?"

He shrugged. "Most wolves are trained in weaponry because there's always a chance we'll go to war. It doesn't necessarily mean what you think."

He had no idea what I was thinking. Heck, I wasn't sure I did either. For now, we needed to sit tight and wait for Graham to clear us. "How long will your father be?"

"Not long." He kissed the tip of my nose and grinned. "Until then, we can play dirty games under the table if you want. I mean ... I'm not suggesting we do that, er, well, unless you want to."

Cyrus glared. "Kill me now," he moaned.

"I wouldn't say that with this crowd present," I argued. "There are a lot of people here who want to take you up on that."

"A lot of people," Gunner agreed.

Cyrus shut his eyes, his face wan. "Oh, shut up. Let me die in peace."

HE DIDN'T DIE. IN FACT, BY THE time the paramedics arrived, he was doing better.

"We've re-inflated the lung," one of them announced. "It looks like a through-and-through."

"Does that mean he'll survive?" I asked, fighting my bitter disappointment.

"He has a good chance," the paramedic replied. "Does anyone want to ride with him to the hospital?"

When no one raised a hand, he shrugged. "We'll be removing him shortly."

"Great." I went to the gurney and looked down at him. He had an oxygen mask on and looked blissed out thanks to the drugs they'd pumped him full of to take the edge off the pain. "Who did this to you?"

Slowly, his eyes tracked to me. "I know what you know," he mumbled behind the mask.

"You know more." I was certain of that. "You didn't come here alone. You had backup in the bushes. Who was it?"

"I don't know what you're talking about." He refused to make eye contact, a dead giveaway.

I decided to play it straight. "Cyrus, I don't want to tell you your business, but one of your own men just tried to kill you. I'm guessing it wasn't Flint because he has other things on his mind. That means it was Drake ... probably. We need you to confirm that if you want to survive."

Cyrus's eyes flashed with impatience. "I don't know anything ... and how do you figure?" he rasped.

"Whoever did this was one of your people. Once news gets out that you didn't die, do you really think the shooter is going to just flee into the night? He or she will come to finish the job. It's not as if you're safe even though you're alive."

I saw the moment the horrific realization hit home. He didn't want to believe I was correct, but he had no choice.

"It was Drake," he said finally, disgust washing over his face. "I thought he would protect me should you attack."

Something occurred to me. "He didn't step in when I started strangling you."

The paramedic arched an eyebrow but remained quiet.

"He didn't," Cyrus confirmed, his eyes sliding shut. "I should've realized something was wrong then. I guess this is on me."

"It is on you." I would never believe otherwise. "You know more about him than you're letting on. You have to tell us. It's the only way you'll survive."

"I don't know as much as you think," Cyrus rasped. "I needed bodies for my army. I didn't run background checks. I couldn't."

"You know something."

"I know that he hates Flint. He tries to hide it, but it's obvious. If he's decided to take me out, he's going after Flint next. You have to save my son."

That sounded like the last thing I wanted to do. Still, Drake was a threat.

"We'll find Drake," I promised. "We won't let him escape."

"Save Flint."

"We'll ... do our best."

GRAHAM WAS A TSUNAMI OF FURY when he burst into The Cauldron five minutes after Cyrus was wheeled off to the ambulance.

"The hills are clear," he announced. "Does someone want to tell me what's going on?"

Rooster took the initiative and delivered his response in measured tones. When he was finished, Graham looked more confused than alarmed. "I don't understand."

"Join the club," I said. "All we know is that Drake is the likely culprit. Cyrus said he was the one parked in the hills, and claims he doesn't know anything about his background."

"You guys were talking for a few minutes," Gunner pointed out. "Is that all he said?"

"He also said that Drake hates Flint."

Rooster furrowed his brow. "How can that be? I thought you said that you've always seen them together. That would indicate they're friends."

"Maybe ... or maybe Flint has something on Drake that forces him to be loyal. Or, quite possibly, there could be something else going on entirely. We won't know until we track down Drake or Flint. Something tells me they're no longer together."

"Especially since, by all the accounts I've heard this morning, Flint looks like a monster," Graham volunteered, his lips twitching when he turned to me. "I hear you're behind that."

I kept my face placid. "I have no idea what you're talking about."

"Uh-huh." Graham shook his head. "I don't know where they're staying. I've had feelers out, but none of them have panned out. They're not registered at any of the hotels, not even in neighboring towns."

I cocked my head, considering. "They probably can't afford to stay in a hotel."

"Can't afford it?" Graham looked amused until he looked to Rooster and they shared a private laugh. Then he sobered. "Wait ... are you serious?"

"It's come to our attention that Cyrus isn't exactly rolling in the dough," Rooster volunteered. "He went up against the wrong enemy not long after the pack split and she absolutely burned his savings. Ever since, they've been taking odd jobs in an effort to build up their coffers. That's gone wrong at least once. I wouldn't be surprised if it happened more than once."

"They're probably cursed," I muttered.

Rooster slid his eyes to me. "What do you mean?"

"Just that. If it was me that he tried to screw over back then, I would've cursed him so he could never get ahead unless he changed his ways. I'm a big believer in karma spells."

Gunner stirred. "You know, that makes sense. Scout enjoys casting karma spells as retribution. Cyrus all but admitted he was trying to rip off the Nexus group when they caught him spying and taught him a lesson. What if they taught him more of a lesson than he realizes?"

"And Scout came from them, whether she remembers it all or not," Rooster added. "The karma spell could be part of her upbringing for all we know."

Graham's face split with a wide smile. "I kind of like the idea of that."

"That's something to dwell on later," I insisted. "We need to find Flint and Drake now. If they're not at a hotel, that means they're in the woods." I searched my memory. "They're not dumb enough to remain close to the area where they killed Fred. I very much doubt they would stay in the same spot where they held their gathering because that would open them up to attack.

"I heard them the first night before I saw them," I continued. "They were howling in the woods. I'm guessing that's because they were visiting the gathering spot, not staying there. They would need access to fresh water and shelter from passing storms. There's a river out there, but no place to shelter. I don't suppose you have any ideas on location?"

"Just one," Gunner replied, thoughtful. "The cove by the lake. He would know it because he used to live here. It's a good place to camp because you can only enter from one side. It's easy to defend."

"Where is it?" I asked.

"About two miles from where you were the other night when you had your adventure with Mama Moon," Rooster replied. "It's a very good location. We used to have training retreats out there. I bet you're right."

I was already moving toward the door. "So, we should head out there."

"Wait." Gunner snagged my arm before I could get too far ahead of him. "We need a plan. You can't run out there half-cocked."

"Maybe I'm fully cocked. You don't know."

He grinned despite the serious nature of the conversation. "We'll discuss that as soon as we have a moment to ourselves. We have to come up with a plan. In fact ... we need more information on Drake. He's clearly much more dangerous than we initially thought."

"Do you still think you've met him?" Rooster queried.

Gunner nodded. "I'm more certain than ever. I don't know where I met him ... or when ... or why he changed his identity, but I've most certainly met him."

"That means he was up here at least once," Graham mused. "It's not like I took you to gatherings across the state. I couldn't because that would mean leaving your mother to her own devices ... which was dangerous."

Gunner turned grim. "That didn't stop you from leaving her to her own devices when you were in town."

"Do you really want to discuss that now?" Graham challenged.

Gunner looked as if he was going to take him up on the offer, but I quickly shook my head.

"Not now," I insisted. "We need to focus on the problem at hand. Drake is out there, and odds are he's going to kill Flint."

"I'm not sure why you care about that," Gunner said. "He's not a good guy. I mean ... I get that Drake isn't either, but he would be doing us a favor if he took out Flint. I guarantee there will come a day when we have to do it ourselves. He's a sexual predator. I already told you that. The world won't miss him."

That was probably true. That didn't mean I could sit back and let him die if I had it in my power to save him. "I would prefer he be locked up. Besides, don't you want to see how long he has to live under the karma spell? If his father is any indication, it could be forever. The back hair will be so long in a few weeks he'll be able to braid it."

Rooster was aghast. "You mean it keeps growing?"

I nodded. "What fun would it be if the spell didn't grow?"

"I just ... remind me to never tick you off."

"Me either," Graham added. "You don't play fair."

"Life isn't fair." I'd learned that a very long time ago. "We have to find Flint. We can't let Drake run around killing people unchecked. Once he takes out

Flint — something none of us would weep over — what's to stop him from coming after us? We have to draw our line in the sand here."

Gunner sighed. "I hate it when you're right."

I beamed at him. "You should probably get used to that."

"Yeah, yeah, yeah." He flicked my ear. "We have to go out to the cove. We can't ignore the very real possibility that Drake is about to kill Flint. We are who we are for a reason. Flint might not be worth saving, but that doesn't mean Drake isn't worth stopping."

"Oh, that was almost poetic," Graham drawled, earning a glare for his efforts. "I can't get involved in this. If you need backup, I can send it, but I can't be involved in a magic battle. You know that."

"We won't need you to be involved," I replied, my attention diverting to the door of The Cauldron as a familiar figure stepped inside.

Irene, her purse clutched against her chest, was all wide eyes and shaking hands as her gaze drifted between faces. "I heard there was a shooting. Ruthie wasn't hurt, was she?" She looked anguished.

"Of course not," Rooster replied, striding in Irene's direction. "I told you I would curb Raisin's time here. You don't want her at a bar. Besides, it's a school day. Shouldn't she be at school?"

"She should be but she's not," Irene said. "The school called an hour ago. She never showed up. I thought she was here with you. She mentioned wanting to talk to Scout last night. I figured she decided to head here rather than go to school this morning." Her eyes were glassy with tears when they locked with mine.

"We've been here all morning," I replied, my mind busy. "Are you sure she didn't go to my cabin?"

"I drove by on my way here. It looked empty."

"We should still check," Gunner said, grabbing his keys from the bar. "We have something to do, but we'll swing out to the cabin on the way and check on her. It won't take us long. When we find her, we'll send her to school."

"I would greatly appreciate that." Irene rubbed her forehead. "I love that girl. You know I do; even though she's a lot of work."

"I'll talk to her," Rooster promised. "She's going to get it together or she won't like what happens. I refuse to let her fall through the cracks."

That was true for all of us.

TWENTY-EIGHT

The front door of the cabin was open when we arrived, and my heart gave a little lurch. Irritation bubbled up as I rushed in. I had every intention of chastising Raisin for skipping school and letting herself into my private sanctuary. All of that fled when I saw the mess waiting for us.

"What the ... ?" Gunner was directly behind me, Rooster in his wake. They both looked flabbergasted at the chaos.

"Raisin wouldn't do this," Rooster offered automatically, his gaze heavy as it scanned the small space. "She wouldn't trash your place. I mean ... why would she scatter toilet paper all over the house?"

"She didn't do that," I replied. "Merlin does that every day." That's when it truly hit me. "Merlin." I started toward the bedroom. He liked to spread out on the bed for naps. With the door open, though, he could've fled outside. I was terrified by the notion. How would I ever find him in the woods?

Gunner went with me while Rooster checked the kitchen. As if sensing what worried me, he dropped to his knees and checked under the bed while I poked through the closet.

"He's not here," I said, anxiety coursing through me. "Do you think he ran outside?"

"No. He's here."

I turned and dropped to my stomach to look under the bed. Sure enough, Merlin was pressed to the far corner, his fur standing on end. He looked as if he'd had a troublesome morning. "He's here." Relief coursed through me ... and then reality set in. "He's here, but Raisin isn't."

I rolled to a sitting position and stared down the hallway, waiting for Rooster to appear. When he did, he was grim.

"Things are a mess in the kitchen, too," he announced. "I think ... I think someone was in here with Raisin."

I'd already come to the same conclusion. "It has to be Drake. He must've come here to stake out my place after he got off only one good shot at The Cauldron. He probably thought he could ambush me, but came across Raisin instead."

"But where is she?" Rooster looked tortured. He was exceedingly fond of Raisin, to the point where he was the father figure she always should've had. He looked out for her, demanded she act responsibly, and doted on her. The fear flitting through his head had to be debilitating.

"If he killed her, he wouldn't have taken her," Gunner noted, earning a harsh glare from our boss. "I didn't mean that the way it sounded," he offered hurriedly. "I just meant ... she's not here."

"Hurting her does nothing for him," I added. "She can't give him what he wants. He has to know that. We're careful with the information we dole out."

"And yet Raisin knows more than she should," Rooster countered. "She listens more than we give her credit for. She managed to trick you the other night. Drake might think she knows more than she does."

That was a sobering thought. "Yeah, well ... we have to go back to our previous assumption. If he has her, they're likely at that cove you mentioned. He won't hurt her because he intends to use her as a bargaining chip."

"For what?" Gunner asked. "What does he want to trade her for?"

"Me."

He stilled. "You? Why would he ... ." He didn't finish the question. The answer was right there. All he had to do was see it. "He wants your magic."

"I think he's always wanted it." I was resigned as I stood. "We need to shut the door and make sure Merlin has water. Then we need to head out to the cove."

Gunner frowned. "No, we need to get the others and plan a formal assault. We need more than the three of us."

"No, we don't." I was firm. "We're not going to fight. I'm going to trade myself for Raisin and you guys are going to take her to safety."

"And leave you behind?" Rooster immediately started shaking his head. "That's not what we do."

"You don't have a choice." I was firm on that. "Raisin is what's important. I can take care of myself."

"We're not leaving you with him." Gunner growled the words. "It's not happening."

"It is." I took pity on him and squeezed his hand. "I know you don't want to. I know you would give your life to stop it. But you can't.

"The truth is, we're in a bad situation," I continued, letting my pragmatic side take over. This is what I was good at, attacking things logically and without emotion. "I can't risk unleashing the full breadth of my magic on Drake while Raisin is around and can be hurt. The same goes for you guys. I don't want to risk it. I have to wait until you're safely away."

Gunner worked his jaw. "I won't leave you."

"You have no choice."

"I do have a choice." He refused to back down. "Rooster can take Raisin to safety. I'll stay with you."

"He'll kill you."

"Well ... he'll have to."

Rooster cleared his throat to get our attention. It was clear he didn't like where the conversation was going. "Scout may be right," he started.

"No!" Gunner shouted. "We can't sacrifice Scout, not even for Raisin."

"You need to think with your head instead of your heart," Rooster insisted. "I understand that you have feelings for her."

"It doesn't matter that I have feelings for her," Gunner exploded. "It matters that we don't abandon a member of our team. We can't just leave her."

"That's not what you'll be doing," I offered gently, wrapping my fingers around his wrist and squeezing tightly. He didn't want to listen, but he didn't have a choice. "I can't risk doing what I need to do with Raisin there. Occasionally I lose my head when unleashing my magic. She could be caught in the crossfire.

"You have to agree to trade me for Raisin and then leave," I insisted. "Drake is smart enough to see the lie in your eyes. I can take care of myself. You have to trust me."

"No." This time when Gunner shook his head it was with minimal effort. He'd lost. He already realized it. He simply didn't want to admit it. "I won't leave you."

"You don't have a choice." I was surprisingly calm given what was about to happen. "We have to do what's right for Raisin. The rest of us ... we signed up for this gig. I'm willing to do what's necessary to save her because she didn't. She's the reason we do what we do."

"No." Gunner stubbornly crossed his arms over his chest. "I won't allow it."

"Yes, you will." My lips quirked at his furious countenance. "You know it's the right thing to do. I'll be okay. You have to trust me."

"It's not about trust. It's about this feeling in the pit of my stomach that I'm doing the wrong thing, and because of that I'll never see you again."

"Oh, you're going to see me." I was certain of that. "You can't get rid of me that easily. I promised to stick around. I meant it."

He looked pained. "I just ... this feels wrong."

"It'll be okay. Have faith."

IT TURNED OUT WE DIDN'T NEED to go to Drake. He wasn't that far away. In fact, he was waiting in the driveway when we exited.

Gunner snarled and moved to attack, but I extended an arm to stop him, my eyes busy as they scanned the trees for hints of movement. Surely Drake wouldn't be stupid enough to come here alone.

"Where's Raisin?" Rooster demanded, stomping his foot as he took a threatening step toward Drake. "If you've hurt her, you have no idea the wrath that I'll rain down on you."

As far as threats went, it was vague but effective. His anguish over Raisin was palpable.

"I can't believe you stayed here," I offered, drawing his attention to me. He looked ragged, exhausted. I was surprised he managed to find the strength to remain upright. "Why didn't you regroup at a more fortified location?"

Drake's gaze bounced between us before finally landing on me. I expected him to start bragging, perhaps make a few demands. Instead, he took me by surprise. "I need your help."

Gunner barked out a hollow laugh. "You need our help? That's rich. Why would we help you?"

"I'm not your enemy." It was a simple and straightforward statement ... and there was truth hidden beneath the words. "You think I took Raisin. I can't blame you. You were meant to think that. It wasn't me, though."

"And we're just supposed to believe you?" Gunner snarled. "Why would we do that?"

That was the question, wasn't it? There was something off about the situation. We were missing something. "You shot Cyrus," I charged. It was a statement, not a question. "Don't bother denying it."

"I *did* shoot Cyrus," he agreed, grim. "I couldn't sit back and wait for an opening any longer. I had to force the situation. I didn't have a choice."

"You know he's still alive, right?"

Drake's expression darkened. "Well, that's depressing. It is what it is, though. I can't go back and take a better shot. I'm surprised I managed to get off the one I did given the angle I had going. I was afraid I was going to hit you." His eyes were on me. "If I'd hit you, all of this would've been for nothing."

"And what is 'this'?" Rooster demanded. "You say you're not our enemy, but you're out here, in the spot Raisin went missing, and you just shot a man in front of us not two hours ago. You're not exactly making the best case for yourself."

"I don't expect you to understand." Drake dragged a hand through his dark hair. It was standing on end, making me believe he'd been swiping at it for hours. "The story is too long, too convoluted. I just ... need your help. I can offer mine in return. If we work together, this will end up okay for everybody."

"We don't care about helping you," Gunner shot back. "We care about Raisin. Where is she?"

"I don't have her."

"Of course you have her." Gunner's fingers twitched, but he kept his hands to himself. "You shot Cyrus and ran out here to take up a position where you could kill Scout. Then you saw Raisin and figured out another plan. Why kill Scout when you can force her to do your bidding by threatening Raisin?"

"That's a solid plan," Drake agreed. "If I'd thought of it, I might actually have tried to pull it off. Here's the thing: I don't kidnap children. Even if I thought I might've been able to pull that off, I wouldn't have touched a child."

"If not you, who?" Rooster demanded, his eyes flashing. "We have one suspect, and you're standing right in front of us."

"It's not him," I announced, taking everybody by surprise and causing three heads to snap in my direction. "He didn't take Raisin. And he didn't kill Fred."

Drake was taken aback. "Of course I didn't kill Fred. Why would you think that?"

"Oh, I don't know," Gunner challenged. "Maybe it's because you've been stalking Scout from the start and he was related to her. Maybe it's because he helped put a curse on Cyrus's merry band of thieves back in the day. Maybe it's because you like playing games."

"Except he's not the one playing games this time," I countered, jabbing a warning finger in his direction when it looked as if he was going to start arguing. "I'm talking now."

He snapped his mouth shut and glowered.

"What is it you believe you've figured out, Scout?" Rooster asked.

"It's Flint. It has always been Flint." Things were slowly slipping into place. "Gunner, one of the first things you said to me when I mentioned his name was that he was known for sexually harassing women. I'm betting the truth is actually worse than that."

Drake's expression was dour. "He's an animal."

"And he has your sister." That was the missing piece. "Cyrus mentioned your sister disappeared. Flint took her. He's been holding her over your head as a bargaining chip. That's why you still hang with him even though you despise him."

"Sarah," Drake confirmed. "He's had her for more than a year. I've tried to find out where, but he's smarter than he looks. He uses her to keep me subservient."

"There's more," I argued. "There's part of the story you're not telling. Your name isn't Drake Frost. Somehow you know Gunner. You used to be someone else. Who?"

Drake grimaced, clearly unhappy with the direction the conversation was taking. "What does that have to do with anything?" he asked finally.

"We're not helping you until we know the whole truth," Rooster answered. "Scout is right. If you're innocent in this ... ."

"I'm not innocent," Drake snapped. "I got involved with Cyrus's group because I needed money, plain and simple. I didn't realize how things would turn out. I thought they were normal pack."

"You're not normal pack, though," I pointed out. "You're something else. You're two things." That's when the final piece slipped into place. "You're a shifter who is magical. That's why you can shutter the way you do."

His eyebrows migrated north on his forehead. "How do you know that?"

"I'm magical, too." It was the simplest answer. "What are you? What do you have to do with Nexus?"

"How do you know about Nexus?"

"Cyrus has a big mouth."

"And he was trying to negotiate with you," Drake surmised, shaking his head. "He thought you would take the curse off Flint in exchange for information."

"Actually, he thought he could bully me into taking the curse off Flint," I countered. "I can't. I wasn't lying about Flint having to deal with the curse himself. Cyrus didn't believe me. When we realized he had financial ties to Fred — or George, the man Fred really was — we offered to make a trade. It was a trade I couldn't hold up my end of the bargain on, but he didn't know that."

"And he just told you about George?" Drake was incredulous. "That doesn't sound like him."

"He seemed desperate to free Flint."

"That's because Flint won't stop crying like a baby," Drake explained. "He acts as if he's dying. Everyone else thinks it's funny. He's furious, though."

"And he took Raisin," Rooster muttered.

"He did, but he won't hurt her," Drake reassured him. "He wants Scout. He knows if he hurts the girl she'll kill him without thinking twice. He's a jerk, a total jackass, but he's not an idiot. He won't hurt the girl. He has specific plans for Scout."

Gunner stirred. "What plans?"

"He wants her magic. He thinks he'll be unstoppable if he gets it."

"What about his ties to Nexus?" I asked. "How does the group play into all of this?"

"From Flint's perspective, they don't play in," Drake replied, grim. "From my perspective ... well ... I used to be part of the group."

I was gobsmacked. "You were? Do you know who I am? Do you know why I was abandoned?"

"I know whispers," he clarified. "I was not high in the group, but I might know something that could be helpful. The fact that I was part of the group and I was trying to hide it is why Flint managed to gain control of me. It's a long story."

"I want to hear it."

Rooster cleared his throat to interrupt us. "We all want to hear it, but we need to get Raisin first. After that, you can talk as long as your tongues hold out."

"And my sister," Drake said. "My sister is innocent, too. He has her ... and he's been mistreating her for a long time. I need to get her back."

His earnest expression was enough to convince me. "If I help you get your sister back, once all this is finished, will you tell me what you know? Will you tell us who you are?"

He nodded without hesitation. "I'm afraid I don't know as much as you would like, but all the information I have will be available to you. I swear it."

"It's still more information than I have." I turned my attention back to Rooster. "The old plan still stands. I'll trade myself to Flint for Raisin. Once it's just the two of us, I'll start getting answers from him."

"No, the old plan doesn't stand," Rooster countered. "The situation is different. Two innocent girls are in trouble. We need to save both of them ... and we'll need the whole team to do it."

"Flint is a wild card. He might hurt Raisin as payback for the curse I set upon him."

"Then he'll regret ever being born." Rooster's eyes flashed with determination. "I let you talk me into a scenario I didn't feel good about before. I've had time to think about it now. We're going a different route. We're bringing in the whole team on this."

I wanted to argue, but it was clear he'd made up his mind. "Fine, but I want to move fast. The more time Flint has Raisin, the more damage he can do. We need to move now."

"You read my mind."

TWENTY-NINE

*W*e hid our bikes near the road. Rooster and Gunner both agreed it was best. If we could get close without anyone noticing, it would be to our benefit. I had an idea about that.

"There's this thing I can do," I offered as we rolled our bikes into the foliage. I felt uncomfortable bringing it up, but it would be helpful. "I can hide us."

Several sets of eyes slid toward me.

"You can hide us?" Gunner asked finally. "How?"

"I'm not sure." I gnawed my bottom lip. "It's just this thing I can do. It works better at night when I can use the stars, but I can make it work during the day, too, especially with so many trees to provide cover."

"What is it?"

"Well ... it's probably better that I show you."

"Wait a second." Marissa's eyes flashed with impatience. "Do we really want to trust some weird idea she has when Raisin is on the line? We don't even know if she can pull it off."

"Absolutely." Rooster bobbed his head without hesitation. "If she says she can do it, I believe her. She wants to save Raisin as much as the rest of us."

Marissa wasn't placated. "I still want to know what it is."

"It's just this thing I can do." She was starting to irritate me. "It will make us invisible, but not silent. If someone stares directly at us as we're moving they might be able to see outlines. It's not a guaranteed solution."

"Nothing is a guaranteed solution," Rooster pointed out. "I'm not looking for guarantees. I'm looking for whatever gives us our best chance of getting Raisin out of here unharmed."

"I think this will do it, but we need to be quiet ... and ready for battle the second I drop the veil. We'll have a few seconds because they'll be confused about how we managed to get into their midst without them realizing, but they'll panic when they see what's happening."

Rooster turned his attention to Drake. "How many men does he have with him?"

"The entire pack is in there, but not all of them will help Flint. They don't like him. Cyrus refuses to see the truth about his own son."

"Is that why you tried to kill him?" I asked. "Do you blame him for what happened to your sister?"

"I blame him for not seeing the truth. He's enabled Flint his entire life. I tried telling him what was going on despite Flint's warnings, but he wouldn't listen to me. He said I was making trouble and threatened me if I didn't stop making waves. In some ways, Cyrus is worse than Flint. At least Flint admits what he is."

I could see that. "You still shouldn't have shot him," I said finally. "You should've come to us for help before Raisin was taken. We could've come up with a better plan if you had."

"I didn't know if I could trust you. I didn't realize you were a Child of the Stars until you froze me the way you did that day in the clearing."

"You mean the clearing where George was killed? That's why I was there."

Drake stilled. "Are you sure?"

"Oh, I'm sure. There was blood everywhere, though someone tried to clean it up. I thought you were part of that."

"No." He shook his head. "Flint did that without me ... I'm not sure why. How would that benefit him?"

That was the question. "I think it's time we find out."

I HADN'T CAST THE SPELL IN a long time. It was more draining than my normal magic, but I thought it was our best chance. Eyes were wide as I dropped the veil. It settled over us like a light blanket, and Bonnie giggled as she felt the magic descend.

"This is neat."

"It's ... something." Rooster looked to be in awe as he reached out to touch the magical boundary. "How close do we have to stick to one another?"

"Fairly close. The bigger I cast the net, the more magic I have to expend."

"And you'll be weak when we get there if we're not careful," Gunner surmised. "I guess that means we should get moving."

"Definitely."

We had to walk two miles to the cove. By the time we started seeing sentries I was already weary. That didn't mean I wanted to take any chances.

"*Sleep*," I murmured, sending out a bolt of magic to cause the nearest sentry to fall. He dropped to his knees and tumbled face first into the brush.

Drake sent me a questioning look, fearful.

"He's not dead," I reassured him with a whisper. "You said not all the pack members would fight with Flint. I'm only interested in hurting those who fight against us."

He nodded and turned forward. "It's only a few more minutes."

"Then we must be silent," I warned. "It's very important now."

No one argued.

The more sentries that appeared, the more dangerous it became to knock them out. Instead, I resorted to another spell.

"Don't let them see," I murmured. "Keep them blind. Let us be."

Gunner's hand moved to my back as we continued walking. It was almost as if he could sense the weariness pervading my soul. The more energy I expended the less I had in the tank for the final fight. "How much longer?" he finally hissed to Drake.

"We're here," Drake replied, inclining his chin toward a rock wall. There looked to be an opening in the back, a cave. "Raisin will be in there ... with Flint."

"How many others?" I asked.

"No more than four or five."

He spoke loud enough this time to cause one of the female pack members to jerk her head in our direction. I made up my mind on the spot.

"Go." I gave Gunner a shove, sending the magical veil with them, and then stepped out from the protective curtain. He fought the effort, tried to move so he could stand with me, but Rooster obviously understood what I was doing and kept a firm hold on him.

The second I became visible the pack members started yelling and circling. The other members of my group were beyond the circle they formed, so they were safe and they had a clear path to the cave.

Gunner desperately fought Rooster, but he couldn't call out to me because Marissa had her hand clamped firmly over his mouth. Drake joined in the effort, and between the two of them kept Gunner from struggling further.

The last thing I saw was his desperate gaze before he disappeared into the cave.

I focused on the pack members. My magic was split until they made the decision to drop the veil. I had to keep funneling power in that direction to give them their best chance. We had too much riding on this to fail now.

"Hello, ladies and gentlemen," I drawled, hoping bravado would win out over most of them. "Lovely day, isn't it?"

One of the men — he was absolutely huge — stepped directly in front of me and glared. "What are you doing here? This is protected land. You weren't invited in."

"Sure I was. Flint sent the invitation himself."

The man was taken aback. "I ... he did?"

Obviously, in this particular case, brawn didn't translate to brains. "He did. He wants me to join your pack."

"Why?"

"Because he's a moron." I saw no reason to lie. "He thinks he can harness my powers for himself. I have news for him. That's not going to happen." The veil was still up. They were still in hiding. Why? They should be moving by now.

"Well, I'm sure you won't mind if we ask him about it," the man supplied with a sneer. "We have security protocols. I'm sure you understand."

I absolutely understood. I also couldn't let anyone enter that cave. That would cut me off from my people. I couldn't have that.

"Listen, I need you guys to back off." I was tired, like "go to bed for an entire weekend" tired. I was also out of patience. "I don't have time for you guys. I don't know if you're evil or just confused. It doesn't really matter, though. I'm going after Flint and you're not going to stop me."

"We're not going to allow that." The man was adamant. "We'll protect Flint with our lives."

A low murmur went through the crowd and I could hear the dissent.

"I don't think the others agree with you," I countered. "Believe it or not, I don't want to hurt you. I only want Flint. He's taken something very valuable and I want it back."

"What has he taken?" This time it was a woman who spoke. She looked to be in her twenties, but the exhaustion permeating her gave the impression she was much older. "We need money."

"It's not money. I wouldn't have risked this for money. It's a girl. He took a teenager and I'm going to get her back. That's not up for debate. You have no say in that. The only thing you have a say in is whether I take you out to get her back."

"A girl?" The woman furrowed her brow and glanced around. "Did anyone see Flint bring in a teenager?"

Most of the pack members shook their heads, seemingly bewildered. Several, though, looked grim. I focused on them.

"The rest of you need to go," I ordered. "I wasn't kidding when I said I didn't want to hurt you. I meant it, but I will kill you if I have to." My voice sounded strained. I would wear out quickly if they didn't step out from the shield. "Don't force me to kill you. It won't make anybody happy ... and it won't stop anything. Flint is going down."

The woman held my gaze for a long beat and then lifted her finger and pointed ... away from the cave. "I won't stop you. In fact, I wish you well. If you kill him, make it hurt."

"Arabella," the alpha male in front of me groaned. "You can't just abandon the cause."

"This isn't my cause, Dorian," she replied with a shrug. "Besides, he's already lost. If you can't see that, I feel sorry for you."

Arabella started for the trees, most of the shifters following. Only three remained; Dorian and two others ... and they were all huge.

"I guess you guys are the idiots, huh?" I heaved out a sigh. "Well, let's do this." I clutched my hands into fists, causing Dorian to smirk. "You think this is funny?"

He nodded. "You can't take us. You're barely standing."

He wasn't wrong. Still, I wouldn't give up. "Looks can be deceiving."

"I guess we'll find out." Dorian took a menacing step in my direction and I braced myself for battle. It would be easier to use magic — in any other situation, I would have — but I was afraid that if I unleashed my power now that I would cause the veil to flicker. If that happened at the wrong moment, all would be lost.

Dorian clearly didn't have a problem fighting a woman, leading with a roundhouse punch directed at my face. I easily sidestepped it while gripping both my fists together and slamming them up into his chin. His eyes went wide and rolled back into his head as he fell backward with a thud. He turned out to be easier than I thought. The other two wouldn't fall for the same ploy.

"You guys need to back off," I ordered, my head going light. I couldn't last much longer. Instead of lessening the power I was pooling into the veil, I doubled it. The magic might be able to last a bit longer even if I fell here. It was all I could hope for.

"We're not going to back off," replied one of the men, a blond with a large scar on his cheek. "We're taking you down ... and then we're going to take that magic for ourselves. Screw Flint. You're the big prize everyone wants, so we're taking you."

"Well, great." This was the end. I couldn't maintain my energy level much longer. "Bring it on."

He stepped forward, mayhem written all over his features, and he almost looked gleeful about what was to come. "This is going to hurt."

I had no doubt, and braced myself for oblivion.

And then it happened. The veil broke ... and all the remnants of the magic I funneled into protecting my friends rushed back into me. It wasn't a full charge, but it was more than enough for what I needed.

The man advanced, his hands outstretched, and I lulled him in. I acted weak, as if I was going to fall down. I gave every impression that I was going to tumble, and then I recovered when he overreached.

"This was a huge mistake," I hissed, grabbing his arm and twisting as hard as I could. I funneled some of the magic I'd regained into the move and the sound of breaking bone filled the air, followed quickly by an agonized cry.

"You broke my arm, you ... !"

I ignored his griping and slammed my foot into his face as he dropped to the ground. He was out quickly, which left only one more.

I was definitely feeling better, but the momentary rush wouldn't last. All I had to do was hold the final guy off long enough for Rooster and Gunner to finish their mission. They could easily take out Flint and whatever comrades he kept close inside the cave. Their battle would ultimately be easy, which is what I wanted.

"It's just you and me," I offered.

The last wolf looked conflicted.

"You can still run," I offered. "No one will ever know that you were bested by a girl."

That was probably a mistake. The remark only doubled his resolve. His eyes filled with fire as he turned back to me.

"Me and my big mouth," I muttered, shaking my head. "Well, you're just as dumb as the others. I should've seen that coming. You guys couldn't even claim a normal IQ collectively."

He let loose a howl and tore toward me. I raised my hands, uprooting the nearest tree and sending it crashing in his direction. He turned at the sound, which allowed me to slam my fist into his face. He was hit with two weapons at the same time – one much bigger than the other – and crumpled to the ground. He didn't as much as twitch after.

"Well, that was entertaining," I wheezed as I listed to the side, my hand immediately grabbing one of the branches from the fallen tree to hold myself up. "That didn't go too poorly."

I was going to pass out. There was no fighting it now. I only hoped that I didn't crash into the tree and inadvertently take out an eye while collapsing.

"Scout!" Gunner's arms were around me from behind as I started to fade, his breath ragged. "Are you okay?"

His eyes were filled with concern, the mark of violence on his cheek telling me he'd participated in a fight of his own, as he lowered both of us to the ground. "I'm okay," I lied. "I'm great." I sent him a thumbs-up.

"You're a moron." He kissed my forehead and cradled me against him. "I'm really mad at you right now."

"I know." I closed my eyes. "Is Raisin okay?"

"She's fine. She's actually excited about what happened. She thinks it'll be good motivation for a chilling performance for her play."

"That's good." I meant it. "Sarah?"

"Not here, but Flint gave Drake her location before ... well, before it was over."

So he was dead. That was good. "Who killed him?"

"Drake. We couldn't stop him."

"Did you want to?"

"No. Flint had it coming."

"Yeah." I rested my head against his chest. "I really need a nap. You won't think less of me if I take one here, will you?"

He chuckled, the sound like a warm blanket as I began to slip under. "No. I'll take care of you. Sleep. I'll buy you the biggest, most expensive dinner in history as long as you wake again."

I realized he was still afraid and tried to comfort him even as the blackness swooped in. "I will. This isn't the first time this has happened."

"That doesn't exactly make me feel better."

"You'll get used to it."

His lips were against my forehead. "I certainly hope not."

That's the last thing I heard before I slipped into dreamless darkness.

THIRTY

I woke to birds chirping, a cat purring, and snoring in my ear. I took a moment to test my muscles by stretching and cringed. I was sorer than I thought, the physical fight combining with the magic overload to make for one wickedly painful morning.

"Ugh."

"Shh." Gunner ran his hands over the back of my head and drew me close. "Go back to sleep."

I had to swallow a laugh. He didn't exactly look as if he was prostrate with worry. "What time is it?"

"Bedtime," he murmured.

Instead of asking again, I turned to study the clock on the nightstand. It was almost ten, which was unbelievable. I'd slept for a good sixteen hours. "I don't want to sleep my life away."

I rolled onto my back and stared at the ceiling. The pedestal fan on the floor was pointed directly at my face and blew my hair, which was clearly too much temptation for Merlin, who pounced.

"Hey." I snagged him around the middle, ignoring the way he wriggled to escape. "You need to chill ... and we also need to have a conversation about the toilet paper. You need to knock that off."

Merlin didn't look impressed with the suggestion.

"I mean it," I added. "This is my serious face."

Beside me, Gunner chuckled and wrenched open an eye. He looked much better than the last time I'd talked to him. "Your serious face, huh?"

I nodded solemnly. "This cat is going to start following the rules."

"Or what?"

"Or no more catnip."

"You're strict." He leaned forward to kiss me, but I immediately pulled away. "Oh, don't even think about pulling the toothbrush thing. I can't take it."

"I'm serious about that rule. I'm not breaking from it no matter what."

"Even though you almost died yesterday?"

That was a gross exaggeration. "I didn't almost die. I passed out. There's a difference."

"And what do you think would've happened if you'd passed out before you took out the shifters? Do you think they would've just left you on the ground and gone on their merry way?"

It was a fair question ... one I didn't want to answer. "I don't want to talk about me." I meant it. "I want to know what happened in the cave. I passed out before I could hear the story."

"It's not that great a story. From what I understand, most of the action happened outside the cave ... which is why I think you sent us ahead and remained behind. You knew that would be the case."

If he expected me to deny it he was about to be massively disappointed. "I knew that Flint would fall. He wasn't smart enough, or strong enough, to take you guys on. He was a coward, and cowards are always easy to beat."

"You shouldn't have stayed outside alone," he chided. "You should've kept me with you."

"Raisin needed you."

"You needed me ... and I need you. I don't want you to ever do that again. I don't care what stakes we're dealing with."

We both knew I couldn't agree to those terms, so I decided to change the subject. "Did Drake find his sister?"

Gunner nodded, his fingers gentle as they brushed my hair from my face. "She was less than an hour away. Marissa and Bonnie went with him. It was an easy takedown."

"And Sarah?" I was almost afraid to ask.

"She's been through a lot," he replied simply. "I think it's going to take some time for her to come around. She's terrified. Flint traumatized her in ways I think we can imagine but won't want to accept."

That's exactly what I was afraid of. "Is Drake staying here?"

"For the time being. Whistler is hooking him up with a job at the bar and

Rooster is giving him one of the Spells Angels cabins for a bit. I don't know for how long, but it's what they both need for the time being."

The information was what I needed to hear. "That means he'll be around."

"Yeah. He knows you have questions. So do I. I'm not telling you your business, but it might be best to give him a few days to recover. I wasn't there, but my understanding is that Flint was keeping his sister in a cage — in an actual freaking cage — and he fell apart when they found her. He's emotionally vulnerable right now."

"Who wouldn't be? I won't go after him right away. But I'll want answers, and I won't forget that."

"I know. I hope he can give them to you."

"But you don't believe he can."

"I don't know what to believe," he clarified. "The thing is ... Cyrus lied to us. He knew more about Nexus than he let on. Flint basically let that slip before he died. He was laughing like a maniac when he admitted that he killed Fred — er, I mean George — in that clearing. Drake might not have been with him, but Cyrus was. My father confirmed it after the fact. That tissue found under George's fingernails? Yeah, it matched Cyrus."

I pulled away enough that I could tip back my head and stare into his eyes. "Are you serious? We need to get to the hospital and question Cyrus."

He stopped me before I could climb out of bed. "He's gone, Scout."

"He died? I thought he was going to make it."

"He's not dead, at least as far as I know. A contingent of wolves led by a woman named Arabella checked him out of the hospital following his surgery. They disappeared while my father was helping us with the cleanup at the cove."

"Arabella?" I propped myself on my elbow. "She took the other wolves away when she realized there was going to be a fight. I thought she was a friend."

"Drake thought the same thing." Gunner hesitated before continuing. "We don't know that she took Cyrus to help him. It's possible she took him to finish what Drake started."

That hadn't even occurred to me. "Do you think that's possible?"

"I don't know." He moved his hands to my back and drew me close. "Stay here with me a little bit. Not all of us slept for sixteen hours. It was after three when I got into bed."

"What were you doing?"

"Helping my father dispose of the dead shifters' bodies. It's not as if we can publicly bury them."

235

That made sense. "What about Drake? Your father isn't going to arrest him for shooting Cyrus, is he?"

"I don't believe so. He's not happy, but he understands what Drake was trying to do."

I wasn't even sure what Drake was trying to do. "How was killing Cyrus going to get him his sister back?"

"Drake believed that the other wolves were loyal to Cyrus rather than Flint, which turned out to be true. Drake thought that once Cyrus was dead the other wolves — many of whom were abused by Flint — would join with him and they would be able to torture Flint into telling him where Sarah was. It kind of worked out that way in the end. Instead of shifters to help with the torture, though, he had us."

"And you're sure Raisin is okay?"

"She's fine. She sat next to you in the clearing while we waited for my father to arrive. I wanted to take you to the hospital, but everyone talked me out of it."

"That was probably smart. There's nothing they could've done for me. I was magically drained, and that's not something they're trained to deal with."

"I get that, but ... you looked so vulnerable." His hands attacked the tight muscles in my back, causing me to groan. "Eventually I agreed to bring you home. Whistler sat with you and cleaned the cabin until I could get back. I hated being away from you, but I'm really glad it was him because he's a neat freak. I believe he also had a talk with Merlin about his toilet paper fetish."

I laughed at the visual. "I'm sorry I missed that."

"Yeah." He exhaled heavily and rested his chin on my forehead. "Flint said they knew that Nexus cast a curse on them. They'd been searching for years to find someone who could lift the spell ... and came up empty."

"Are they the ones who killed the people watching me throughout my childhood?"

"Flint says no."

"Do you believe him?"

"I ... don't know. Flint said they were aware of the bodies that were dropped throughout the years but didn't realize it had anything to do with you. They were following someone else who happened to be in the same locations with you. A woman."

I jerked up my head. "What woman?"

"All he knew was that her name was Claudette."

There was that name again. "So Claudette was in the same locations I was.

They were following her and bodies dropped in each location. That can't be a coincidence. They had to be responsible."

"I tend to agree, but Flint denied it. Given what was happening at the time, I'm not sure what he gained by lying."

"It doesn't make any sense otherwise."

"Unless we're still missing a piece of the puzzle, which is entirely possible. Flint said they modeled George's death on the other bodies because they thought it would help them get away with it. They threatened George to remove the spell, but he either couldn't or wouldn't, and they killed him in a rage.

"They had one of the witches in the pack cast a spell to keep him awake for the torture. It was a terrible death," he continued. "They used your name because they thought it would distract me, which was their ultimate goal. Flint swore up and down that he had no idea you were affiliated with Nexus as it was going down. I tend to believe him because he misunderstood what we said to him and swore he was going to torture you to remove the curse."

"He was nothing if not predictable," I muttered.

"I don't know that he's lying in this particular instance. We need more information. Drake is hanging around, so he might be able to provide some answers. We also have a name — Claudette — which is more than we had a week ago. I know it doesn't feel like much, but it's better than nothing."

"It definitely doesn't feel like much," I agreed, pursing my lips. "I thought we would get more answers out of all this. It felt like we were close."

"We still might get answers."

"Not with Cyrus gone."

"I admit that's a blow. I thought he was telling the truth. I should've insisted my father put a guard on him. But at the time we assumed Drake was guilty."

"Because Cyrus told us he was."

"He was also technically guilty."

That was true. "I can't help looking at it as a disappointment," I admitted as I rubbed my forehead. "I wanted answers."

"You'll get them. I promise. I'll be there with you when it happens. What we really need to do is write all of this down and go through it from beginning to end. I'm not suggesting we do that today, but once you're feeling better we'll find a new angle. I guarantee we're not done here."

I was thankful for his enthusiasm, even if I couldn't join in. Instead of prolonging the conversation, I rolled to look at his face ... and caught sight of something plush out of the corner of my eye. When I focused on it, I realized it was a stuffed wolf, one that reminded me of the one I coveted as a child.

"What's that?"

Gunner grinned when he saw where my eyes went. "That's your first toy. I bought it for you yesterday. It's a get-well gift."

I didn't know what to say. "You didn't have to do that."

"Sometimes it's not about 'have to' as much as 'want to' and I wanted to get you something. Besides, now you'll have that to sleep with every night. You can name it Gunner Jr."

I had to press my lips together to keep from laughing. "I see." I ran my hand over the wolf's soft head. "Thank you."

He hugged me tight. "You're welcome."

For the next few minutes, we eased into comfortable silence. I was the first to break it. "What do think we should do with our day? I mean ... we can't grill Drake for information and Cyrus is gone. It seems we have an open day with nothing to do."

A sly smile spread over his face. "I'm glad you asked, because I have a few ideas." He edged lower on the bed so he was staring directly into my eyes.

"I bet I can guess what those ideas consist of."

"I bet you can, too. I thought we would start with breakfast. I can cook — Whistler filled your refrigerator with every sort of food you could possibly want — and then we'll eat in bed. Then we'll watch some television and wrestle."

I cocked an eyebrow. "Wrestle? Is that what we're calling it?"

"For now. Then we'll have lunch in bed and repeat the process throughout the entire day. This is after you shower and brush your teeth, of course. Oh ... and shave your legs. We can't have leg stubble in this bed."

I laughed despite myself at his reaction. "And that's what you want to do with your entire day?"

He nodded. "As long as we spend it together, I honestly don't care what we do. I think that's a marvelous idea, though. I don't know how you could possibly argue with it."

That made two of us. "I want pancakes and bacon for breakfast. Like, a big pile of bacon."

Merlin perked up and meowed.

"I think the entire family wants bacon," Gunner agreed, leaning forward and resting his forehead against mine. "I want something else, too, but you won't allow it until you brush your teeth. By the way, I'm going to break you of that habit."

"You wouldn't be the first to try. They all failed."

"Yes, but I'm special."

Ah, another thing we agreed upon. "You can try. It'll be harder than you imagine."

"I happen to love a challenge."

"Then we'll get along fine."

"I already knew that."

We both did, which only proved that we were in for a magical adventure – and I was looking forward to it.

Made in the USA
Coppell, TX
11 March 2020

16717007R00141